Frank's new house was just about finished. The new barn was completed, so Frank forked hay into Horse's stall, put some grain into the feed box, then went into his house.

He fed Dog, fixed a pot of coffee, filled a cup, and went out onto the front porch to sit for a time, enjoying the quiet of late afternoon. He was rolling a cigarette just as Dog came out and laid down beside his chair.

"We're getting to be regular land barons, Dog," Frank said with a smile, reaching down and petting Dog. "I believe we might have actually found us a home. What do you think about that?"

Dog looked up at him for a few seconds, then went back to sleep.

"I thought that would impress you," Frank said with a laugh.

*Do I want to spend the rest of my life here?* Frank asked himself. Well, why not? The people—most of them anyway—are nice and don't really give a damn about my past.

And there is that nice young widow to think about, too.

Thinking of Julie filled Frank with a warm, comfortable feeling. A feeling he had thought he could never dredge up again.

But could he really ever put his past behind him? There were still a lot of punks looking for a gun reputation, and they would find him. They always did. Then he would have to kill again—or be killed.

"Damn," Frank whispered. "It ain't easy being Frank Morgan."

He went inside and lit a lamp. He'd read for a time, then go to bed. He had bought a book of poems written by a fellow named Poe. What a strange, dark, and lonely mind that man had. Frank refilled his coffee cup and began reading about the beautiful Annabel Lee.

# THE LAST GUNFIGHTER:

# THE FORBIDDEN

## WILLIAM W. JOHNSTONE

PINNACLE BOOKS
Kensington Publishing Corp.
www.pinnaclebooks.com

PINNACLE BOOKS are published by

Kensington Publishing Corp.
850 Third Avenue
New York, NY 10022

Dear Readers,

When I first began thinking of a new western series, I wanted it to be a bit different. Then I thought: Why not do a series on the fading glory of the Old West, a series about the final days of the wild frontier? But who should be featured in these books, other than a middle-aged gunhandler who just wants to live out his days in peace and quiet but can't because his reputation won't let him?

That's when I came up with Frank Morgan. The man known as the Drifter—the Last Gunfighter.

*William W. Johnstone*

"I seen my duty and I done it."

—Anonymous

# ONE

Someone had taken paint and covered the names of the two towns on the signpost at the crossroads. Beneath one of the painted-out names was printed HEAVEN. Beneath the other was printed HELL.

From where Frank sat his saddle at the crossroads, Heaven was five miles to the south, Hell was five miles to the north.

Frank looked at Dog, sitting off to the right, at the edge of the road. "Want to go to Heaven or Hell, Dog?"

Dog growled softly.

"Well, in some ways Hell might be more interesting, but Heaven sure sounds peaceful to me," Frank said.

Dog sat and stared unblinkingly at him.

"Let's try Heaven, Dog. It's probably about as close as I'll ever get to the real thing."

Before Frank could lift the reins and head for the town of Heaven, the rattling and rumbling of a wagon turned his head. A heavily loaded freight wagon was approaching from the east. The driver pulled alongside Frank and halted his team.

"Howdy," the driver said.

"Afternoon," Frank replied. "You going to Heaven or Hell?"

The driver chuckled and shifted his wad of chewing tobacco from one side of his mouth to the other. Then he spat. "Accordin' to the preacher, I'm hell-bound for my final haul. But today, I'm goin' to Heaven."

"Mind if I ride along with you?"

"Not a-tall. Glad to have the company." He looked at Dog. "That your dog?"

"He is. Name is Dog."

"Fittin' name, I reckon. Looks mean."

Frank smiled. "He'll bite a biscuit if you'll butter it."

"Let me guess: your horse's name is Horse?"

"That's right."

The driver chuckled. "Mind if I ask your name?"

"Frank."

"I'm Luke, Frank. Glad to meet you and Dog and Horse. When we get to Heaven I'll let you buy me a drink. How's that sound?"

"They serve whiskey in Heaven?"

"Sounds strange, don't it? Yep, they do. They got everything a regular town has, 'ceptin' soiled doves."

"No whores, huh?"

"Not nary a one." He grinned. "'Lessin' you know where to look, that is."

Frank laughed, lifted the reins, and proceeded on toward Heaven, putting Hell behind him, for the time being.

Heaven was a pleasant little town with a single long street

and a half dozen or so shops and stores on each side: two saloons—one on each side of the street, a hotel, a cafe, a huge general store, a livery, a ladies' dress and hat shop, a leather and gun shop, a barber and bath place, and several other smaller shops. There was nothing to distinguish it from dozens of other small Western towns Frank had ridden into and out of over the years.

"Folks is real friendly in Heaven," Luke told Frank. "If you ain't workin' for them people over in Hell, that is."

"I'm not working for anybody," Frank told him. "Just drifting."

"You shore look familiar to me, Frank. And you seem like a right nice feller. I hope I'm right on that last count."

"Luke, all I want is a bath and haircut, a meal I don't have to cook myself, somebody to wash and press my clothes, and a soft bed to sleep in. Then I'm gone."

"You can get all them things done in Heaven, Frank. I got to pull around back of the general store and unload. I'll see you around maybe."

"I reckon so, Luke."

Frank rode over to the livery, very conscious of many eyes on him. Not unfriendly eyes, just curious.

"Rub him down and feed him good," Frank told the liveryman. "Dog will stay in the stall with him. Don't try to pet Dog unless he comes up to you and acts like he wants to be petted. He might snap at you. And don't get behind Horse. He kicks." Frank paused, then added, "Matter of fact, he bites too."

"Is there anything else them critters do I need to be warned about?" the liveryman asked.

"No, that's about it."

"That's enough."

"You got a secure place for my gear?"

"Sure. I got a storeroom yonder that I keep locked."

"Fine. I'll check back later."

"Gonna be in town long?"

"Couple of days."

"Lookin' for anyone special?"

"No. Just a quiet place to relax for a day or two."

"You look familiar to me. You ever been here before?"

"Never have."

"It'll come to me. I never forget a face."

"Maybe so." Frank gathered up his trail-worn clothes and walked across the street to the Chinese laundry, which was next to the bath and barbershop.

*So far, so good,* Frank thought as he walked across the street. *I've found a place where no one knows me. For a time anyway. But somebody will ride up who recognizes me. They always do. So I'd better enjoy the peace while it lasts.*

Frank Morgan was just about the last of a vanishing breed: a gunfighter. But it was a title he never wanted and had never actively sought. There were a few men like him still around. Smoke Jensen, Louis Longmont, to name a couple. But for the most part, many of the West's gunfighters either were dead or had dropped out of sight and changed their names. Mostly dead.

Frank dropped his clothes off to be washed and pressed, and then walked over to the general store and bought some new black britches and a red and white checkered shirt, with a black bandanna to top it all off. Then he went next door to the barbershop and had a good, hot bath, washing days of trail dust off him, then had a haircut and a shave while a boy polished up his boots. Frank buckled on his gunbelt and left the shop smelling and looking better than he had in days. His hat had just about lost its shape, but Frank figured he could work on that himself and get it back looking halfway decent. If he couldn't, he'd throw the damn thing away and go buy a new one.

Frank certainly didn't need to watch his pennies. He was a wealthy man for the time, due to his late wife's leaving him a percentage of her company's earnings in her will. And the company, left to her by her father, was vast, with various holdings all over North America. Frank had a trusted attorney and banker handling all his money, and they were doing a wonderful job of it.

Frank got a room at the hotel, registering under the name Moran, enjoyed an early, quiet, and very good supper at the Blue Moon Cafe, and then lingered over several cups of really good coffee. He complimented the waitress on how good the meal was.

"Most everything is homegrown, sir," she told him. "The south part of the long series of valleys is all farm and sheep country, with a few small ranches here and there, mostly owned by men who also farm."

Frank tensed at the word "sheep." He hoped the waitress had not noticed.

She hadn't, just went right on continuing her praise of the south end of the series of valleys, ending with: "The north end, past the crossroads, is all cattle ranches."

"Whose idea was it to change the names of the towns to Heaven and Hell?"

She smiled and shook her head. "I don't know. That was done several years ago and the names just sort of stuck."

She refilled Frank's coffee cup and went off to wait on other customers who were coming in for an early supper. Frank rolled a cigarette and sat for a time, very conscious of the furtive glances he was receiving from the men who had taken seats in the cafe. He finally met the eyes of a man who was staring at him.

"Afternoon," Frank said.

"Howdy," the man said. "Forgive me for staring. We don't

get many visitors to our town. Any new face draws attention. But we don't mean to be impolite."

"That's all right. Doesn't bother me at all. You have a nice town."

"Thank you. Our town is very peaceful. Just the way we like it."

"I can appreciate that. I need to thank the freight driver for turning me south instead of north at the crossroads."

"North would have taken you straight to Hell. It's a nice enough town, I suppose. But it can get rowdy sometimes."

Frank smiled at the play on words. "Lives up to its name, hey?"

"At times, yes. It's a cattle town. But I suppose you already knew that."

"I guessed, from what the waitress told me."

"You just passin' through?"

"Yep. I needed some supplies and a bath." Frank left it at that, wondering how far the citizen would push it. Frank hoped not far, for pushing was something he didn't like. Frank Morgan had a habit of pushing back, verbally or physically.

"I'm the banker," the citizen said. "John Simmons."

"Frank."

The banker blinked. "Just Frank?"

"No, I have a last name."

"Well, what is it?" one of the men seated at the table with the banker demanded in a very hard tone of voice.

"I don't figure that's any of your business," Frank told him as his hackles began to rise. "But if you're that nosy you can go look at the hotel register."

"I might just do that," the citizen said.

"Go right ahead," Frank replied, jerking his thumb. "The hotel is right over yonder across the street. Any fool can find it."

The citizen flushed at that. "Are you calling me a fool?"

"No. I just said any fool can find the hotel."

"Settle down, George," the banker told his friend. He looked at Frank. "We're a little edgy, Frank." He smiled. "I guess strangers bring that out in us."

"Oh? Why is that?"

"Stay around, Frank," another citizen told him. "And you'll find out."

"I just might do that."

"Told you he was workin' for them," George said.

"I'm not working for anybody," Frank told the table of men. "And I'm not looking for a job. So put that out of your mind."

"You say," George sneered.

Frank had just about had enough of George and his mouth. He pushed back his chair, ready to stand up. "You calling me a liar, George?"

John Simmons held up a hand. "Steady, men. This is getting out of hand."

Frank laid both hands on the table. "I'll take an apology."

"You'll take nothin', drifter," George said. "'Cause that's what I'm givin'."

Frank abruptly stood up, and the table of men all stared at the .45-caliber Peacemaker slung low in leather and tied down.

"Gunfighter," George breathed. "I knew it."

"Are you?" John asked.

"I'm just a man with a tired horse who is looking for a warm bed and some relaxation. Nothing more. I'm sure as hell not looking for any gun trouble. I have a sore-pawed, worn-out dog with me and he'd like to rest for a time too." Frank dropped some coins on the table for his meal and stepped back, away from the table. "Now if you gentlemen will excuse me, I'll be on my way to the hotel."

Frank walked to the counter and ordered another full meal to go.

"You really must be hungry," the waitress said.

"It's for my dog," Frank told her.

The waitress blinked a couple of times, then smiled. "I'll get it for you."

The customers watched as Frank left the cafe, Dog's supper in a sack, and walked toward the livery.

"I don't trust him," George said. "He's workin' for the cattlemen."

"You don't know that for sure," John said.

"Tied-down gun," George said. "That's a dead giveaway."

"A lot of men tie down their pistols," another citizen said. "Keeps the holster from flappin' around."

"What do you know about gun-handlers, Paul?" George questioned. "You're still new out here. Have you ever even seen a gunfight?"

"I was in the war, George. I seen plenty of men die."

"No pretty uniforms in this war, Paul. No bugles blowin' and fancy generals givin' orders. This is a different kind of war."

"Let's give the man a chance," John said. "But I have to say this: He sure looks familiar to me."


"Same ol' crap, Dog," Frank said as he unwrapped Dog's supper and set it down in the stall. Dog began eating the meat and bread. Frank found a bucket and filled it with fresh water from the pump. "Looks like we rode into a hornet's nest. We'll get rested up here and then hit the trail. I got to find us another packhorse 'fore we do, though. Then I'll provision up and we'll be on our way. You stay close to the livery now, you hear me?"

Dog looked up for a moment, then resumed his eating.

Frank patted Horse and then walked across the wide street to the saloon. He'd listen to the talk and maybe find out what was going on in the area. But he felt he knew pretty well already. Cattlemen and farmers nose-to-nose over land use. Add sheep to that and you had a damn explosive situation.

Most of the men in the saloon wore low-heeled clodhopper boots or work shoes, pegging them as farmers right off the mark. Several of the men wore business suits with high shirt collars and neck pieces. Bankers and lawyers and store owners and such, Frank figured.

The saloon fell silent when Frank entered.

He walked to the long bar and ordered a whiskey. Men began moving away from him, and Frank had to secretly smile at that. *Nothing ever changes,* he thought. *A stranger shows up in a tense town and citizen reaction is always the same.*

The bartender poured his whiskey and then moved away from him.

Frank sipped his whiskey slowly, enjoying the bite of the after-supper drink. Frank Morgan was not much of a drinker, but he did enjoy a shot of whiskey or a cool glass of beer every now and then.

"Damn that Circle Snake bunch," a man said, his voice almost shrill with anger. "They'll not get away with it, boys. Bet on that."

*Circle Snake,* Frank thought. *Strange. That must be an interesting-looking brand. Can't recall ever hearing anything like that before.*

"Settle down, Peter," another man said, his words drifting to Frank. "There might be unfriendly ears close by."

Frank knew they were referring to him.

"I don't care," Peter said. "They can hire all the gunfighters they want. Don't make a bit of difference to me."

"He don't look so damn tough to me," yet another voice added. "Got some gray in his hair too."

"For a fact, he's no youngster."

This time, Frank made no attempt to hide his smile. *No youngster,* he thought. *Well, you've sure got that right.*

Frank was in his mid-forties, just a bit over six feet tall. He was lean-hipped and broad-shouldered. His hands were big and callused and his arms were packed with muscle. His hair was brown and thick, graying at the temples. His eyes were a strange pale gray color. Women considered him a very handsome man.

Frank pushed back his hat and leaned on the polished bar, nursing his whiskey and listening as the talk continued.

"I looked at the hotel registry," a man said, intentionally loud enough for Frank to hear. "Frank Moran is the name he signed in the book."

"I never heard of no gunslick by that name."

"Probably isn't his real name."

The barkeep walked over to Frank. "Another drink, mister?"

"I'm all right with this one," Frank told him.

The barkeep leaned on the bar and whispered. "I knew I'd seen you somewhere, mister. It finally come to me. You're Frank Morgan."

"That's right. But I'm not here to cause any trouble."

"I'd be surprised if you was. That ain't your style."

"With any kind of luck, I'll be provisioned up and out of here in the morning. I don't want anything to do with the trouble in this valley."

"Actually, it's half a dozen connectin' valleys. But for a fact, trouble is comin'."

"Cattlemen and farmers. Same old story."

"And now we got sheep."

"More trouble. Cattlemen won't stand for that."

"You're tellin' me? I have to listen to it, day after day."

"Hey, Chubby!" one the men at the table called. "Who's your friend?"

"A customer, Ben."

"Y'all gettin' mighty close over there."

Chubby straightened and gave the man a hard glance. "You got a problem with me talkin' to a customer?"

"Don't get all hot under the collar, Chubby."

"Then mind your own business, Wallace."

"All right, Chubby, all right. Sorry."

"I shouldn't get mad at any of them," Chubby said, again speaking to Frank in low tones. "Things are really beginnin' to get nasty around here."

"How?"

"Farmhouses and barns are gettin' burned by night riders. Shots have been fired at farmers in the field. Pretty soon it'll be crops gettin' destroyed. No one's been killed yet, but it's comin'. Bet on it."

"How about the law?"

"Frank, we never had any need for much law here in this town. We have a marshal, but he's only part-time and he's old. He don't even carry a gun."

"Well, don't look at me, Chub. I don't want the job."

"I was kinda hopin' . . ."

"Forget it."

The batwings suddenly were slammed open and three cowboys walked in.

"Oh, hell," Chubby said. "Snake riders."

"What arc thcy doing in this town?" Frank asked.

"It's a free country, Frank. They can come and go as they please."

"Well, lookie here," one of the cowboys said. "Someone

in this damn stinkin' sheep-crap town is wearin' a gun, boys. Reckon he knows how to use it?"

"Here we go," Chubby said.

Frank turned slowly to face the three cowboys.

# TWO

"The man shore ain't no sheep farmer," a cowboy said. "I think the clodhoppers done gone and hired themselves a gunhand."

The third cowhand had not yet spoken. He was intently studying Frank's face. "Back off, Eddie," he finally said.

"We haven't hired anybody," one of the men seated in the saloon said.

"Why should I back off, Tom?" Eddie asked. "It's just one man and he don't look like much to me. What do you think, Carl?"

"Come to think of it," Carl replied, "he looks sort of familiar to me."

"You got a name, mister?" Tom asked.

"Frank."

"Frank what?"

"Just Frank."

"Hell," Eddie said with a laugh. "The man don't even know his last name."

"Morgan," Tom said softly. "That's Frank Morgan."

"Aw, hell," Eddie said. "Frank Morgan's been retired for years. Or dead. That ain't Frank Morgan, Tom."

"Frank Morgan?" one of the men at a table breathed. "Here, in Heaven?"

"Are you really Frank Morgan?" another farmer asked.

"Yes," Frank said without taking his eyes off the three Snake riders. "I am. But I'm not looking for any trouble and I'm not looking for a job."

"Then what the hell are you doin' here?" Eddie challenged.

"Minding my own business, boy," Frank replied. "Something that you obviously can't or won't do."

"I ain't no boy!"

"I'm going to finish my drink," Frank said. "Leave me alone."

"I just might decide to finish *you.*" Eddie almost yelled the words.

"You're a damn fool," Frank told him. He looked at the older of the Snake riders. "You better put a leash on that pup."

"He's a man growed up," Tom said. "He's got a right to speak his mind."

Frank turned away and picked up his shot glass with his left hand.

"Don't you turn your damn ass to me, Morgan!" Eddie shouted. "By God, I don't take that from no man."

Frank ignored him.

"Do you hear me, you old bastard?" Eddie yelled.

"Shut up, Eddie," Tom said. "Morgan ain't here to bother none of us."

"He's botherin' me, by God!" Eddie said.

"Settle down, boy," Chubby cautioned him.

"You shut your mouth, fat man!" Eddie snapped at him. "This here is between me and Morgan. Ain't none of your affair."

"There is nothing at all between us, Eddie," Frank said. "Have a drink on me and settle down."

"To hell with you and your drink, old man! By God, I think you're tryin' to worm out of this. I think you've lost your damn guts."

"Don't push it, Eddie," Frank warned.

"Or you'll do what, Morgan?" Eddie challenged.

"Eddie," Tom said. "Let's get out of here. Drop this."

"You may be the foreman on the job, Tom. But we ain't on the job. This is my business. None of yours."

Tom held up a hand. "I'm out of this, Morgan."

"Good," Frank replied.

"By God, I ain't out of it," Carl said, stepping forward. "I'm with you, Eddie."

The batwings pushed open and a man who looked to be in his late sixties or early seventies stepped in. There was a star on his chest and no gun on his hip.

"What's going on here?" the old marshal said.

"None of your damn business, old man," Carl said. "Stay out of it."

"I'm the duly appointed law in this town, young man," the marshal said. "This certainly is my business."

"Come on, Eddie," the foreman urged him. "This is stupid. If Morgan don't kill you, the colonel is sure to fire you over this."

"This has-been ain't gonna kill me, Tom. No way. I can shoot his eyes out anytime I take a notion to."

Frank sighed and put down his drink. He knew the time for talking was nearly over. He'd been through this too many times in the past. Eddie was not going to back down. Frank turned slowly to face Eddie and Carl.

"Now just a minute here," the marshal said.

"Stand clear, Marshal," Frank told him.

"Morgan?" the marshal said. "Frank Morgan?"

"Yeah, Marshal," Chubby said. "That's right."

"Dear God in Heaven," the marshal said, shaking his head. "Frank Morgan."

"He ain't jack-crap, Marshal," Eddie said. "He's an old used-up has-been. Nothin' else. But you best stand clear. If Morgan manages to clear leather, ain't no tellin' where he's liable to throw lead after I shoot him. He'll be like a dog, bitin' at himself when he's dyin'."

Frank sized up the situation fast: figuring he'd better take Eddie out first, then Carl. Carl was getting edgy, maybe figuring he'd gotten himself into something he was now quickly realizing he'd been better off leaving alone. Eddie was ready for a fight, standing tense, his right hand hovering over the butt of his pistol.

"I won't stand for this," the old marshal protested.

"Shut up," Eddie told him.

Frank stood silent and waiting and ready.

"Come on, Morgan!" Eddie shouted. "Let's see how good you are."

"It's your play, boy," Frank told him. "I won't start this."

"Yellow!" Eddie said. "That's what you are. Just plain yellow."

Frank stood silent.

"Drag iron!" Eddie yelled.

Frank didn't make a move.

"Damn you!" Eddie shouted. "Draw on me."

"You've got to start it, boy," Frank said softly.

"This is the man you clodhoppers hired?" Eddie said. "He's a coward. Just like the rest of you pig farmers."

"You got it all wrong, cowboy," a man said. "We didn't hire Morgan."

"You're a damn liar!" Eddie snapped. "Why else would a man like him come to this nothin' town?"

"Just passing through, Eddie," Frank told him.

"Liar! You're all damn liars. Every one of you."

Eddie had worked himself into a killing rage. Nothing was going to stop him now. Tom had backed up, out of the line of fire. He was holding his hand away from his gun.

Frank waited. He was not going to pull on Eddie. Eddie would have to start this deadly showdown.

"Damn you, Morgan!" Eddie yelled. "I'll make you hook and draw." His hand closed around the butt of his pistol. "Now, you coward! Pull iron!"

Frank shot him, drawing and firing in one fast and smooth movement. The .45-caliber slug hit Eddie in the center of his chest. His feet flew out from under him and he stretched out on the floor, his right hand still gripping the butt of his six-gun. He had just cleared leather when Frank's bullet knocked him down.

"Good Lord!" Tom said, his voice awe-filled at Frank's lightning speed.

"Morgan was so fast I didn't even see him draw," a farmer said in a hushed tone.

Carl was shaking his head. "Don't shoot me, Morgan! I ain't gonna draw on you. I'm out of this."

"Suits me," Frank replied. "I didn't want any of this."

Eddie groaned in shock and pain.

"I'll go fetch the doctor," the old marshal said, heading for the batwings.

Tom knelt down beside the fallen Snake rider. But he had seen many gunshot wounds in his time, and knew there was nothing the doctor would be able to do. Eddie was near death and fading fast.

"Did I get him?" Eddie asked.

"Are you kiddin'?" Tom said.

"I got him, didn't I?" Eddie asked.

"Eddie, you just barely got your gun out of leather. Now lay quiet until the doc gets here."

"It's really beginnin' to hurt, Tom. I'm hard hit, ain't I?"

"Yes, you are, Eddie. I ain't gonna lie to you."

"I done messed up bad, didn't I?"

"I reckon you did."

Frank had holstered his Peacemaker and was leaning up against the bar.

"It always happens, don't it, Frank?" Chubby said. "Folks just won't leave you alone, will they?"

"Seems that way, Chub."

"You want another whiskey?"

"How about some coffee?"

"Comin' right up."

Tom looked up from the dying young Snake rider. "All hell's gonna break loose because of this, Morgan."

"I didn't start it," Frank replied.

"That don't make no difference. Nobody kills a Snake rider and walks scot-free away from it."

"I don't intend to walk away. I intend to ride away."

"Then you better saddle up and get out right now, Morgan."

"And nobody runs me out of any town." Frank's words were cold, with a hard edge to them.

"Don't bet on that, gunfighter." Tom's words were just as cold and hard. "I'm tellin' you for your own good."

"Tom?" Eddie said. "I'm really hurtin' something bad, Tom."

"You're a dead man, Morgan!" Carl had decided to stick his penny's worth into it. "I'll kill you myself."

"Don't let your butt overload your mouth, boy," Frank

told him. "Eddie was a damn trouble-hunter. He came look-ing for trouble, and he found it. He brought all this on him-self. There is no need for revenge talk."

"I'd like to hear you tell the colonel that!"

"I will if he has the grit to face me."

"The colonel?" Carl questioned. "He's got the grit, Morgan. He was a hero in the war. Won all kinds of medals."

"What war?"

"The Civil War."

"Which side?"

"The right side, Morgan," Tom said. "The same side I was on. The Union side."

"I was on the other side."

"Figures. A damn Reb."

"Tom?" Eddie called. "Where's the doc?"

"Right here," a man said from the batwings. "I'm Dr. Everett." He looked at Morgan. "And you'd be Frank Morgan."

"That's right."

"I worked on what was left of two men who braced you down in Arizona some years back."

"Did they live?" Frank asked.

"No." The doctor knelt down beside Eddie and opened his bloody shirt. After quickly examining him, he took off his stethoscope and dropped it back into his bag, standing up.

"Am I gonna live, Doc?" Eddie asked.

"Not damn likely."

"Well . . . that's a hell of a thing to tell a man!" Eddie pro-tested.

"I'm not going to lie to you, boy. The bullet went right through a lung and nicked the heart. You're filling up with blood and there isn't a damn thing I can do. Your heart's going to stop beating any minute now."

"Damn!" Eddie said weakly.

"You best make your peace with God. You want me to get the preacher?"

"I want you to get me a doc that knows what the hell he's doin'," Eddie said, his voice very weak. "That's what I want."

"I'm the only one in town, boy. And I know what I'm doing." He turned to the foreman. "You damn Snake riders finally met up with a man you can't push around, hey, Tom?"

"You go to hell, Everett," the foreman replied. "The Snake ranch has got as much right to these valleys as anyone."

"Nonsense, Tom. Everything the people here in the south end did was legal. They filed on their land and proved it up. Your brand and the other ranchers are in the wrong. And the sad thing is, you know it."

"Has everyone done forgot about me?" Eddie asked as his lifeblood leaked from him, staining the floor. "I'm dyin' and no one gives a damn."

Frank sipped his coffee and listened.

"Bah!" Dr. Everett snorted his contempt and turned to the bartender. "Chubby, pour me a whiskey, please."

"Where's the preacher?" Eddie asked.

"The marshal's gone to get him," one of the men seated at a table said.

"I wish he'd hurry," Eddie said. "I need some comfortin'. How much time do I have, Doc?"

"A few minutes. Maybe half an hour. Hell, you might live until dawn." Everett took a tiny sip of whiskey.

"You a damn cold doctor," Carl said. "'Bout the coldest I ever seen."

Everett did not reply to that, just shook his head and looked disgusted. He cut his eyes to Frank. "Are you planning on staying in town long, Morgan?"

"My plans are to pull out tomorrow, after I provision up."

"Maybe you should postpone your departure date," the doctor suggested.

"Why?"

"Oh, things might get interesting around here if you'd stay."

"I'm sure they would." Frank's reply was very dry.

Dr. Everett smiled and took another tiny sip of whiskey. "You have a reputation of fighting for the underdog, Morgan."

"Only when pushed into it, Doctor."

The batwings squeaked and pushed open. A very large man lumbered into the saloon and looked around him, disapproval in his eyes. "What a horrid place," he said.

"Reverend Philpot," Everett said. He pointed to Eddie. "He needs your gentle words of comfort, Preacher. He is a sinner of the first degree and he's not long for this world."

"Go to hell, you old quack!" Eddie said.

"Here now, son," Philpot said, as he walked over to the dying Eddie. "Don't let your spirit approach the glorious gates of forever with a curse on your lips."

"Say a prayer, or something," Tom said.

The marshal pushed a chair over for Philpot to sit in. *Good thing,* Frank thought. If Philpot tried to squat down, it would take a dozen men to get him back on his feet.

"Have you been saved, son?" Philpot asked.

"I reckon," Eddie said. "I was dunked in a crick by a lay preacher once."

"Did you give your heart to God then?"

"I was in love with Druilla Simpson at the time."

"That's not exactly what I meant, boy."

"We used to meet every Sunday behind the outhouse at the church," Eddie replied.

Philpot sighed. "This is going to take a lot of preaching."

"He doesn't have that much time," Everett said. "Can you make it the short version?"

"You're a heathen, Everett!" Philpot said. "And a disgrace to your most honorable calling."

"Is that coffee fresh, Morgan?" Everett asked, ignoring Philpot.

"Tastes good to me."

"I'll have some," Everett told Chubby.

"I brought the choir with me," Philpot said. "But I forbade any of the good ladies to enter this den of inebriety and impiousness."

"This what?" Chubby asked. "This ain't no whorehouse, Preacher."

"Be quiet," Philpot said. "I'm preparing to ask the Lord to forgive this evil wretch on the floor and allow him entrance into his final home in the great beyond. Ladies!" he yelled. "Some Christian music, if you will."

The choir outside began softly singing "When the Roll Is Called Up Yonder."

"That's a little traveling music, Eddie," Doc Everett said.

Frank had to grimace and shake his head at that. The doctor certainly had a wicked sense of humor.

"That isn't at all amusing, Doctor," Preacher Philpot admonished him.

"It wasn't meant to be."

"Quiet now." Philpot began to pray, and Frank took off his hat in respect.

Eddie began to gurgle.

"Won't be long now," the doctor whispered.

Eddie suddenly stiffened and beat his hands on the floor. Then he died.

"Damn!" Tom said.

Just then the batwings pushed open and the front of the saloon filled with men.

"Colonel Trainor," Tom said.

"Oh, hell," Chubby said. "Now it's shore gonna break loose."

"I'll sure drink to that," Dr. Everett said.

"That's Frank Morgan!" Carl yelled, pointing at Frank. "He's workin' for the sodbusters!"

# THREE

The rancher looked over at Eddie. "Is he dead?"

"Yes," Philpot said.

"Then somebody cover him up until we can remove the body." He turned his gaze toward Frank. "You're the infamous Frank Morgan?"

"I'm Frank Morgan," Frank acknowledged. "Who are you?"

"Colonel Trainor. I own the Circle Snake."

"Congratulations."

Trainor could not miss the sarcasm in Frank's voice. He smiled. "Thank you, Morgan."

Frank turned away, facing the bar. He picked up his coffee cup and took a sip.

"Don't turn your back to me, Morgan!" Trainor's voice held a hard edge.

"Why not?" Frank asked without turning around. "I don't have anything else to say to you."

"You just gunned down one of my hands."

"He started it. I finished it." He motioned to the bartender. "Some more coffee, Chubby. Hotten this up for me."

"You picked the wrong side in this fight, Morgan."

"I haven't picked any side, Trainor."

"You say."

"No one else speaks for me."

"Colonel," the foreman said. "You want me to hire a buckboard and carry Eddie's body back to the ranch?"

"Yes, Tom. Do that. We'll bury him tomorrow. Go with him, Carl. I'll question you about this incident in the morning."

"Yes, sir."

Trainor walked to the bar and stood beside Morgan for a moment. "A whiskey for me, Chubby."

Frank straightened up and looked at the rancher. Colonel Trainor was about Frank's height, but heavier and stocky, square-jawed and solid. Frank concluded the man would be hard to handle in a fight.

Trainor was taking that time to size up Frank more closely. He basically reached the same conclusion.

"You're younger than I imagined you would be," the rancher said.

"I 'spect we're about the same age."

"I was in the war."

"So was I."

"I was on the winning side."

Frank smiled. "I was on the right side."

"A damn traitorous Rebel."

Frank sipped his coffee and said nothing.

"You really haven't hired on with the farmers, Morgan?"

"No, Trainor, I haven't. And I don't plan on hiring on . . . with anybody. I plan on pulling out in the morning."

"Have they offered you a job?"

"Not yet."

"They will."

"I was going to suggest that," Dr. Everett said. "Since the Snake brand is hiring gunslicks."

Colonel Trainor stiffened at that. He set his whiskey down and looked at the doctor. "I'm hiring hands to work cattle, Doctor. Not gunhands."

"When did Jess Malone ever work cattle, Trainor?"

"Jess Malone?" Frank asked. "From New Mexico?"

"That's him," Everett said. "He rode in with four others a week ago. One of them is called Carson."

"That would be Peck Carson," Frank said. "He runs with a man name of Rondel. No-goods, both of them. Back-shooters. Jess is not much better."

"You know them?"

"We've crossed trails a time or two. They generally fight shy of me."

"I'll be sure and tell them you said that, Morgan," Trainor said.

"You do that."

The foreman pushed open the batwings. "We've got Eddie loaded up, Colonel."

"All right, Tom. We'll all ride back together." Trainor drained his glass and glared at Frank. "You be gone by noon tomorrow, Morgan."

"You go to hell, Trainor."

"You've been warned, Drifter."

"And you heard my reply."

Trainor pushed away from the bar and walked out of the saloon, his men trooping out behind him.

Frank made no mention of it, but he had recognized one of the Circle Snake hands as a paid gun who sometimes went by the name Brooks. There certainly was no doubt in Frank's mind that Trainor was hiring gunfighters . . . but was that any concern of *his?*

"We need a town marshal, Morgan." Dr. Everett broke into Frank's thoughts.

"Sorry, Doc. I don't want the job. You have a telegraph here in town. Start sending wires around. You'll find a man for the job."

"We are a prosperous town, Morgan." Everett just wouldn't give up. "We could pay you well."

Frank smiled at that. "I really don't need the money, Doc." Frank carried several thousand dollars in paper and gold in a money belt. He also had money stashed away in a secret pocket in his saddle.

"So what I heard from some lawyer friends of mine over in Denver is true?"

"Depends on what you heard."

"That you're a rich man."

"I'm very comfortable."

"Yet you drift aimlessly."

"I like to see the country. While I still can. Won't be many more years before barbed wire will be strung up all over the place."

"I see. So you just drifted into this part of Montana?"

"Yes, as a matter of fact I did. I never dreamed anyplace like this was in this part of the territory."

"It's unique, Morgan. And so are the people. About ten or so miles farther on south, there is a colony, or settlement if you will, of Hutterites."

"A settlement of what?"

"Religious people. Nice folks, but they don't socialize much and they don't bear arms. At all."

"They'll be the first to go then, if or when the shooting starts."

"And that will be sad, for they're good people, model citizens. You'll know them when you see them . . . when they come to town. The men are dressed in suits and the women in dark dresses and scarves. Good people. I like them."

"Have any of them been harmed?"

"Not yet. But it's coming."

"I wish you lots of luck in dealing with this problem."

Dr. Everett smiled. "Well, to tell the truth, I was sort of hoping I could change your mind about leaving."

Frank shook his head. "It isn't my fight, Doctor."

"Well, if I don't see you again, best of luck, Drifter."

"Same to you."

Frank checked on Dog and Horse and then walked over to the hotel. He sat in a chair on the boardwalk in front of the hotel for a time, smoking and watching the town slowly shut down for the rapidly approaching night. A pretty little town, Frank thought. Probably filled with good, hardworking people, here and in the southern section of the valleys.

*But it isn't my fight and I don't want to get involved in it. I'll just keep . . . keep doing what, Frank? Drifting aimlessly?*

*Yeah.*

*Why? Wouldn't this be a nice place to settle down and build a home?*

*Probably.*

*Then?*

*I'd get myself involved in the middle of this damn war,* Frank realized, adding: *And I don't want any more trouble in my life.*

*That's a good reason to leave,* another silent inner voice said. *Just ride off and leave these good people at the not-so-*

*tender mercies of Colonel Trainor and the other ranchers in the valleys.*

"Damn!" Frank muttered, pushing himself out of the chair. He decided to take a walk around town; maybe that would clear his head. He looked across the street at the marshal's office and saw the old marshal standing out front. He'd go have a chat with the man.

The shadows were getting long as he stepped off the boardwalk and walked across the street. "Marshal," Frank said in greeting.

"Morgan," the marshal said. "Taking the air?"

"Yes. It's going to be a nice night. What is your name, Marshal? No one told me."

"Handlen."

"Been marshal long?"

"Too damn long. It's just a part-time job. I can't work the land no more so the people hung this badge on me and gave me a livable salary. My wife died some years back. No one but me to worry about."

"This job is likely to get dangerous before long."

"I know it. And I'm too damn old for a lot of rough stuff."

"I told the doc to start sending out wires to find a man for the job."

"So he didn't tell you?"

"Tell me what?"

"We've been trying to hire a new marshal for several months. No one wants to lock horns with Colonel Trainor."

"I see. What is Trainor's first name?"

"Colonel is all I ever heard."

"If he was a colonel in the war, he's got to be a few years older than me. I was in the war too."

"I think he's fifty. I've heard that a couple of times. Did the doc ask you if you wanted the marshal's job?"

"Yes. I told him no."

"I don't blame you. This end of the valley is filled with good people, but they're not fighters. They're farmers, and good ones too, but they're family men, with wives and kids to worry about. Most of them don't even own a pistol. I've never seen any carry one."

"And you've got that religious bunch."

"The Hutterites. Yes. Good hardworking folks. But they won't fight. They don't believe in it."

"Don't believe in defending themselves?"

"Don't believe in taking a human life."

Frank had heard of those types of religious people, but had never actually met any. Personally, he didn't believe that any-one would just stand by and let another person kill him or a loved one . . . unless he was some sort of a fool.

"Are there any ranchers in the north end of the valleys who want to live in peace?" Frank asked.

"Oh, sure. Most of the smaller spreads. But the Snake is the biggest spread and the colonel is the top dog. No one wants to buck him."

"What are some of the others?"

"The Lightning spread is just about as big as the Snake. It's owned by Ken Gilmar. The Diamond .45 is right up there too. It's owned by Don Bullard. Those are the big three. And all three men are greedy and mean as hell."

"And those three you named are gobbling up the smaller ranches."

"You got it. Just as fast as they can grab them."

"Nice bunch of men. Are they married, have families?"

"All of them. They've got a whole passel of kids."

"Do any of the wives or kids ever come to town? This town, I mean?"

"They used to. But now?" He shrugged his shoulders. "Not very often. Too much hard feelings on both sides for that."

"A couple of Snake riders came here today."

"Looking for trouble." Marshal Handlen smiled. "And they found it, didn't they?"

"One of them sure did."

"I'm going to make my early rounds, Morgan. Nice talking with you."

"See you around, Marshal." Frank watched as the marshal walked slowly away. An old man caught up in a really bad situation that was sure to get worse. "But it's none of my business," he muttered.

Frank walked around the small town until it was full dark, then decided to make one final check on Horse and Dog before heading back to the hotel and an early turn-in.

He was walking past an alley when he caught a glimpse of someone standing in the darkness. Frank tensed, his hand closing around the butt of his pistol.

"Stand still and listen and live or grab iron and die, Morgan," the voice said. "It's your choice."

# FOUR

"I'm standing easy," Frank said.

"Stay that way, Morgan. I'll do the talkin'."

"I'm listening."

"You done me a good turn once, way back years ago, down in Texas. It don't matter what my name is, or was back then. I ain't forgot the favor. Now it's my turn to do you a favor, and this is it. You listen up good."

Frank waited, standing in the mouth of the alley.

"There ain't nothin' but trouble for you here, Morgan. These valleys is fixin' to bust wide open with trouble."

"I know that," Frank said.

"Good that you do. I heared you was fixin' to pull out come mornin'. You do that. Ride out and don't look back."

"That's my plan."

"Good. 'Cause if you stay, them big ranchers up at the

north end is hirin' gunhawks. And you'll be in a world of trouble. They'll kill you, Morgan. You probably still 'bout the fastest man in the West with a short gun. But the odds will be stacked way agin' you in this fight. You understand what I'm sayin'?"

"Yes."

"And they's still big money on your head and some folks lookin' for revenge for things long done and over."

"I know that too."

"Then get out of this part of Montana, Morgan. Rattle your hocks, Drifter. This just ain't your fight. This ain't nothin' but a death trap waitin' to spring on you. Now, I done you a favor. We're even. I'm gone."

Frank heard a whisper of movement that quickly faded away.

He walked on past the alley and stepped up to the boardwalk. There he paused for a moment. Frank did not try to recall the favor the voice had mentioned. He had done a lot of favors for a lot of people over the years, everything from a simple handout for someone down on his luck to saving a life. Nor did he feel he would ever know the identity of the voice. Not that it really mattered, for if didn't.

Frank watched as the street lamps were being lighted. They cast a very pretty glow on the pleasant evening.

He walked over to the livery and once again checked on Horse and Dog, then returned to the hotel and went to bed. He planned to buy a packhorse, provision up, and be gone by midmorning.

Frank was jarred out of bed by the sounds of shouting in the street below his hotel room. The shouting increased in intensity. He lit the lamp and checked his watch. Four o'clock. He bathed his face and slicked his hair down, then dressed quickly, put on his hat, and buckled his gunbelt around his waist, stepping out into the hall.

"What's going on?" a sleepy traveling man dressed in a long nightshirt called from his open room door.

"Don't know," Frank replied. "But you'd better get some clothes on."

The door closed.

Frank walked down the stairs and into the dark lobby. He looked around, could find no one, and stepped out to the boardwalk. The street was rapidly filling up with men, in various stages of hurried dress.

"What's going on?" Frank asked a citizen.

"The Jefferson family," the citizen replied. "They been burned out. They're all dead. Killed by night riders."

"The bastards killed the kids too!" another citizen said, walking up. "Looks like the night riders set the house on fire and burned up the whole family."

*It's started,* Frank thought. *All hell's going to break loose now.*

"The Jeffersons had a little baby," the citizen said, slipping his galluses straps up on his shoulders. "'Bout five months old."

"The baby's dead too?" the other man asked.

"Burnt to a crisp, I was told."

"Who found them?" another man asked.

"A neighbor heard the shots. By the time he could get dressed and saddled up and get over there, it was too late. He couldn't do nothin' 'ceptin' watch it burn."

Frank moved on up the street, listening to the men talk. Handheld torchlights flickered up and down the street. By now a number of women had joined the crowd, and they were crying and kicking up a fuss. Frank stepped back and melted into the darkness as Preacher Philpot joined the milling crowd.

"It's time to fight!" the preacher shouted. "Gird your loins and pick up your sword and shield."

"We've got to do something!" a woman shouted. "Those murdering night riders will attack the town next."

Frank sat down on the edge of the boardwalk and rolled himself a smoke. What he really wanted was a hot cup of coffee, but the Blue Moon Cafe was still dark.

"Where is Marshal Handlen?" a man shouted.

"He rode out to the Jefferson place," someone called.

"Alone?"

"I reckon so."

"That ain't smart. Them night riders might be layin' for him."

Frank turned away and spotted the man who ran the livery stable. He walked over to him. "Can you rent me a good horse? Mine is tired and I don't like the idea of Marshal Handlen out by himself after all that's happened this night."

"That's a good idea. Come on. You can take mine. He's a good one."

Frank was gone in five minutes, after telling Dog to stay put and then getting directions from the livery owner out to the Jefferson place. The liveryman was sure right about his personal mount: He was a good one and liked to travel. Frank let him trot for a while and then slowed him down. He caught up with the old marshal several miles before the turnoff to the Jefferson farm.

"You mind some company, Marshal?"

"I'd welcome it. The folks in town send you out to look after me?"

"No. It was my own idea."

"You're not as ornery as folks make you out to be, Frank. There's a decent streak in you a yard wide."

"Don't let it get out, Marshal. It would ruin my reputation."

"I'll keep it to myself."

They both could smell the smoke long before they reached the burned-out farmhouse and barn . . . that and the unmistakable odor of seared human flesh.

"Takes some real lowlifes to do something like this," Handlen remarked.

"And a lower type to send them out to do it," Frank added.

"Agreed, and Colonel Trainor is definitely a low-life son of a bitch."

Frank glanced at the marshal. There had been considerable heat in the man's voice. "The colonel do you a wrong sometime?"

"Not really. He's just a no-good, that's all. I knew that first time I set eyes on him. Thinks he's better than anyone else. Come in here right after the war like some sort of hero, expecting everyone to bow down and lick his boots. A few did, most didn't. I was one who told him to go right straight to hell." Handlen smiled. "'Course I was some younger then. He hasn't cared much for me since that time."

"Were you in the war, Marshal?"

"No. I came West before the war started. Me and the wife and kids. The war had been going on for a year or more before we knew anything about it. We were too busy fighting Indians anyway. It was wild out here back then. Town was mostly burned down twice."

"Where are your kids?"

"All of them went back East soon as they was old enough. The West wasn't for them. Too hard a life, I reckon. I haven't seen any of them in years. Wouldn't know any of them now if I was to come face-to-face with them."

"That's sad."

"In a way, yes. But you got to believe that everything is done for a reason. Those kids didn't have what it took to live out here." He pointed. "There's lights up ahead. That would be Phil Wilson probably. Jeffersons' nearest neighbor."

"Farmer?"

"Yes. Has a small connecting ranch too. Nice fellow. Real pretty wife and several kids. There's a story behind the two oldest kids. I'll tell it to you sometime."

"Marshal," Wilson greeted them. "It's still too hot to try to find the bodies. It's pretty bad. Horses was burned up too." He looked at Frank in the lantern light.

"This here is Frank Morgan, Phil. He's just passing through this area and agreed to help me this awful night."

"Nice of you," Phil said, glancing at Frank. "Come on. But there isn't much left 'ceptin' ashes." Phil started to walk on, then paused and turned around to face the two men. "*Frank Morgan?*"

"That's right," Frank told him.

"But you're a . . ." Phil let that trail off into the silent darkness.

"He's all right," Marshal Handlen said. "Lead on, Phil."

As the men drew closer, the smell of burned human flesh grew stronger in the night air.

"They burned everything," the marshal said, then looked over at what remained of the barn. "Those poor animals."

"I'll look for tracks," Frank said. "Might find a hoofprint that stands out."

"I'll help," Handlen said. "Nothing else we can do."

"It's going to be several hours before we can try to retrieve what's left of the bodies," Frank said. "You live far from here, Phil?"

"Just a hop, skip, and a jump, Mr. Morgan."

"You reckon your wife could make up a big pot of coffee?"

"She sure could. Be glad to. I'll ride on over and get it going."

"It'll give him something to do," Frank said when the farmer had ridden away. "And one less person stomping around."

"It's still too dark to see very good," Handlen said.

"Be light enough in a few minutes," Frank told him. "Let's hold off until then."

"That smell is gonna make me sick, Frank."

"Wash your face with water out of your canteen. That might help."

"You're not feeling sick?"

"No. I've smelled it before."

"I have too. But that was years ago, after a band of bucks burned out a farmer way north of here."

"Before the ranchers moved in?"

"Oh, yeah. These connecting valleys used to be all farms. Colonel Trainor and his men came in and the farmers began being forced out. About ten years ago we made the crossroads the line. I knew it would be only a matter of time before the big ranchers would start something like this."

"And now it's happened."

"Yes."

The dawning came slowly, pushing the night away, and Frank began a slow circling of the ruins of the farmhouse and barn. He finally found a track he could identify if he ever saw it again. He pointed it out to Marshal Handlen.

"It's a big horse, carrying a big man, looks like to me," Handlen said. "And it's got a strange mark on that right front shoe."

"And the riders all headed back north."

"That goes without saying," Handlen said dryly.

"Here comes a wagon," Frank said, standing up.

Handlen squinted into the early morning light. "Phil and his wife, Julie. She's about the best-lookin' woman in this area. Thank God they left their kids to home."

Frank stared hard as the wagon drew nearer. "She doesn't look old enough to have many kids."

"They have three. Twins, a boy and a girl, 'bout fourteen or fifteen, and a younger girl, 'bout eight or nine. I reckon Julie's 'bout thirty-five. But you're right: she don't look it."

"Phil's some older, seems like."

"Yes. He's in his mid-forties. They come out here when the twins was just babies. He's a good farmer and a good father. But those twins . . ." He shook his head. "I'll tell you about them later on. It's a story."

The couple got down from the wagon seat, and Julie pulled a big pot of coffee from the bed of the wagon while Phil got the tin cups.

"It's still plenty hot," Phil said. "And Julie had just made some biscuits. I brung butter and honey."

"Sounds good," Frank said.

"This here is Frank Morgan, Julie."

Julie put her blue eyes on Frank and smiled. "Pleasure to meet you, Mr. Morgan."

"Frank, please. That coffee smells good."

"I'll put the biscuits and the butter in the back of the wagon," Julie said. "Help yourselves whenever you like." She waved a hand in front of her nose. "But that smell is really awfully bad. Is that? . . ."

"Yes," Frank told her. "The Jefferson family."

"What a terrible thing."

"Yes, ma'am. It really is." Frank poured himself a cup of coffee and went over to a tree and squatted down. He rolled a cigarette and enjoyed a quiet smoke while sipping his cup of really good coffee.

Julie came over and sat down on the ground beside him.

"You'll get your dress all dirty," Frank said.

"It's just an old thing I wear when I'm doing chores."

"Looks pretty to me."

"Thank you, sir. Are you really Frank Morgan the famous gunfighter?"

"I guess so, Julie. But the title of gunfighter was never something I wanted."

"I've read a number of books and articles about you. A lot of the articles made you out to be a vicious killer."

Frank smiled. "Well . . . I hope now that you've met me you can see I don't quite fit that role."

She laughed and tossed her blond curls. "I do, Mr. Morgan."

"Frank?" Marshal Handlen called. "I got some shovels out of the shed. It wasn't burned that bad. You want to try to find the bodies?"

Frank stood up. "Be right there, Marshal." He looked at Julie. "You might not want to see this, Miss Julie. It'll be pretty grim."

"You're right," she said, holding out a hand for Frank to help her up. "I'd better get back and see to the kids. They have chores to do." She stood up and stood very close to Frank. Close enough to make Frank sort of uncomfortable, for Julie was a very well endowed woman. "And you know kids: they can find all sorts of ways to shirk their chores."

"Yes," Frank said. "I was the same way when I was a kid." Frank stood looking at her for a moment. Julie Wilson was really a beautiful woman. Smelled good too. He was reluctant to release her hand, and didn't until Marshal Handlen called again for him.

"Come on, Frank. I spotted the bodies."

"Be right there, Marshal."

"I hope I see you again, Mr. Morgan," Julie said. "And my children would be just thrilled to meet you."

"Perhaps we'll see each other again, Miss Julie."

"Bye, Mr. Morgan."

Frank walked over to the ruins of the house and picked up one of the shovels Handlen had found.

"Right over there," Phil Wilson said, pointing to a spot in the ashes and still-smouldering rubble.

"Let's do it," Frank said.

# FIVE

The bodies were finally dug out—the entire family and the dog. The smell was awful, and the men had to stop several times to bathe their faces in cold well water to refresh themselves. Wilson and Marshal Handlen both got sick, and had to stop and vomit when the body of Mrs. Jefferson literally fell apart while they were picking it up. Frank dragged the several sections of the woman to the side of the burned-out house and covered the pieces with a blanket.

"I hope to God I never see anything like that again," Wilson said.

"I hope the men who did this burn in hell forever," Handlen said, wiping the sweat from his forehead. "Goddamn them all to the hellfires."

"Mount up and go get your wagon, Phil," Frank said. "We'll load them up and take them into town for burial."

"Good idea," the farmer said. "I'll be back in a few minutes."

"Go with him, Marshal," Frank said softly. "I'll wrap the bodies in that old sacking you found in the shed."

"You don't mind, Frank?"

"I've seen worse, Marshal. Much worse."

"We'll be back as soon as possible."

"Take your time. I'm going to take mine in doing this, believe me."

Handlen gave him a wan smile and walked to his horse and mounted up, following Wilson back to his farm.

Frank gathered up the raggedy blankets and sacking from the shed and went to work. He almost lost his biscuits and coffee several times, but managed to get the job done just as the Wilson wagon came rattling up the road, Handlen riding along beside the wagon.

"I'm sure glad you left your wife at home," Frank told the farmer. "This is not something she should see."

"That's what I told her," Phil said. "Then we had sort of a fuss about it. She will be coming into town later on. Riding with some of our neighbors. Several of the older boys and girls in the area will keep all the kids safe."

"Word's already gone out through the south end of the valleys," Handlen said. "They'll be a big town meeting tonight."

"Better leave some men behind with the kids," Frank cautioned. "Men who know how to use guns."

"Good idea," Phil said. "I'll see to it personal."

The men loaded the burned bodies in the bed of the wagon, and Wilson and Marshal Handlen made ready to head back to town.

"Coming with us?" Handlen asked Frank.

"Not yet. I'll be a few minutes behind you," Frank told him. "I'm going to look around a little more."

Frank slowly circled the cleared area around the burned house and barn, and found a couple more hoofprints that stood out from the others. He would be able to recognize them if he ever saw them again. There was nothing else for him to do, so he mounted up and headed back to town, catching up with Handlen and Wilson a few miles later.

They met half a dozen farm families standing solemnly by the road as they rolled along toward town. The men and women didn't say a word, just stood silently and watched as the death wagon rolled past, the men standing with hats in hand.

Wilson pulled the wagon behind the undertaker's office. Frank headed back to the hotel to wash up and get the smell of death off him, then shave and get into some clean clothes.

"They all dead, Mr. Morgan?" the desk clerk asked.

"All dead," Frank said. "Including the dog and some of the horses."

"Damn!" the clerk whispered.

"Get some hot water up to my room, please," Frank requested.

"Yes, sir. Right away."

A half hour later Frank was cleaned up, packed up, and ready to go. He figured Horse would be rested enough for the trail and Dog would be ready to go. Now all he had to do was buy a packhorse and packsaddle, provision up, and get moving. He stopped by the cafe and bought a half dozen biscuits for Dog.

Dog was glad to see him and the biscuits, and Horse looked fit and trail-ready. The liveryman did not question Frank about the Jefferson family, sensing that Frank did not want to talk about that morning's events. Frank bought a packhorse and then walked over to the general store for supplies. He bought coffee, beans, salt, bacon, potatoes, flour, and cartridges for pistol and rifle. Back at the livery, he paid his bill, then packed up and was ready to swing into the saddle.

"You're not going to stay with us, Mr. Morgan?" the liveryman asked.

"No."

"Heaven's a nice town."

"Yes, it is. Very pleasant."

"Be a nice place to settle down in."

"I've sure seen a lot worse."

"Maybe you'll come back."

"Might do that."

Frank mounted up and headed out without another word. People gathered on the boardwalk on both sides of the street to watch the gunfighter ride out. A few raised their hands in fare-well, including Marshal Handlen.

"Come back and see us, Frank," the marshal called.

Frank touched the brim of his hat in reply and headed for the crossroads, putting the town of Heaven behind him. There was nothing else for him here. Nothing else for him to do . . . except get involved in a war, and that was not something he wanted.

He looked down at Dog, padding along beside him. "Let's go see some country, Dog."


Weeks later found Frank in the copper and gold mining town of Butte. The town was wide-open and roaring, with dozens of saloons that stayed open around the clock. Painted-up soiled doves were hanging out of windows above the saloons and in homes with a red lantern on the front porch, inviting any and all to come sample their wares.

Frank was camped on the edge of town, since there were no hotel rooms to be had at any price. But that was all right with Frank, for he didn't plan to spend much time in the town; just long enough to buy supplies and then get away from all the smoke and noise and hustle and bustle of too damn many people. Frank had found a couple of very nice families who were opening businesses in Butte. Due to the housing shortage, both families were living in and under their wagons until houses could be built for them. The women and kids agreed to look after Dog while Frank went into town for a bath, a haircut, and supplies.

"And new boots," Frank reminded himself as he rode into town. His old boots were literally coming apart on his feet, and Frank decided to treat himself to a new pair, and a new hat as well.

"Might as well," he muttered. "I can damn sure afford it."

Frank bought his supplies, told the clerk he'd be back for them, then toted a sack full of dirty clothes over to a laundry. He had himself a shave, a haircut, and a bath, dressed in clean long handles, jeans, and shirt, then went in search of a boot and hat shop. He bought new boots and a new Stetson. He felt like a brand-new man as he walked over to a saloon to have a drink before he found a cafe and had something to eat.

The saloon had plenty of customers but there was room at the long bar, and Frank bellied up and ordered a whiskey— the first drink of whiskey he'd had in weeks—and listened to the gossip around him. It was mostly about mining, and Frank paid no attention. Then he heard his name mentioned and he perked up and listened.

"I heard some big rancher down some south and east here run Frank Morgan out," a man said.

"Do tell?" his drinking companion said.

"Yes, sir, he did. Man by the name of Colonel Trainor. Runs the Circle Snake spread. Made ol' Frank Morgan tuck his tail 'tween his legs and run, he did."

"Where'd you hear that?"

"Some cowboy passin' through yesterday. Seems this Trainor feller is hirin' guns for his spread. Payin' big money too. Gonna run all the farmers and sheep herders out of the valley."

"Hard to believe that Frank Morgan would run from anybody."

"Well, hell . . . Frank's gettin' old, I reckon."

" 'Bout forty-five, so I understand from an article I read once. That ain't old."

"Maybe he just lost his nerve. It happens, you know."

Frank smiled into his shot glass. The rumor came as no surprise to him. Others like Trainor, full of arrogance and self-importance, had made the same type of claim against other men. A few, a very few, had laid those remarks on Frank in the past. Frank had always ignored them. But this time the charge of cowardice rankled in him. Perhaps it was because he had taken such an instant dislike to Colonel Trainor.

"I'd like to run into that damn Morgan!" another voice shouted, rising above the crowd of men at the end of the bar.

"Oh, hell, Rob," a man said. "What do you think you'd do if you did see him? You think you'd maybe crowd him into a fight?"

"Damn right I would," Rob said. "I'm tired of reading all them books and newspaper stories about him. I want to see firsthand if he's got the backbone to face a really fast gun."

"Like you, Rob?" yet another citizen asked.

"Yes, sir, just like me. I'm the fastest gun in these parts and you all know it. Anybody here want to say I ain't?"

Frank was hemmed in by the crowd at the other end of the

bar. If he tried to leave, this punk Rob might recognize him and call his hand. Frank decided to nurse his drink and try to blend in with the crowd around him.

"Ain't nobody callin' you nothin', Rob," a man said. "We're just tryin' to relax and have a drink, that's all."

"Fine," Rob said, an edge of anger in his voice. "Gimmie another beer, Jake."

"Comin' right up, Rob," the bartender called. "Keep your pants on."

"Yeah, please do that!" a burly man dressed in dusty miner's clothing said with a laugh.

"Who said that?" Rob yelled amid all the sudden and raucous laughter from others in the saloon.

*Damn!* Frank thought. *The crowd is going to make this fellow mad, and that's the wrong thing to do at this time.*

Frank took a tiny sip of his drink.

The barkeep slid a foamy mug of beer down the bar toward Rob.

"I wonder how much this Trainor guy is payin'," Rob tossed out. "If the money's right, I might take me a ride down there and sign on."

"Then you're not goin' to run into Frank Morgan, Rob," a drinker said. "Not if this Trainor run him off."

"Oh, hell," Rob replied. "Frank Morgan's probably in Texas by now, runnin' like a scared rabbit."

"I wouldn't count on that, boy," a voice called from a table close to the door.

"Oh?" Rob turned to face the man. "How come you say that?"

"Morgan ain't never run from no one in his life, that's how come. This Colonel Trainor is just blowin' smoke, that's all."

"You know Frank Morgan?" Rob asked.

"I seen him a time or two, yeah."

"What's he look like?" Rob laughed. "Raggedy and gray-headed and probably a damn drunk too?"

"I wouldn't say that," the man replied. "But was I you, I'd back off with the mouth some. Frank just might hear about your comments and come here and make you eat them."

"Huh?" Rob yelled. "If he ever come to Butte, I'd kick his ass from one end of town to the other."

"I'd give a hundred dollars to see you try that, Rob!" a patron said.

"I wouldn't try," Rob said. "I'd do it."

The saloon customers all burst into laughter at that.

"By God, I would!"

That brought even more laughter.

Rob turned around and picked up his beer, all the while muttering vile obscenities. "I ever run into Morgan," Rob whispered, "I'll show all of you. I swear I will."

Frank waved to the bartender for another shot of whiskey. The barkeep walked down, filled his glass, and then locked eyes with Frank. His mouth dropped open as his eyes widened with sudden recognition. "Jesus Christ!" he muttered.

"Keep it to yourself," Frank told him in a low voice. "I'm not looking for any trouble."

But his words came too late. Jake stepped back and stared at the West's most famous gunfighter for a few seconds. "My God, boys!" he hollered. "It's him. He's here. Right in this saloon."

"Who's here?" someone called.

"Who's him?" another yelled.

*"Frank Morgan!"* Jake shouted. "Standin' right in front of me at this bar."

The men on both sides of Frank suddenly moved to one side in a hurry. The men standing by Rob did the same. Only the long, empty expanse of bar was now between the gun-fighter and the bigmouth.

Frank sipped his whiskey and stared straight ahead.

"Well, there he is, Rob," a man called. "Poor old gray-headed, raggedy Frank Morgan." He began to laugh. "Are you drunk and shaking in your boots, Mr. Morgan?"

"Not likely," Frank said softly.

"Well, I think you're a coward," Rob said. "What do you think about that, Morgan?"

"I think you ought to run back home and get your mama to change your diaper and tuck you into your little bed," Frank said, turning to face Rob. "Either that, or shut your goddamn flapping mouth."

# SIX

Frank began to walk slowly toward Rob. The young man backed up a few steps.

"Now you hold it right there, Morgan!" Rob said.

"Or you'll do what?" Frank challenged him.

"I'll have to deal hard with you, that's what."

Frank took another step. "All right, Rob. Shuffle the cards and deal."

"I mean it, Morgan."

Another step from Frank. Another step back from Rob. The saloon patrons were silent, watching, with only a few men whispering.

"Is that really Frank Morgan?"

"Damn sure is. Now shut up."

"I don't want to have to hurt you, Morgan!" Rob said. "But by God, I will if you don't hold it right there."

Frank took another step. "I'd hate for you to try to hurt me, Rob. Because if you try that, I'm going to take those guns off you and beat you half to death with them."

"I'd like to see that," a man said.

Rob was scared and sweating as he backed up another step. Frank Morgan didn't look anything like Rob had imagined he would. Frank Morgan looked big and powerful and just plain mean.

"Take off those guns, boy," Frank said.

"Do what?"

"I said take off those guns. Lay them on the bar and walk out of here."

"I ain't gonna do no damn such of a thing!"

"You're mighty young to have to die." Frank's words were spoken with a touch of ice in his tone.

"Die?" Rob questioned. "No, not me, Morgan. You don't stop pushin' me, I'm gonna have to draw on you. I mean it."

"I hope you don't drag iron on me, Rob. 'Cause if you do, it's going to be the last thing you ever do on this earth. Now take off those guns and lay them on the bar."

"You go to hell, Morgan!"

Frank took another step.

"Morgan! Stop it."

"Think about death, boy," Frank told him. "Give it some hard thought. Dead is forever, boy. Do you realize that?"

"Huh? You the one who's gonna be dead, Morgan. I'm fast, man. I'm the fastest gunslick in this part of Montana."

"But you're not fast enough, Rob. Believe me, you're not."

Frank took another step forward. Rob took another step backward.

"I don't think the boy's got enough grit in his craw to jerk iron," someone said from the crowd.

"Shut up," Frank told the unknown voice. "Unless you want to step up here and take Rob's place."

The man had nothing to say in reply to that.

Frank started walking toward Rob.

"Now you just hold on!" Rob yelled, the blood draining from his face. Sweat was dripping from his forehead.

Frank didn't stop until he had backed the young would-be gunfighter up against the wall. Then Frank slapped him open-handed, twice across the face.

"What? . . ." Rob gasped. "Why are you doin' this to me? I ain't never done you no hurt."

Frank reached down and tore the gunbelt from Rob's waist, jerking so hard he broke the buckle. He tossed the rig onto the bar.

"You put gunfighting out of your mind, boy," Frank told him. "You're not a gunhand and never will be. And that's a good thing. You'll live a lot longer."

"You . . ." Rob sputtered.

"Shut up and listen to me," Frank said sharply. "You go be a cowboy or a farmer or run a store or sell ladies' corsets or men's hats. But you put gun-handling out of your mind. You hear me?"

"Yes, sir," Rob said meekly.

"You come back in here tomorrow, sometime after I'm gone, and pick up your guns and sell them or store them away in a trunk. But don't wear them. Somebody will kill you if you do. Understand?"

"Yes, sir."

"Fine. Now get out of here."

Rob hit the boards without looking back.

Frank walked back down the bar and picked up his drink.

"Good advice you give that young feller, Mr. Morgan," Jake said. "His smart mouth was sure gonna get him hurt."

"He'll be all right," Frank replied. "As long as he leaves those guns alone. I wish somebody had done that to me when I was his age . . . or younger."

"You gonna be in town long?"

"I'll be pulling out come the morning."

"Town could sure use a lawman like you."

"Not interested. Thanks just the same."

"Why didn't you just kill the loudmouth, Morgan?" The question was thrown out from a group of men sitting at a table.

Frank turned from the bar. "Because it wasn't necessary."

"Too bad," the unidentified man said. "I really wanted to see just how fast you are."

Frank chose to ignore the questioner and turned back to the bar, picking up his drink and taking a sip. But he picked up the shot glass with his left hand, leaving his right hand free. There was something in the man's voice that was troubling. Frank had a hunch the man just might be looking for trouble.

Behind him, Frank heard the sounds of chairs being pushed back. He finished his drink and set the empty glass on the bar.

"Turn around, Morgan," the man said.

"I can hear you," Frank said.

"I said turn around, you bastard!"

Frank turned around. The man was standing up, facing him, maybe thirty feet away. He was dressed all in black. The men who had been seated at tables close by had moved away. "If you have a problem with me, mister, state it," Frank said. "But don't call me names."

"Yeah, I got a problem, Morgan. And I'll call you anything I damn well please."

"Mister, you're about to buy into a high-stakes game here. And I don't know why. You want to tell me?"

"You know."

Frank sighed. He hated those kinds of answers. If he knew what the problem was, he wouldn't be asking. "No, I don't know, mister. If I knew, I wouldn't have asked."

"You and me, we got a debt between us."

"I owe you money? I don't think so."

"You owe me a life."

"How do you figure that?"

"My older brother."

"You're not giving me much to go on. What's his name?"

"His name was Guy. Guy Perkins."

"I don't recall ever meeting anyone by that name."

The man in black laughed bitterly. "I guess you don't, since you shot him down in cold blood."

"You want to explain that?"

"It was in Arizona. Down along the border. At a tradin' post near Fort Huachuca."

"I was there, years ago." Frank shook his head. "But I don't recall any trouble. You sure you got the right man?"

"I'm sure."

There was no talk among the saloon's many patrons. The men were all silent, listening and watching intently.

"You got the wrong man, mister," Frank told him.

"Time for you to pay for killin' my brother, Morgan. I been lookin' all over for you for years. Now you pay your debt."

Frank suddenly was weary of the talk. He had been wrongly blamed for a hundred deaths over the years . . . probably more than that. And it was certainly possible this man in black didn't even have a brother. He was just looking for a name.

"You ready, Morgan?"

"I guess so," Frank replied. "But I'm not looking forward to killing a man for no good reason."

"You killed my brother, damn you!"

"I don't think so. I think you're just a damn fool looking to make a name for himself. And I'm not going to draw on you."

"Stand real still, mister," a voice said from the entrance to the bar. "You, all dressed in black. Don't move a muscle or I'll cut you in half with this shotgun."

Frank shifted his gaze for just a second. A man wearing a badge on his shirt was standing near the batwings, a sawed-off shotgun in his hand, the barrels pointed at the man in black.

"I ain't done nothing, Marshal," the black-dressed man said.

"You were just about to get yourself killed, that's what you were about to do. And if that's what you want to do, go somewhere else to do it."

"This bastard killed my brother, Marshal!"

"Did you, Morgan?" the marshal asked.

"Not to my knowledge."

"That's good enough for me. You take off that gunbelt, mister. Lay it on the table."

"The hell I will," the man said.

"You'll be dead if you don't," the marshal said coldly, then eared back both hammers on the Greener.

The man in black slowly unbuckled his gunbelt and laid it on the table. "What now, Marshal?"

"Back up, away from the table. All the way to the back of the saloon. Then you sit down, both hands on the table."

The man backed up and carefully made his way to the rear of the saloon. He sat down and put both hands on the table.

"Now you stay there." The marshal cut his eyes to Frank. "How long are you going to be in town, Morgan?"

"I plan on pulling out first thing in the morning, Marshal."

"Good. I'll make sure that young punk Rob and this stranger here don't follow you out."

"I appreciate that. Rob's guns are over here on the bar."

"They can stay there until they rust, far as I'm concerned."

"That would be best, I'm thinking. All right, Marshal," Frank said. "I'm going. Thanks for your help."

"Don't mention it. Have a good trip."

Frank walked out of the saloon and headed for the general store. He picked up his supplies and carried them to the livery, telling the liveryman to keep an eye on them. The woman who ran the laundry said his clothes wouldn't be ready for several more hours. Frank walked over to a cafe and had a good meal, lingering long over several cups of coffee. The news that Frank Morgan was in town had spread fast, and dozens of people walked past the cafe for a looksee at the famous gunfighter. Frank finally got tired of it and went back to the livery. The crowds of curious followed him over there. Frank finally said to hell with it, went back to the general store, and bought a couple of new outfits and rode out of town, avoiding the main street as he did. Early the next morning, he left Butte for good, just wandering.

A month later, Frank was on the Montana/Wyoming border, buying coffee and bacon at a general store in a tiny town. He wasn't certain if he was in Montana or Wyoming and wasn't interested enough to ask.

Frank's appearance was rough after a month on the trail. He was dusty and hadn't shaved for several days. He looked like a drifting out-of-work puncher.

"Headin' up north a ways, are you?" the clerk asked after Frank had placed his order.

"Beg pardon?" Frank said.

"I'm told several ranchers up north and west a ways is hirin' men. Thought you might be headin' that way, that's all."

"I'm just drifting. No place in particular in mind."

"Seein' the country, are you?"

"That's right."

"Well, if you're not lookin' for work, I'd fight shy of that area I mentioned. Goin' be trouble aplenty up there 'fore long."

"Oh?"

"Yep. Ranchers and farmers."

"Where is this place?"

"North and some west of here. Two towns named Heaven and Hell, of all things. Farmers' town is called Heaven. Ranchers' town is Hell. It'd be funny if people weren't gettin' killed."

"Who's winning the fight so far?"

"No one yet. But the farmers will lose. You can bet on that."

"The law's on their side, isn't it?"

"Law? No law up there to speak of. The county sheriff is fifty or seventy-five miles away. And he's probably in this Colonel Trainor's pocket. Trainor owns the Circle Snake brand. Big moneyman. He's hirin' any man who wants to make some good money and ain't particular how he uses his gun."

"Sounds like a good place to stay clear of."

"You bet it is."

Frank paid for his supplies and asked where the nearest telegraph office was located.

"'Bout twenty-five miles north of here. Just follow this road," he said, pointing. "Take you right to it."

"Is there a hotel in that town?"

"Rooms for rent over the saloon is all."

"That'll do. Thanks."

Frank headed north. He had some wires to send to his attorneys in Denver. And he had an idea too. He was tired of drifting. Maybe Heaven would be a good place to settle down in.

# SEVEN

Frank reined up at the burned-out ruins of the Jefferson place and swung down from the saddle. He stretched for a moment, then walked around. "Well, Dog, what do you think about it? I think it'll be a right nice place once we get the cabin up."

Dog looked at him and wagged his tail in agreement.

"You want to stay here or ride into town with me?"

Dog walked to the shed out back of the house and lay down.

"All right. I guess that answers that. I'll get you a pail of water 'fore I go."

Frank found an old bucket and filled it with water from the well. The corral was still up, and Frank made sure the water trough had water in it, then put his packhorse in the corral. He pulled several handfuls of grass and hand-fed the packhorse. "I'll bring you back some hay, girl," he said. "If I can arrange for a wagon and team, that is. If not, I'll bring a bag of oats." He walked over to the shed and told Dog, "You stay put."

Dog growled.

"I mean it, boy. Stay put."

Frank rode toward the town of Heaven. He had already been to the county seat and signed all the papers his lawyers had sent to a lawyer there. The old Jefferson place was his. Hundreds of acres of prime farm and grazing land, with good water aplenty. And just to be ornery about it, and to be perfectly honest, to further irritate Trainor, Frank had bought several hundred acres both east and west of his new property.

As he approached the cutoff to the Wilson farm, a wagon came rattling out driven by Julie, with a young girl, maybe eight or so, sitting beside her. Frank caught up with the wagon and Julie reined up.

"Mr. Morgan," she said. "I never thought I would see you again."

"Like a bad penny, Miss Julie, I came back."

"I'm so glad you did. I guess, ah, you haven't heard what happened since you've been gone, have you?"

"Just that Trainor is hiring a lot of gunhands."

"Phil was killed about a week after you left."

"Phil? Your husband?"

"Yes."

"How?"

"A couple of Snake riders goaded him into a fight. One of them knocked him down and Phil hit his head on a rock. His skull was fractured. He died a few days later. He never regained consciousness."

"I . . . I'm sorry. What happened to the Snake riders?"

"Nothing. Both of Trainor's men said Phil started the

fight and they were only protecting themselves. Which is a lie, of course, but . . ." She shrugged her shoulders. "The sheriff is in Trainor's pocket."

"Are you making out all right?"

"I guess. I hired a fellow to help bring in the crops this fall. And Phil Junior and Katie and I can work the garden and put up the vegetables."

"How about the cattle Phil was running?"

"They've been pretty much on their own, I'm sorry to say."

"I can take care of them, since we're going to be neighbors."

"Neighbors?"

"I bought the Jefferson place."

"Frank! That's wonderful!"

"I think it's a good investment."

"You can come over for dinner then."

"I'd like that, Julie. I sure would."

"How about sometime this week?"

"That would be fine. Come on, I'll ride with you into town. But first, who's that beautiful young lady sitting next to you?"

The young girl blushed and Julie said, "This is my youngest, Shelley. This is Mr. Morgan, baby."

"How are you, sir?" the girl asked very politely.

"I'm doing well, Shelley. Tell you what. When we get to town, I'll buy you some candy and a sarsaparilla. Would you like that?"

"Yes, sir!"

"It's a deal then. Come on."

Frank rode alongside the wagon to town, he and Julie chatting. Frank had been gone from the area for several months and a lot had occurred during his absence.

"Colonel Trainor and Don Bullard—he owns the Diamond .45—and Ken Gilmar—he owns the Lightning spread—have been hiring gunfighters. They say they're cowboys, but everyone knows they're not. Trainor has about thirty new men now working for him, and the others have hired about twenty each."

"That's in addition to their regular hands?"

"Yes."

Frank whistled softly. "That's costing them a lot of money each month. How can they afford it?"

"They're all rich men. All of them have stock in the mines up in Butte and they're making more money than they know what to do with."

"And Phil is sweet on Betty Lou Gilmar and Katie's stuck on Donnie Bullard," Shelley blurted out.

"You hush now!" Julie told her.

"But it's true, Mama!"

"That don't make no nevermind. Just be quiet about it."

"Yes, ma'am."

"Are there good carpenters in town?" Frank asked, quickly changing the subject.

"Oh, yes. Several of them. They do good work."

"I'll need them. I can do rough work, but I'm no skilled house builder."

"Phil Junior can help," Shelley said. "He used to help Daddy build things."

"He can't do much," Julie said.

"Anything would be a help," said Frank. "I'd sure pay him."

"I'll tell him. He needs to be around a man who will make him watch his p's and q's."

Frank laughed at that. "I'm not much good at that. Don't have any experience with kids."

"You were never married, Frank?"

"Yes, I was. Right after the war. But we separated before my son was born. I didn't even know I had a son until last year. He doesn't have much use for me, I'm afraid."

"That's sad."

"It's life, Julie. You got to be ready for the thorns along with the roses."

"You have a poetic streak in you, Frank."

"First time anyone ever said that to me."

Conversation came to a halt at the sound of several men riding up behind them. "Mama," Shelley said. "It's that awful Wells Langford and his men."

"Who is Wells Langford?" Frank asked, taking a quick look behind him at the six mounted men.

"The Diamond .45 foreman," Julie said. "He's killed several men in gunfights. He's a really dreadful person."

"And the men with him?"

"I don't know them," Julie said, looking behind her.

The Diamond .45 hands reined up alongside Frank and the wagon.

"Got you a new hand, Mrs. Wilson?" Wells asked, giving Frank a quick visual once-over. From the expression on his face, he didn't much like what he saw.

"A friend of mine, Mr. Langford," Julie said stiffly.

"Where did you come from and who the hell are you?" Wells asked Frank in a very demanding tone.

"Watch your mouth around the ladies," Frank said.

"Or you'll do what, mister?" Wells asked.

"Close it for you . . . permanently."

That shut Langford's mouth for a few seconds. He stared at Frank. "You must think you're really something, cowboy!"

"He is," one of the other .45 hands said. "That's Frank Morgan, Wells."

Frank cut his eyes to the hand who had identified him. He

knew him. A bad one who went by the name of Davis. "Haven't seen you in a long time, Davis."

"About five years or so, Morgan. Since that night you killed my saddle pard down in Colorado."

"He needed killing."

"He shouldn't have braced you, that's a fact. You didn't start it. But he'd had a few drinks too many."

"That's no excuse, Davis."

Davis had nothing to add to that.

"I thought Colonel Trainor told you to get out of this area and stay out, Morgan," Langford said.

"I don't take orders from Trainor," Frank replied. "Or from anyone else, for that matter."

"What brought you back, Morgan?"

"I like the people . . . those that live in the south end of the valleys, that is."

"These valleys belong to the ranchers, Morgan. And that's a hard fact."

"That's nonsense, Langford. And courts have said as much. The farmers are here to stay and you'd better get used to it."

"When hell freezes over, Morgan."

"Hell can't freeze," Shelley piped up. "It's too hot down there."

Julie smiled at her daughter's words and said nothing.

"Let's get to town, boys," the Diamond .45 foreman said, and spurred his horse.

The men rode ahead, leaving a cloud of dust behind them.

Julie and Shelley fanned themselves until the dust cloud dissipated. "I don't like that man," Julie said.

"I can certainly see why," Frank replied. "Let's get to town, ladies. I'll buy you both a sarsaparilla."

# EIGHT

When the wagon, with Frank riding alongside, rolled into town, a lot of heads turned to gawk and whisper.

"The rumor mill has started," Frank said.

"Let them talk," Julie said. "It'll take their minds off of the big trouble."

Frank reined up in the front of the store and went inside, while Julie pulled around to the rear of the general store and backed the wagon up to the loading dock. He bought Shelley some hard candy and a bottle of sarsaparilla, and then went in search of a wagon and team he could rent or buy. He found a wagon and team at the livery and arranged for its purchase. He told the liveryman to get the team into harness, he'd be back.

He walked back over to the general store and started buying the basic supplies he figured he'd need until the house was built. Then he went to the bank and deposited several large bank drafts. Frank was suddenly Mr. Morgan to Banker Simmons. He then went looking for the carpenters Julie had told him about. After speaking with them, he set up a line of credit at the sawmill.

"You going to farm, Mr. Morgan?" the sawmill owner asked.

"I'll plant some wheat and corn and oats, for sure."

"You'll need farmin' implements."

"When the time comes, I'll get them."

"And a good mule or two."

"I'm sure you'll be able to get them for me," Frank said dryly.

"You just say the word."

Smiling, Frank went back to the general store to check on Julie and Shelley. He wanted to convoy back with them. It seemed to him that they were looking at every item in the store . . . and buying very little. Julie said they'd be ready to go in about an hour. Frank walked over to the saloon to listen to the gossip. He wasn't in the mood for hard liquor or a beer, so he ordered coffee. The .45 crew was there, sprawled all around two tables, halfheartedly playing penny-ante poker. Frank ignored them.

"The famous Frank Morgan," the foreman of the .45 spread said in a sneering tone of voice. "Gonna be a sodbuster now. You gonna raise sheep too, Morgan?"

Frank did not turn around. He sipped his coffee and smiled.

"I'm talkin' to you, Morgan!"

Frank knew he should just walk away from this. But running away was not something that set well with Frank Morgan. He set his coffee cup on the bar and turned around to face the .45 crew. "What brings you boys to this end of the valley, Langford?"

"It's a free country, Morgan. Ain't it?"

"So I'm told."

"'Sides, we like to come down here. It's a nice friendly town."

"Unlike the town at the north end?"

Langford frowned. "There ain't nothin' wrong with Hell." Then he scowled at his own words.

Frank laughed. "I bet the preachers in your town would disagree with that, Wells."

"There ain't no preachers in Hell, Frank," a local said. "They got an empty church and that's all. They can't get a preacher to come to Hell."

"I wonder why," a local said. "Could it be the name?"

Langford glanced at the local. "You shet your damn mouth, farmer."

"Why should he, Wells?" Frank stepped in. "This is his town. You boys are just visiting here. And I doubt you were invited."

"You tellin' us to get out, Morgan?"

Frank shrugged his shoulders. "Nope. You don't see any badge on me, do you? I'm just a private citizen."

"Nobody runs us out of nowhere, Morgan," Davis said. "Especially you."

"I don't recall anyone asking you to leave, Davis."

"Just makin' things plain."

"Tell me this, Wells. Why do you boys want to come to a place where you know you're not welcome?"

The foreman smiled. "Oh, I think you know the answer to that."

"Yes, I suppose I do. So you can strut around and shoot anybody who dares challenge you, right, Wells?"

The .45 foreman stared at him and offered no reply.

"Now let me add this," Frank said. "I just bought the old Jefferson place. The place where night riders burned the whole family to death a few months back. And I bought land surrounding the place. If I find any of you Diamond .45 people, or Circle Snake riders, or Lightning hands on my property, I'll kill you and I won't ask questions before I do it. I'll just blow you out of the saddle and leave you for the buzzards and the bears. You understand all that?"

Wells's eyes bugged out and his face flushed from sudden rage. His hands gripped both arms of the chair until the knuckles turned white. "That's hard talk, Morgan."

"You are damn right it is. And I mean every word of it. I'm no helpless woman or child. Or a man who isn't used to guns. And if you doubt it, stand up and get ready to drag iron."

Wells slowly relaxed and leaned back in the chair, being careful to keep his hands away from his pistol. "You'd like that, wouldn't you, Drifter?"

"I'm no drifter anymore, Wells. I own a farm and a small ranch, and I'm also looking after the cattle that belong to the Wilson family. The same rules apply to the Wilson property."

"That's mighty nice of you, Morgan," a .45 hand said. "You liftin' the skirts of that fine-lookin' woman for payment? She give you a good roll in bed for all your help?"

Frank was away from the bar in a heartbeat. He reached the mouthy cowboy in the next heartbeat, just as the man was getting to his boots, both hands balled into fists.

"Finish him, Cort!" one of the hands yelled.

Frank hit Cort in the mouth with one big fist. Cort's boots flew out from under him and he landed on the table behind where he'd been sitting. He rolled and got to his feet, his lips dripping blood.

"I'll kill you for that, Drifter," he said, calling Frank the nickname that an Eastern writer had hung on him in an article.

"Come do it," Frank told him.

Cort charged him and Frank met him square on with both fists, a series of lefts and rights to the stomach and face that sent Cort stumbling backward. Frank pressed the .45 hand hard, hitting him solidly on the side of the jaw with a right fist that glazed the man's eyes and caused his knees to buckle a bit.

Cort backed up, shaking his head and spitting out blood. Frank came on without hesitation, coldly and mercilessly. He slammed a left to the man's belly and a right to his face. Cort's nose flattened and the blood and snot flew. He backed up, hurt and dazed and shaking his head, splattering blood.

"You son of a bitch!" Cort said, taking a swing at Frank.

Frank grabbed the man's arm, just at the wrist, and using his forward momentum, threw the man out one of the front windows of the saloon. Cort bounced on the boardwalk and rolled off into the dirt of the street.

Frank was out the batwings after him before Cort could get up and get his shaky legs under him. The Diamond .45 hand was bleeding from a dozen cuts from the broken glass, but he was still game. He tried to climb up on the boardwalk. He didn't make it. Frank kicked him in the belly, and Cort doubled over and went to the ground, both hands holding his belly and horrible gasping, choking sounds coming from his mouth.

Frank stepped off the boardwalk and then for the next several minutes, methodically beat the man to a bloody pulp. Like a steam-driven piledriver, Frank's fists smashed Cort's face and belly. When he finished, Cort was unconscious, his face torn, bloody, and unrecognizable. The Diamond .45 puncher was slumped against a water trough, his chin resting on his chest. Incredibly, Cort had not landed even one blow on Frank.

Frank splashed water from the trough on his face and

stepped back onto the boardwalk, walking up to the Diamond .45 foreman. "Have I made my point, Langford?"

"Yeah, I reckon you did, Morgan," Wells said tightly. "But it ain't gonna be forgot no time soon."

"I hope you never forget it. And be sure and tell your boss about it. I'll do the same damn thing to him if his actions or remarks ever warrant it."

"You're a fool, Morgan," Wells said in a low voice. "You can't fight every rancher on the north end of the valleys."

"You want to bet your life on that?"

The foreman elected not to respond. He turned away with a muttered curse and said, "One of you boys get a buckboard from the livery to haul Cort back to the ranch."

"You want me to get Doc Everett to look at him 'fore we do?" another hand asked.

"No. I don't want that mean-mouthed bastard to look at him. We'll get Doc Woods."

Frank stood on the boardwalk and listened to the Circle .45 hands talk, all the while flexing his fingers to help keep them from stiffening up. They would be sore from the pounding against Cort's face, but nothing was broken. He would soak both hands in hot water and salt later on.

He glanced up and across the street at the crowd that had gathered on the boardwalk, Julie and Shelley among them. He started to step off the boardwalk and walk across to them when Cort suddenly moaned.

"I'll . . . kill you . . . for this," the busted-up cowboy mumbled through loose teeth and smashed gums. "That's a . . . promise."

"And if he don't, I will!" another Circle .45 hand blurted out.

"Shut up, Dick," Langford said. "We'll get our evens 'fore long, you can bet on that."

"I'll sure be around," Frank informed them. "And you

boys best keep in mind what I said about staying off my property and Miss Julie's property."

Both of Cort's eyes were almost swollen shut, but Frank could see the hate shining through the swelling. *I'll have to kill that man someday,* Frank thought.

Doc Everett strolled up and glanced at Cort, then over at Langford. "You want me to take a look at him, Wells?"

"I want you to keep your damn hands off him!" the foreman lashed out.

"With pleasure," the doctor replied. "Maybe the community will get lucky and he'll die."

"You're a mean bastard, Doc," Dick said.

"I'm a realist."

"Huh?" Dick asked.

"Never mind. It would take the rest of the day trying to explain it to you." He looked at Frank. "Heard you were back in town. Julie told me moments before the fight. She seems quite fond of you."

"She's a nice lady."

"Yes. That she is. I hope your intentions are honorable."

"They are."

"Are you unscathed after this brief battle?"

Frank smiled. "I know what that means, Doc. Yes, I'm fine."

"That's good to hear. Oddly enough, I believe you." Doc Everett stuck the stub of a cigar into his mouth and walked away.

"Here comes Luke with the buckboard," a hand said. "Looks like he put some hay in the back to soften the ride."

Cort was loaded into the buckboard and the Circle .45 hands rode out, after they all gave Frank dirty looks. Frank walked across the street to stand beside Julie and Shelley.

"Are you all right?" Julie asked.

"Oh, yes."

"What was all that fighting about?"

"I got upset about some ugly comments he made about you."

She looked up at Frank. "I won't ask what they were."

"Best you don't."

"Your hands look swollen."

"A mite. But they'll be all right. I'll heat water and soak them this afternoon."

"You'll stop by the house and I'll heat water for you."

Frank smiled. "Yes, ma'am."

# NINE

Once Frank outlined for the builders what he wanted, he left them to their sawing and hammering and nailing and started rounding up what was left of the cattle. Jefferson had not registered any brand, so Frank marked them with his own brand, one he had registered at the county seat after checking the Montana brand book. His was an F bar M. He branded Julie's cattle with a J bar W.

It was midsummer, too late to do anything with what was left of Jefferson's unattended and weed-choked beet and potato crop, and too late to plant his own, so Frank just left it alone. The wheat crop looked good, and he made arrangements with another farmer to bring that in when it was time—for shares of whatever the crop brought.

For the most part the ranchers on the north side of the crossroads stayed in their part of the multiconnecting valleys. Frank had never been to the town of Hell, and really had no desire to go. He didn't think he'd be too welcome there.

Frank heard that Cort had recovered from his beating, at least physically, but that the hand talked daily about his hatred of Frank Morgan and how someday he'd kill him. Frank felt that someday, probably sooner than later, he'd have to face Cort in a showdown.

On a hot, midsummer day, Frank was taking a break, relaxing under the shade of trees by the banks of a creek. The creek was one of the dividing lines between his property and the Wilson property. Horse had wandered down to the creek for a drink. Dog was back at the home site, watching the carpenters at work. Frank heard the sound of horses, a couple of them, he thought, coming from different directions. He perked up, watching and listening.

The first horse he saw was Katie's paint pony. Julie had said the girl rode nearly every day after her chores, sometimes staying away for hours at a time.

"Now where is she going?" Frank muttered just a heartbeat before he spotted the other rider. "Oh, hell," Frank said, recognizing the second rider: Donnie Bullard, son of the owner of the Diamond .45 spread, whom Frank had seen a couple of times in town.

Frank watched the boy and girl meet, then ride off into a stand of timber. "Young love," he muttered.

Julie had forbidden her daughter to have anything to do with Donnie, but as she had told Frank, "I might as well be talking to a stump. She's going to do what she wants to do, no matter what I say. And Phil Junior is seeing Betty Lou Gilmar whenever both of them can slip away. It's becoming a big mess."

"What do the ranchers have to say about it?"

"The same thing I say. But their kids are just as hard-headed."

"Are they . . . ah . . . doing anything . . . ah . . . you know what I mean?"

"I don't know. I rather doubt it. They're still awfully young to be thinking about, you know, *that.*"

"They're all about fifteen, aren't they?"

"Yes."

"That's old enough. How old were you when you married Phillip?"

Julie sighed. "Fifteen."

"Enough said, I reckon."

"I'll chain her to the bed!" Julie said.

"I think I'd pick another object to chain her to," Frank said very dryly.

Julie giggled. "You're awful, Frank!"

Frank stared at the stand of timber, wondering what the kids were doing in there. Then he decided he really didn't want to know. He slipped down to the creek and swung into the saddle, heading back to his house. If the kids were doing what comes naturally, Frank hoped they were being careful about it.

"I seen that damn snooty Betty Lou Gilmar 'bout two hours ago," one of the workmen told Frank as soon as he dismounted. "Ridin' that fancy horse of her'n."

"Where?"

"I was up to the crossroads, directin' a wagon load of lumber here. I seen her cross the road, headin' south."

"All them kids is up to no good," another man said after taking a dipper of water from the bucket. "When one of them girls gets in a family way, it's gonna be really bad."

"I don't believe they're doin' anything but smoochin'," another workman said.

"You probably still believe in Santa Claus too," his friend replied.

"Maybe if the kids of the ranchers and the farmers can get along," Frank said, "the adults might follow suit."

"The folks on this end of the valley would be happy to make peace," the workman said. "But we're not the ones hirin' gunfighters and sendin' out night riders to burn and kill, Mr. Morgan. All we want to do is live in peace and raise our kids and crops." He looked toward the southwest and his tanned face paled. "Oh, God, look!" He pointed.

Frank turned and looked. A huge cloud of smoke was visible, rising from a fire several miles away. Someone's wheat field was burning and he doubted it was an accident.

"I'll check it out," Frank said, heading for the corral.

By the time Frank reached the field, neighbors had set up a fire break and the fire was nearly out. But the flames had destroyed the entire wheat field of a man named Clay. Frank rode up to the gathering of men and women and sat his saddle. There was no point in dismounting; there was nothing he could do. The farm families stood in silence and looked out over the ruined field.

"That's it for me," Clay said, leaning on his shovel. "I'm busted. Flat busted. The goddamn ranchers have beat me."

"Did anyone see who started it?" Frank asked.

No one had.

Frank looked at Clay. "Don't start packing yet."

"Why not?" the farmer asked. "I don't even have the money to get through the winter, much less buy seed and equipment for next year. The fire got all my implements. They was down on the end where the fire started."

"I'll stake you," Frank said. "And you work for me the rest of this summer and fall. I'll pay good wages. Deal?"

Clay blinked a couple of times. "Why would you do that?" he questioned.

"Because I want to," Frank replied.

Clay nodded his head. "All right, Mr. Morgan. Deal."

Frank lifted the reins. "I'm going to do some checking; see if I can find anything about why this fire started, or who started it. I'll be back." He looked at the woman standing beside Clay and smiled. "I'd appreciate a pot of coffee when I get back, ma'am."

She returned his smile. "It'll sure be ready, Mr. Morgan."

Frank found a number of hoofprints and an empty kerosene can that had been tossed in a ditch near where the fire started. He followed the tracks for a time, all the way back to the river that marked the boundary of one side of the valley. Frank did not cross the small river. He had seen enough to know the fire had been deliberately set, but had no proof as to who started it. Or paid to have it started.

But he knew from carefully checking the hoofprints that at least one of the riders had been a part of the group that had killed the Jefferson family a few months back.

"Getting bolder," Frank muttered. "Striking in broad daylight." He turned and rode back to the burn site.

"What'd you find, Mr. Morgan?" one of the neighbors asked.

"The riders headed back to the north end of the valley. I didn't follow them."

"They might have been waitin' in ambush," another man said.

"I thought about that," Frank replied. "But even if I had caught up with them, I had no proof that would directly link them to the fire. And I'm not the law."

"You could be," another farmer said.

Frank shook his head. "Forget that. My days of totin' a badge are over."

Mrs. Clay poured Frank a cup of fresh brewed coffee and he took it. "Thank you, ma'am. Smells wonderful."

Julie Wilson came rattling up in a buckboard, Shelley on the seat beside her. Julie walked over to Mrs. Clay and the two women hugged each other, while the other farmers' wives gathered around. The men grouped together away from the women.

"You men have got to arm yourselves," Frank said. "And you've got to be ready and willing to use those guns. If you don't, you're going to lose this war."

"We're farmers, Mr. Morgan," Clay said. "Not gunfighters."

"You all hunt, don't you?" Frank challenged.

The men all solemnly nodded.

"Then you all know how to use guns. That's half the battle."

"I never took a man's life," a farmer said. "I don't know if I could shoot a man."

"By God, I could," a woman shouted from the crowd of females. "And you men are going to teach us how to shoot."

"Now, Frances," a man Frank had heard called Hunt said.

"Don't you now, Frances me, Daniel!" his wife said. "I mean it."

"All right," Daniel said. "Settle down, Frances." He looked at Frank. "I got a rifle and a shotgun."

"Get a pistol too," Frank said. "All of you men get a pistol and learn how to use it. Get used to carrying it around."

"No point in notifying Sheriff Wilcox about this," a man said. "He's in Trainor's pocket. And so is Judge Broadhurst."

"For a fact, we're all alone in this fight," another said.

"We've got each other, Josh," Clay said gently.

"That's right," Mrs. Clay said, walking to her husband's side and putting an arm around his waist. "We sure do."

Clay smiled at the woman. "All right, Edna. I'll teach you how to use a rifle."

"And a pistol," she added.

"It's a start," Frank said. "Once the ranchers learn we've gotten organized and will fight, they might back off."

"They're not going to back off, Mr. Morgan," Josh said. "They'll never back off until they've run us out or killed us all. But this way . . . well, we'll go down fighting. Like growed-up men and women."

"Don't start talking about defeat," Frank admonished. "I don't like to lose. And we're not going to lose this fight."

"But some of us are going to get hurt or killed," another man said. "That's a hard fact of the matter. And I got a whole house full of young'uns to think about. I'm gettin' out of here. There's land aplenty elsewheres. I ain't dyin' for no piece of dirt."

"I figured you'd quit, Jamison," a farmer said, his mouth full of scorn. "You ain't done nothin' 'ceptin' gripe and moan since you got here."

"Be that as it may," Jamison said. "I'm shore packin' up and leavin'. I'll be gone in the mornin'."

"What about your land?" Frank asked. "And the home you built? How much do you own and where is it?"

"I got me a section down by the creek." He pointed. "Over yonder. Ain't much of a house, but it's good land."

"All right. I'll give you a fair price for it," Frank told him. "At least enough to get you going and started elsewhere. That is, if you've really got a mind to go. But I wish you'd stay and join us in this fight."

"It ain't my fight, Mr. Morgan. Not no more. I'm done."

Frank studied Jamison's face. The man had the mark of a loser on him. Frank suspected Jamison would drift until his dying day, never being content anywhere. "All right, Jamison. I'll ride over to your place now, look it over, and we'll settle on a price. I'll have the papers drawn up in the morning and pay you then. Is that all right with you?"

"You gonna bring the money to me or do I have to meet you in town to do it?"

"We have to meet at the bank to sign papers."

"I'll be there when it opens."

After Jamison had rattled away in his wagon, Clay said, "No one's going to miss him, Mr. Morgan. You'll see why when you ride over to his place. Ranchers have a word for people like Jamison. They call them rawhiders."

"I suspected as much. And it's Frank, not Mr. Morgan."

"All right, Frank. My name is Harry."

"I'll see you in the morning, Harry." He glanced at the man's wife. "Thanks for the coffee, Mrs. Clay. It was delicious."

"It's Edna, please."

Frank smiled and tipped his hat. He waved at Julie and then rode off after Jamison.

"He's nothing like the articles I've read about him and the stories I've heard," a woman said. "He's a nice man."

"Yes, he is," Julie said. "He's good with kids and he's very well read."

"He's still a gunfighter," said a man who had not spoken since Frank joined the farmers that day. "He's gonna get a lot of us hurt or killed."

"Oh, shut up, Maynard," Josh said. "Frank's all right. The men who's working over at his place say he's a nice fella."

"I don't like him," Maynard said. "And nothin' you nor nobody else can say is gonna change that."

"Fine, Maynard," Dan Hunt said. "You're entitled to your opinion. But you're wrong about Frank Morgan."

"Doubt it," Maynard said stubbornly.

"Are you going to join us in arming ourselves?" a farmer asked.

"I'm armed. Got me a good rifle, a good shotgun, and a pistol. I'll defend myself when the time comes."

"Then go on home to Louise, Maynard," Josh said. "If you're not going to join us, you can stand alone."

"I'll do that. Hell with you all." Maynard stalked over to his horse and rode away, his back stiff with anger.

"What brought all that on, you reckon?" Josh asked.

"Who knows," a farmer called Ned said. "Maynard's always been a strange duck."

"For a fact," Harry Clay said. "All right, folks. I reckon I've got me a new job and we've all got us a good neighbor."

Jamison's house was nothing but a shack. There were half a dozen kids, ranging in age from just walking to midteens. Mrs. Jamison looked worn out. Frank checked Jamison's equipment, and found it ill-kept and practically worthless. But the 640 acres that Jamison owned were prime farmland, with good water and drainage.

Frank told Jamison he'd see him in town in the morning, and headed back to his place. The workmen had already left for the day. The house was just about finished, with most of the remaining work to be done on the outside. Frank rubbed down Horse and turned him into the corral for a time. The new barn was completed, and Frank forked hay into Horse's stall, put some grain into the feed box, then went into his house.

He fed Dog and fixed a pot of coffee, filled a cup, and went out onto the front porch to sit for a time, enjoying the quiet of late afternoon. He was rolling a cigarette just as Dog came out and lay down beside his chair.

"We're getting to be regular land barons, Dog," Frank said with a smile, reaching down and petting Dog. "I believe we might have actually found us a home. That'd be nice, wouldn't it? What do you think about that?"

Dog looked up at him for a few seconds, then went back to sleep.

"I thought that would impress you," Frank said with a laugh.

*Do I want to spend the rest of my life here?* Frank pondered the question. *Well, why not?* he silently answered. *The people, most of them anyway, are nice, and don't really give a damn about my past.*

*And there is that nice young widow to think about too.*

Thinking of Julie filled Frank with a warm, comfortable feeling. A feeling he had not thought he could ever dredge up again.

But there it was.

The difference in their ages of ten years or so was not that great. Nothing that couldn't be overcome.

But could Frank ever successfully put his past behind him?

That worried him, for there were still a lot of young punks looking for a gun reputation, and they would find him. They always did. Then he would have to kill again, or be killed.

"Damn," Frank whispered. Then he smiled. "It ain't easy being Frank Morgan," he said aloud.

He went inside and lit a lamp. He'd read for a time, then go to bed. He had bought a book of poems written by a fellow named Poe. What a strange, dark, and lonely mind that man had. Frank refilled his coffee cup and began reading about the beautiful Annabel Lee.

# TEN

Frank met Jamison in town the following morning and told him how much he would give him for the land, after checking to see the title was free and clear. Jamison took the offer and signed the papers. Frank paid him in cash and the land was his.

"When are you planning on pulling out?" Frank asked.

"Right now," Jamison said. "Everything we're takin' is in the wagons."

"Where will you go?"

"California," Jamison said. "I hear it's the land of plenty."

"Losers," Banker Simmons said, standing beside Frank as the wagons pulled out. "The whole woebegone lot of them."

"I reckon you're right, John. But I can't help but feel sorry for them."

"You'd be wasting your time and your sympathies, Frank.

Nearly everyone in this end of the valley has helped that family at one time or another. I think all of them had gotten used to people helping them long before they arrived here."

Frank watched as a carriage came rolling onto the main street, followed by a couple of mounted men. Their horses wore the Snake brand.

"Mrs. Viola Trainor," Simmons said. "She comes to this end of the valley about once every two or three months."

"To shop?" Frank asked.

Simmons smiled. "In a manner of speaking. She's addicted to laudanum. Sam Bickman at the apothecary shop gets it for her. She buys it a case at a time."

"She can't get it in Hell?"

"The colonel won't allow the druggist there to sell it to her. So she comes over here and buys it."

"Surely he knows that."

"Oh, he knows it but he can't do much of anything about it. Viola has money of her own." Simmons chuckled. "She keeps some of it in my bank."

"Who are those riders with her?"

"The one with the fancy vest is her baby boy, Julian. Called Jules. He's about nineteen, I believe. And he's a cruel bastard. There's a real twisted streak in that young man. The other rider is Viola's personal bodyguard, Ortiz."

"The Nogales gunfighter," Frank said. "I haven't seen or heard anything about him in years. I wondered whatever became of him."

"He was hired by Trainor. I guess, oh, six or seven years ago. Wherever you see Viola, you'll see Ortiz."

"Has anyone crossed him in that time?"

"Two men that I know of. Right out there in that street in front of us. They didn't have a prayer when it came time to draw. He's fast, Frank. He's so fast it's scary."

"I know. Mutual respect is just one of the reasons we've avoided each other over the years."

"What are some of the others?"

Frank smiled. "Another is that both of us know if it comes to a showdown, we'll both take some lead. I got shot in the shoulder last year. I don't heal as fast as I used to."

Simmons was called into the bank, and Frank walked across the street to the cafe for a cup of coffee and a plate of biscuits, if they had any left from the breakfast crowd.

He was halfway across the street when he heard his name called. Frank turned to face the .45 hand Cort, standing about thirty feet away.

"I told you I'd kill you someday, Morgan," Cort said. "Well, that day has come."

"Don't be a fool."

"You ready, Morgan?"

"No, I'm not. I don't want to have to kill you. The remarks you made about the lady were out of line and you got a beating for it. It was deserved and you know it."

Out of the corner of his eye, Frank saw Ortiz and Jules Trainor step out onto the boardwalk to stand and watch. The Mexican gunhand was staring and listening intently.

Frank heard Jules say, "I bet Cort kills him, Ortiz."

"Don't be a fool when you bet, boy," the Nogales gunhand replied.

"But I can see some gray in his hair," Jules said.

"Gray in my hair too, boy," Ortiz said with a slight smile. "The business we're in grays a man's hair quickly."

Frank pulled all his attention back to Cort. He felt a calmness slowly spread over him. Any tenseness left him. He stood quite still and faced the angry .45 hand. Frank's right hand hung near the butt of his Peacemaker.

"What's it take to make you pull on me, Morgan?" Cort shouted.

"I'm not going to start this, Cort. I don't want to kill you. So why don't you just turn around, get on your horse, and ride out of here?"

"I ain't a-feared of you, Morgan!"

"I never said you were."

"By God, I think you've lost your speed," Cort said with a nasty smile. "I think age has done caught up with you and you're doin' nothin' 'ceptin' livin' a big bluff."

"I don't care what you think, Cort."

"You're a damn clodhoppin' piece of sheep-dip."

Despite the life-and-death situation, Frank could not contain a short laugh at the juvenile charge.

"Don't you laugh at me, Morgan!" Cort yelled.

The boardwalk on both sides of the street was filling with men and women and kids, standing silently and watching.

"Can't help it, Cort," Frank said. "What you said struck me as funny."

"Huh?"

"You eat potatoes and corn and such, Cort?"

"Do I do what?"

"Do you eat corn and potatoes and beans and such?"

"Why . . . hell yes, I do."

"Where do you think it comes from, Cort?"

"Well . . . how the hell do I know!"

Several of the men on the boardwalk smiled as they realized where Frank was going with his questioning. Ortiz smiled as he rolled a cigarette. He felt no rancor toward Frank Morgan. Ortiz's job was to protect Mrs. Trainor. He took no part in any night riding.

"They come from farmers, Cort. Think about it."

"What the hell are you talking about?"

"I'm talking about what you eat, Cort. And where it comes from."

Cort shook his head. "What damn business is it of yours what I eat, Morgan? I think you've turned loony on me."

"I'm trying to save your life, that's all." Frank told him.

"Are you gonna fight me?" Cort yelled.

"Not unless you force me to do it."

Sweat was beginning to trickle down the .45 rider's face. This just wasn't working out the way he'd planned it. "All right, Morgan. I'm forcin' you. Pull iron, you bastard."

"After you, Cort."

Cort began cussing him, long and loud. Frank stood calm and unmoving in the center of the street.

"Draw on me, Morgan!" Cort yelled, his words tinged with frustration and desperation. "Damn you, drag iron!"

Morgan yawned.

Ortiz was highly amused as he watched the drama in the street turn into a dark comedy.

"Morgan's yellow," Jules whispered.

"No, boy," Ortiz said. "He's a very smart man who doesn't want to kill anyone. Believe me, I know the feeling well."

"All right, Morgan," Cort said, the sweat dripping from his face to plop in the dirt at his feet. "You forcin' me to call your hand."

"I wish you wouldn't, Cort."

"I ain't got no choice in the matter!" Cort's words were practically a scream. "I ain't gonna stand here and have you make a fool of me."

"You're doing that all by yourself," Frank said.

"Huh? I ain't doin' no sich of a thing neither."

"I think it's over, boy," Ortiz said.

"What do you mean?" Jules asked.

"I just have a feeling, that's all. It's something you develop after a few years in this business."

"I'm going to walk away now, Cort," Frank said. "If you shoot me, it'll be in the back. Are you a back-shooter?"

"Hell, no, I ain't no back-shooter."

"Then you go back to the ranch and cool down."

"Morgan?" Cort hollered. "You got to fight me."

"Why, Cort?"

"Why? 'Cause I done made up my mind to, that's why."

"Then change your mind. See you." Frank turned his back and walked the rest of the way across the street, stepping up on the boardwalk. "Howdy, Ortiz," he said to the man. "I hadn't seen you in so long I didn't recognize you at first."

"Morgan," Ortiz said. "You're looking fit."

"What's Cort doing, Ortiz?"

"He's walking away. Heading for the saloon, I think."

"Good. I didn't want to have to kill him."

"I know the feeling, Morgan. Only too well."

"I'm farming and running a little ranch now," Frank said.

"So I heard. Think you can really settle down after all these years?"

"I'm going to give it a good try."

"I wish you luck."

Jules Trainor had walked away, disappointed there had been no gunplay.

There was not much else for the two gunfighters to talk about—they had never been friends—so Frank stepped into the cafe for a cup of coffee. Dr. Everett was sitting alone at a table, a pot of coffee in front of him, and he waved Frank over to join him.

"You could have easily killed that cowboy, Frank," the doctor said, pouring Frank a mug of coffee.

"I didn't want to kill him, Doc. It would suit me just fine if I never had to draw on another man."

"The reluctant gunfighter," Everett said with a smile. "I guess some of the articles I've read about you are true."

"Which ones are those? I must have missed them."

"The ones that say you were forced to kill a man when you were just a boy and from that moment on the title gun-fighter was nothing that you wanted."

"That's true, Doc. I was just a kid."

The doctor nodded his head. "You're buying a lot of land, Frank. You really going to try to settle down in this area?"

"I'm going to try."

"I hope you make it. How are you and Miss Julie getting on? And tell me to go to hell if you think I'm getting too personal."

Frank smiled. "We're taking it slow, Doc. Just one step at a time."

"Those kids of hers giving you any trouble?"

"I know where this is going, and no, they mind quite well, except when it comes to their puppy love."

"It might not be puppy love, Frank. Have you thought about that?"

"I try not to think about it at all."

"Nice safe answer."

Before Frank could reply, a man rushed into the cafe and yelled, "There's some man here from over Butte way. Says he's come to kill Frank Morgan."

"What's his name?" Frank asked.

"Rob something or another."

"Damn," Frank said, pushing back his chair. "Twice in one day is too much."

"You know this person, Frank?" Doc Everett asked.

"He's a punk kid who thinks he's a gunslick. I ran into him in Butte. I thought it was over between us." He looked at the man who had run into the cafe. "Where is the .45 hand I just talked out of a gunfight?"

"He got his horse and rode out of town."

"At least I got him going home alive." Frank slipped the leather thong off the hammer of his Peacemaker. "I don't think I'll be able to talk Rob out of a fight."

"Morgan!" the kid from Butte hollered. "Get out here in the street and face me. Your time has come."

Frank picked up his coffee mug and took a long pull. "That's real good coffee," he said, setting the mug back on the table. "Doc, you go out the back way and tell Marshal Handlen to stay out of this. This kid's kill-crazy, I'm thinking."

"Handlen's out of town, Frank. He left early this morning heading back East. One of his kids is near death. Hell, he might be dead by now."

Frank headed for the door. "Might as well get this over with."

"A crowd is gathering on the boardwalks," a customer said.

"I see them," Frank said, a slight note of bitterness in his voice. "Hell, folks, it's time for the show."

# ELEVEN

Frank stepped out of the cafe. Rob, the young man from the saloon in Butte, was standing in the middle of the street.

"I seen you walk away from that other feller, Morgan," Rob shouted. "But by God you're gonna face me and we're gonna settle this thing."

"What thing, boy?"

"The quarrel between us, Morgan. Damn you, you know what."

"I got no quarrel with you, boy."

"I ain't no boy, you old bastard!" He was wearing twin .45s, hung low and tied down, his hands hovering over the butts of his guns.

"I'm not going to argue with you, Rob. It's hot out here. If you want to kill me, have at it. Now's your chance."

"I'm gonna make you sweat some, you old has-been."

"The only thing you're going to do is piss me off. And you've just about reached that point."

Rob grabbed for his guns, both of them. Frank shot him before Rob could get either gun clear of leather, and his aim was perfect, the bullet slamming into the young man's hip and spinning the would-be gunslick around in the street and depositing him on his butt in the dirt. Rob tried to lift and cock his right-hand .45 just as Frank reached him and jerked the pistol from his hand, tossing it to one side. Frank stepped on Rob's left hand hard, preventing him from pulling his other pistol.

"It's over, boy," Frank told him, reaching down and removing Rob's left-hand pistol. "And you're alive. Be thankful for that."

"I'm crippled!"

"I doubt it. But even if you are, you're alive."

"I hurt somethin' fierce, you bastard."

"Good. Maybe the pain will help you get your mind off gunplay and onto something constructive."

While Rob lay in the dirt, bleeding and cussing, Doc Everett walked up and motioned to several men standing on the boardwalk. "You boys help me get him over to my office so I can dig that lead out."

"Is it gonna hurt, Doc?" Rob asked.

"Not as much as it should. I'll give you something to dull the pain. Come on, boys, lift him up and get him out of the street."

Rob was toted off to the doc's office, hollering about how bad he was hurting all the way. Frank picked up the young man's guns and carried them over to the gun and saddle shop, giving them to the owner.

"Stow these away, will you?"

"I sure will, Mr. Morgan."

Frank walked over to the bank, and Simmons waved him into his office. "You should have killed that young hoodlum, Frank."

"You're probably right, John. But I'm tired of killing, tired of men trying to make a name for themselves at my expense."

"You'll never be able to take off that pistol and put it away, will you, Frank?"

"Not anytime soon, that's for sure."

The men looked at each other in silence for a moment, Frank finally saying, "The workmen will be finishing up for this week by early afternoon today. Pay them off when they get here, will you, John?"

"Of course I will. I'll have the receipt waiting for you when you come in."

Frank stood up. "I'm going home and do some work on my new property this afternoon." He smiled. "I think I'll just tear down that shack that passed for a home. See you."

Frank headed for home, arriving just as the workmen were finishing up for the weekend. He made sure Dog had food and water, and then headed over to the place Jamison had just sold him. He walked into the house and shook his head at the squalor left behind.

Frank backed out, his mind quickly made up. He'd arrange for a team of mules— the man at the livery had some big Missouri Reds—and have Harry Clay go into town after them, hook them up, and just pull the damn shack down. Whatever lumber there was that could be salvaged and reused, he'd give to Harry.

He walked over to the ramshackle barn and once again looked at the farming equipment. Much of it was just plain junk, beyond repair. Harry could have whatever equipment he could fix and use. But the land was prime, with good water. Even though Frank was far from being an expert at farming, he knew from just looking the property over that Jamison had not used the land properly and was not a good farmer.

Frank knew one thing for certain. He had a lot of work to do.

"I don't know what I'm going to do about the twins," Julie said to Frank, refilling his coffee cup.

Frank looked up from the plate of food Julie had prepared for him. Noon mealtime at the Wilson farm, and the twins were not at home. They both had been gone since early that morning. Shelley had been fed and was in her room, reading. "You want me to talk to them?"

"They resent you, Frank," Julie said, sitting down. "Oh, they both like you. But they both say you're not their father and you have no right to tell them to do anything."

"They have a point."

"But Shelley obeys you."

"Shelley is a child. She's used to grown-ups telling her what to do. Phil and Katie are near'bouts grown up. In body, if not in mind."

"It's body I'm worried about," Julie said, rolling her eyes. "Especially Katie's body. What if those kids are doing . . . well, you know."

Talk such as that made Frank very uncomfortable. "You want me to try to arrange a meeting with Bullard and Gilmar?"

"Do you think it would do any good?"

"What could it hurt? It would be concerned parents talking about their kids."

"Frank, have you ever been across the line to rancher territory?"

"No," he admitted. "I haven't had any reason to go over there."

"They might shoot you on sight over there."

Frank smiled. "That would be unpleasant."

"Don't joke about it! Just the thought of something happening to you scares me."

"Well, if you don't want me to ride over there, we could always send them a telegram," Frank suggested, struggling to hide a smile.

Julie sighed and gave him a very jaundiced look.

"Or, we could hitch up the buckboard and go together."

"I think that might be best. If you don't mind."

"We'll go tomorrow."

"You're sure you don't mind?"

"Not a bit."

Julie smiled. "That takes a real weight off my mind, Frank."

"Think nothing of it."

She leaned over and kissed him, and Frank returned the affection. Just as they were pulling apart, Shelley stepped out of her room and said, "I'm going to play outside, Mother."

Red-faced at nearly getting caught smooching, Julie jerked away from Frank and replied, "All right, baby. Stay close to the house."

"I want to go down to the creek!"

"Shelley . . ." Julie said, then shook her head. "All right, you can play down by the creek. Just don't get all wet and muddy. You hear me?"

"Yes, ma'am." She was out the door in a blur of calico.

"That dress will be filthy when she comes back," Julie said, then smiled. "Oh, well. It needs washing anyway."

"What time do you want to go over to see the ranchers?"

"We'd best leave early. I'll fix us a fried-chicken lunch."

"With biscuits?" Frank asked, smiling.

She playfully reached out and ruffled his hair. "With biscuits, Frank."

Frank had another cup of coffee and then puttered around the house for a time, fixing this and that. He had just finished repairing a harness when the faint sound of a shot reached him. He stepped out of the barn and listened, but no more shots came.

"What the hell was that?" Frank muttered, heading for Horse and swinging into the saddle.

Julie had stepped out of the house and called to him. "Was that a shot, Frank?"

"Yes. But I don't know where it came from. I'll check it out."

"You wait a minute. Saddle me a horse. I'm coming with you."

"In a dress?"

"Saddle the damn horse, Frank!"

Frank tossed a saddle on a little gentle mare, and Julie hiked up her skirt and swung into the saddle. "Let's go," she said, and took off for the creek.

Frank spotted the still form of Shelley, lying beside the creek bank, before Julie did, and reached out and grabbed the bridle of her horse. "You wait here, Julie. I mean it. Let me check this out. Wait right here!"

Frank jumped from the saddle and ran to Shelley's side, but he knew she was dead. The bullet had slammed into her chest and blown out the back. She was dead before she had hit the ground and there was little blood. He knelt down and touched her face, closing her sightless eyes. The little girl was gone.

"Goddamnit!" Frank said.

"Frank?" Julie called from the hill. "Did you find her, Frank?"

Frank stood up and walked to where she could see him. "Yes, Julie. I found her. Don't come down here."

"Why? Why shouldn't I come down? I'm coming down there, Frank."

"Julie!"

It was too late. Julie came down the hill at a gallop and jumped out of the saddle, almost tripping on the hem of her dress. She ran to her daughter's side and stood for a moment, looking first at Shelley, then at Frank.

Then she collapsed.

# TWELVE

Frank wrapped Shelley's body in a blanket, and then wet his bandanna and bathed Julie's face until she came out of her faint.

"It was a dream, wasn't it?" Julie asked, her eyes unfocused and still glazed over from shock.

"No," Frank said gently. "It was real."

"Shelley's dead?"

"Yes."

Julie put her hands to her face and began weeping.

Frank didn't have a lot of experience with grief-stricken mothers. All he could do was stand helplessly by and listen to Julie sob over the loss of her child. When there didn't appear to be any letup in Julie's weeping, Frank walked away and got their horses.

"Come on, Julie," he urged. "We've got to take Shelley

into town. You mount up and I'll carry the girl. We'll go back to the house and hitch up the buckboard."

When there was no immediate response, Frank pulled the woman to her feet. "Julie!" he said as gently as he could. "All this won't bring the girl back."

Julie pulled away and stood glaring at him, tears streaming down her face. "Did you look for any signs of who might have done this?"

"No, not yet."

"But you will?"

"You want me to do that now?"

"Yes. I want to be alone with my child for a moment."

"All right. Julie, don't take the blanket off her. Don't look at her again."

"Why not?"

"Because it's a dreadful wound, that's why. You don't want to keep that picture in your mind."

"She has to be dressed before we take her into town."

"No, she doesn't. You can pick out a dress when we get back to the house."

"I've got to comb her hair."

Frank grabbed her arms. "Julie, damnit! Listen to me."

She struggled away from him. "Leave me alone with my Shelley! Go look for . . . go look for something! Leave me alone."

"All right, Julie. All right. I'll leave you alone for a few minutes."

"I'm going to look at my child, Frank."

"I won't try to stop you." Frank walked away, stepping across the small creek. He walked about a hundred yards up a gently sloping rise toward a stand of timber and began casting about for a sign. It didn't take him long to find it.

It was the same hoofprint he'd seen at the Jefferson place

after the fire, the same print he'd seen when the fields of Harry Clay had been set afire. The horse had an odd way of stepping that any experienced tracker would pick up on immediately. Frank found some boot prints in the stand of timber where the shooter had knelt to fire. Whoever it was was no small fellow. The bootprints were deep in the ground. He was a good-sized man.

Frank followed the boot tracks and found where the man had mounted up, riding off toward the north. He searched for, but could not find any shell casings that would help identify the type of rifle used.

Frank walked back to the other side of the creek. Julie was sitting beside the blanket-wrapped body of Shelley. Her eyes were red and puffy from crying. "Let's get back to the house, Julie," he said. "I'll carry Shelley. I'll hitch up the buckboard; then we'll go into town."

She nodded her head and rose to her feet without speaking. She walked to her horse and climbed into the saddle. Frank picked Shelley up and as gently and gracefully as possible got into the saddle. They headed for the house.

The twins had not yet returned home, and that infuriated Julie. She stormed around for a couple of minutes, then calmed down enough to go into the house to change clothes and get clean clothing for Shelley while Frank hitched up the team.

Frank had a hunch Julie was not going to leave her daughter's side until the service was over and the girl was buried, so after he placed Shelley in the buckboard and pulled around to the front of the house, he tied the reins of his horse to the back of the buckboard.

Julie left a brief note for the twins, placed a traveling bag in the buckboard, and climbed onto the seat beside Frank.

"You ready?" Frank asked.

She nodded her head.

Frank picked up the reins, clucked at the team, and they headed for town. It was going to be a silent trip.

The news of Shelley's death spread like an unchecked prairie fire. When the townspeople began gathering at the undertaker's, Frank slipped out and headed for the saloon.

Chubby was behind the bar and he set a bottle and glass in front of Frank. Frank poured himself a couple of fingers of rye and took a sip.

"Sorrowful time, Frank," Chubby said.

"It is that."

"This is liable to light the fuse to this powder keg."

"I 'spect it will, Chubby. Tell me, what good do you think it would do to notify the county sheriff?"

"None a-tall. Sheriff Wilcox is solidly behind the ranchers. Oh, he'd send one of his deputies over here, a report would be taken, and that would be the end of it. Wilcox is a sorry-assed sheriff, for sure. When's the funeral goin' to be?"

"Tomorrow, I reckon."

"Whole town'll be showin' up for sure."

" 'Magine so." Frank took a sip of his drink, thinking: *And every farm family in the valley will be there. What a great opportunity for some hired guns to strike and do some house and barn burning.*

Frank shoved his drink away. "I'll see you, Chubby."

"All right. Take care."

Frank walked over to the undertaker's and pushed his way through the crowd gathered outside. He found Julie sitting alone with Shelley's body. She had been crying. She looked up as Frank walked in.

"Frank? Will you ride back to the house and check on Phil and Katie?"

"Yes, of course. You want me to send them into town?"

"If you don't mind. I'm sure we can spend the night with someone here in town."

"I'll do better than that. I'll rent you rooms at the hotel. That sound all right with you?"

"That would be nice, Frank."

"When are the services?"

"Tomorrow, at one o'clock, at the church."

"I'll pay my respects now, Julie, if you don't mind. I think I'd better do some scouting up near the crossroads in case some of the hired guns go on the prowl with everyone in town, away from their farms."

"I hadn't thought of that. You're right, of course. I'll pass the word to some of the other farmers as I see them and tell them what you're doing. Some of them may want to stay home too."

"It might be a good thing if they did. Do that, Julie."

Frank walked over to the hotel and reserved two rooms, explaining to the clerk what he was doing.

"They'll be no charge for the rooms, Mr. Morgan. It's my way of saying how sorry I am that this happened."

Frank thanked him and stepped outside just as several riders on horses wearing the Lightning brand were reining up in front of the saloon. Frank stood in front of the hotel, under the awning, for a moment, then stepped out into the street and paused as the riders came hurriedly out of the saloon. They stopped when they spotted Frank.

"Now you wait just a minute, Morgan," one said. "We just now heard what happened to the girl. We're regular hands, not hired guns. We didn't have nothin' to do with no killin' of a child. Don't none of us hold with that sort of thing."

"Your boss does," Frank said coldly.

"Maybe he does," another Lightning hand said. "But we don't."

"Was I you boys," Frank said, "I'd get on those horses and get the hell out of this town. The mood the townfolk are in, you might be in for a lot of trouble if you stay around."

"We was just leavin', Morgan."

"Good. Do that."

Frank watched them mount up and ride out. He believed they had told the truth. They were only cowhands, not hired guns, but whether or not they had taken part in any of the night riding against the farmers was still unclear.

He looked back at the undertaker's place: the crowd was getting larger, the women weepy-looking and the men sullen. Frank stepped into the saddle and rode out. He passed the town's cemetery; grave-diggers were already digging the small hole for Shelley's coffin. It was a lonesome ride back to his place.

Frank awakened long before dawn, as was his custom, fed Dog, and made certain there was plenty of fresh water available for him. He fixed a couple of sandwiches, filled up his canteen, then saddled up a big Appaloosa he'd bought recently at the livery. He had cleaned his rifle, a .44-40, before going to bed, and he slipped it into the saddle boot. He put a couple of boxes of ammunition for both rifle and pistol into his saddlebags.

"You stay here," he told Dog. "You hear me?"

Dog looked up at him and wagged his tail.

"I'll take that as a yes," Frank said, squatting down and petting the dog for a moment. "You be good and stay out of trouble."

Frank rode out, heading for a range of high hills that

would give him a commanding view of a good portion of both sides of the long series of valleys. It had been dry in this area for several weeks, and any group of riders would kick up enough dust to be seen a long ways off. The Ap was a stepper and loved to travel. Frank reached his vantage point about an hour after daylight flooded the landscape, and got his field glasses out of the saddlebags.

Frank figured the farmers in this part of the south end of the valley would be leaving about midmorning for the journey into town. He checked his rifle, making sure the tube was full of cartridges, then settled down under the shade of a tree.

He didn't have a long wait before he saw the dust rising from under the hooves of many horses. They were coming straight through the pass, heading right at Frank. As they drew closer, Frank picked up his field glasses and studied the riders. He immediately picked out four men he personally knew were hired guns, not cowboys.

"Okay, boys," Frank muttered. "You rolled the dice."

He picked up his rifle.

# THIRTEEN

Taking a last look through his field glasses, Frank spotted what appeared to be heavy containers dangling from several saddle horns. They sure weren't canteens, and Frank didn't think they were jugs of lemonade the hired guns were taking to a picnic.

"Kerosene, most likely," he muttered, casing his field glasses.

When the riders were in good range, Frank put several slugs into the ground well ahead of the hired guns, then stood up on the ridge. He stood silently, letting the gunhands get a good look at him.

The hired guns sat their saddles for a moment, talking among themselves. Then they spread out, forming a single line, twenty or thirty feet between them. Frank smiled, shoving fresh loads into his .44-40. "Gonna charge me, are you?

Figured you boys would do something like that," he muttered. "Real stupid of you."

The line of riders pulled their rifles from saddle boots and charged the hill, coming at a full gallop. "Dumb," Frank said. "Just plain dumb." He lifted his rifle and waited for the riders to open fire.

Lead began zinging and howling around Frank, none of the bullets coming anywhere close to him.

Frank took aim, compensating for the fact he was shooting downhill, and gently squeezed the trigger. One hired gun fell from his saddle and bounced on the ground. Frank got another shot off and missed his target, before the line of gunhands broke apart and scattered, half a dozen going one way, half a dozen heading off to Frank's right.

Frank ran for his horse and headed off toward the east, keeping the crossroads, a few miles away, to his left. The hired guns, once they figured out where he was going and regrouped, followed en masse.

Frank galloped into a small stand of timber, jumped off his horse, and knelt down, pulling his .44-40 to his shoulder and taking careful aim. The shot knocked a rider from his horse. The hired gun hit the ground and rolled. He got to his feet and staggered off, one hand holding his wounded side.

The older and more experienced of the hired guns stopped their advance and turned around, quickly getting out of range of Frank's rifle. One rider charged on, shouting and waving his rifle as he rode.

Frank shook his head at the rider's stupidity and levered another round into the chamber. He took aim and squeezed the trigger. The bullet hit the gunhand in the chest and slammed him out of the saddle. He rolled on the ground and did not move. His horse galloped on for a few seconds, then stopped and began grazing.

That did it for the hired guns. They headed back north, riding hard for the road, leaving their dead behind them. The wounded man got to his horse and struggled into the saddle, riding off behind the main group.

Frank waited for a couple of minutes, tracking the paid gunhands with his field glasses until he was sure they were leaving for good . . . at least for this day. He booted his rifle and stepped into the saddle, riding down to the nearest fallen rider. He checked the man, confirming his death, then rounded up the man's horse and tied the gunhand across the saddle. He rode back to the first man of the bunch to hit the ground and checked him. He was dead too. Frank muscled him across his saddle, tied him down, and leading the horse, which had a jug of kerosene tied to the saddle horn, headed for town.

A couple of miles later, he ran into a small group of farmers who had elected to stay behind on this funeral day and protect their farms. They were carrying rifles and shotguns.

"We heard shots," a farmer called Job said.

Frank gestured toward the dead men and the jug of kerosene. "The guns were planning to do some burning this day."

"Just these two?" another asked.

"There were about a dozen of them. I wounded at least one other before the group decided they'd had enough."

"What do you think we should do now?" Job asked. "Go on back home?"

"No. I'd continue patrolling, just to be on the safe side."

"You takin' those bodies into town, Mr. Morgan?"

"Yes. And just so you'll know . . ." He pointed to the brands on the horses carrying the dead men. "Snake brand."

The men stared at the brands for a moment. Job said, "A little girl is shot to death and the very next day the ranchers try to burn some of us out. That takes a sorry son of a bitch!"

There was nothing left to say after that. Frank lifted the reins and rode on toward town.

He stowed the bodies in the livery, and walked down the boardwalk of the seemingly deserted town. Only a few businesses were open: the saloon, the hotel, the general store with one clerk on duty. Everyone was gathering early at the church for Shelley's funeral.

Frank stepped into the saloon and Chubby greeted him. "Seen you ride in with them bodies, Mr. Morgan. Whiskey or beer?"

"Beer."

Chubby pulled a mug and slid it down to Frank. "Where'd you nail them boys?"

"Just this side of the road. Coming through the pass." Frank took a swig of beer. It was cool and refreshing.

"Sorry bunch of bastards," Chubby muttered. "On the very day the little girl they killed is bein' buried."

Frank sipped his beer and said nothing.

"It's gettin' on toward lunchtime, Mr. Morgan. Can I fix you something to eat? We got cold meat and cheese and pickles and hard-boiled eggs. The bread is fresh too."

Frank looked at the wall clock behind the bar. Eleven-thirty. "Not yet, Chub. But thanks."

Frank stood alone at the bar and finished his mug of beer. He declined Chubby's offer of another. "Chub, I thought the funeral was scheduled to be held at one o'clock?"

"Time was changed, Mr. Morgan. High noon."

"Any word from Marshal Handlen?"

"Not that I know of. You reckon he'll even come back out here?"

Frank shrugged his shoulders. "You never know. Man gets back with family he hasn't seen in years . . ." He let that trail off into silence.

"You got any family, Mr. Morgan?"

Frank shook his head. "I 'spect I've got some cousins and such scattered here and there. But I don't know where. You?"

"I got some folks back East, but I ain't seen or heard from none of them in years. I come out here right after the war." He paused for a moment. "Man ought to have some family to grieve for him when he goes to meet his Maker, don't you think?"

"Laying in the casket, you think the dead knows who's at his burying?"

"That's deep thinkin', Mr. Morgan. Goes over my head. I don't rightly know. Who would know?"

"The Good Lord, I reckon. But He don't talk to me."

"Me neither. Least in no way that I understand."

Frank walked outside and stood on the boardwalk, looking up and down the silent empty street. He knew he should walk over to the church, but he just couldn't bring himself to do it. It had been a long time since he had stepped inside a church and felt comfortable doing so. He turned his head at the sounds of footsteps on the boardwalk. Doc Everett was heading toward him.

"Howdy, Doc," Frank said. "You going to the funeral?"

"No. I hate them. Barbaric things. You?"

"No." The two men stood without speaking for a moment. Frank said, "I would offer to buy you lunch, but the cafe is closed."

"No matter. I saw you ride in with the bodies hung over the saddles. Snake riders?"

"Yes. They were going to burn down some farmhouses."

Doc Everett cussed for a few seconds. "Whole damn fight is senseless. Plenty of land for everybody in these valleys."

"But the colonel wants to be king, right?"

"That's as good a way to put it as any, I suppose."

"With him out of the way, would Bullard and Gilmar settle down?"

"I doubt it. They're both envious of the colonel's holdings. With him out of the picture, they'd turn on each other, and the winner of that would turn on the farmers. Hell, it might even be worse than now."

The men stood for a moment and watched as three riders came into view from the edge of town.

"Can you see the brands?" Doc Everett asked.

"Yes, but I don't recognize them."

The three riders drew closer.

"Ah," Doc Everett said. "I know who they are now. They're cowhands, not gunfighters. Two work for the Snake, one for the .45."

"Surely they know about the funeral."

"I'm sure they do."

Frank took note of the fat saddlebags and the thick bedrolls behind the saddles. "I think they're pulling out, Doc."

"If so, that's not a good sign."

"No. It isn't."

Doc waved the men over and greeted them. "You know Frank Morgan?"

"Not personal," the cowboy Doc had addressed as Fred said. "Sure heard of him."

"You boys look like you're pulling out," the doctor said.

"For a fact," the .45 rider replied. "We don't want no part of this war that's shapin' up. It's gonna be bad."

"Bullard paying fighting wages?" Frank asked.

"Sure is. First-rate. And he's gettin' some real bad boys signin' on."

"Most of the old Lightnin' hands is gone," Fred said. "Drifted out last week. I reckon we're about the last of the regular hands on the Snake."

"You heard about Shelley Wilson?"

"Yes," said the .45 rider. "Late last night we did. That done it for me."

"And us," the third rider said, jerking a thumb toward Fred. "I ain't makin' war on kids."

"Who killed the child?" Frank asked.

The three men exchanged quick glances before Fred spoke. "The bushwhacker from Kansas, we heard. Goes by the name of Orin."

"Orin Mathison?" Frank asked.

"That's him. Big ol' boy. Uses one of them bolt-action rifles."

"He's been around for a time," the third rider said. "He's gettin' paid good by all three of the big ranchers. Top money for killin'."

"You know him, Frank?" Doc Everett asked.

"Never met him. But I've heard about him for years. Mainly that he's a sorry son of a bitch."

"That's him, all right," Fred said. "He's about the most disagreeable feller I ever met, for a fact. Don't nobody like him."

"Hell, why should they?" the third rider said. "He won't socialize with nobody. Never smiles or kids around. And he don't bathe much neither."

"Sounds like a delightful fellow," Doc Everett said dryly.

"A stone-cold killer, Doc," Frank said. "Absolutely no conscience. He'll kill anything or anybody for money."

"From hiding, though," Doc replied.

"Usually. But he's damn quick with a pistol too. Never sell him short in that way."

The three drifting cowboys said good-bye and rode on south.

"That about tells how this situation is shaping up, Frank," Doc Everett said. "It's going to get plenty bloody."

"Sure looks that way."

Slow, sad music began inside the church, the sound drifting faintly to Doc Everett and Frank. Frank did not recognize the song.

"You going to the burying ground, Frank?" Doc asked.

"I don't plan to. You?"

"No. I see enough of death in my work."

"You believe in God, Doc?"

"I believe there is a higher power. That answer your question?"

"I reckon so."

"You were probably asking about heaven and hell, right?"

"I guess so."

"Well . . . I think there might be a heaven. You see, I don't believe the soul dies. Just the shell that contained the soul for a brief period of time."

"Where does the soul go?"

"Beats the hell out of me, Frank," the doctor said, then lifted his hat and walked off, a smile on his lips.

Frank smiled faintly and walked over to the undertaker's. No one answered his knock on the door and the door was locked.

Frank sat down on the edge of the boardwalk and rolled a cigarette. He'd wait until the service was over and then escort Julie and the kids back home.

The service was a long one and Frank had smoked several cigarettes before it ended. The church emptied and the mourners headed for their wagons and buggies and horses for the ride over to the graveyard. Frank walked the short distance to the graveside services, and stood by the fence until it was over. When John Simmons walked up, Frank waved him over and told him about the riders he'd intercepted that morning.

"You put the bodies in the livery?" the banker asked.

"Yes. Tell the undertaker he can have their guns and saddles and whatever's in their pockets for burying them. The horses are wearing the Snake brand."

"I doubt that Trainor will ever come in to lay claim to them."

"Probably not. I just wanted you to know that."

"I'll take care of it. Are you going to see Miss Julie home?"

"That was my intention."

"Good. She's going to need some tender care for a time."

"I'll do my best, John."

"I know you will, Frank. There she comes now. I'll be getting along."

"See you."

Julie walked to Frank's side, and he put an arm around her and held her for a moment. "The kids riding back alone?"

"Yes. But not to the house."

"You mean? . . ." Frank let that dangle.

"They've got to go see their sweethearts. They both told me and openly dared me to do something about it!"

"Settle down, Julie. You want me to talk to them?"

"No, Frank. I want you to take me back to the house and stay with me for a time."

"What about Phil and Katie?"

She looked at him in silence for a moment, and then walked away, toward the buggy parked at the edge of the graveyard.

"I ought to find those damn kids and beat their butts," Frank muttered. Then he shook that thought out of his head and walked toward Julie. He caught up with her and took her arm. "They're just kids, Julie. They don't understand the finality of death or what Shelley's death has done to you. Times are changing. It's not like the way it was when we were kids. Kids are softer now. Times are so much better."

"If you say so."

"Maybe you should visit your sister in California, Julie. Get away for a time."

"I don't think so. We never got along. We haven't written in years. I don't even know if she's still in California or if she's still alive."

Frank helped her into the buggy and drove down to the livery. He tied the Ap to the rear of the buggy and headed for home.

Julie was silent and stone-faced.

Frank gave up on conversation after the first mile.

# FOURTEEN

Frank stayed with Julie the rest of the afternoon, then stayed for supper. As nightfall approached, even Frank was getting worried about the twins.

"I'd better go look for them," he said, reaching for his hat.

"Let me change and I'll go with you," Julie said.

"We can't take the buckboard, Julie. I'll be headed cross-country."

"I'll change into britches and ride my horse."

*"Men's* britches?"

"Certainly."

Frank stared at her for a moment, then shrugged his shoulders. "Times sure are moving fast," he muttered.

Julie turned to leave the room. Then both of them paused as the sounds of a galloping horse reached them. They both headed for the door, and stepped out into the waning light just as Katie reined up and almost fell out of the saddle. Frank grabbed her and steadied her, helping her to the ground.

"Phil!" the girl sobbed. "They've got him."

"Who's got him?" Frank asked.

"Mr. Gilmar and his men. He broke away from them once and yelled for me and Donnie to run. Then one of the hands roped him. Mama, they're going to horsewhip him."

"Why?" Julie shouted.

"One of the hands caught Phil and Betty Lou in the woods."

"Doing what?" Julie snapped the question.

"You know," Katie said. "Without any clothes."

"Oh, God!" Julie whispered.

"Where are they?" Frank asked.

"Just south of the crossroads, Mr. Morgan. Where that spring bubbles up and starts the creek."

Frank pushed the girl toward her mother. "Take care of her. I'll find Phil and bring him back."

Phil was still tied to a tree when Frank got to the spring. He had been stripped naked and horsewhipped, his back, buttocks, and legs a maze of bloody welts and cuts. Before he was horsewhipped, somebody had beaten him savagely. Phil was unconscious.

Young Phil's horse was nearby, where he'd been ground-reined. Frank got the horse and led him over before he freed Phil and gently laid him on the ground. He found the boy's pants and got them on him, then hoisted him into the saddle and tied him there.

"Stay unconscious, boy," Frank said. "It'll be easier on you if you do."

Phil moaned several times on the long, slow ride back to the farm, but mercifully, he didn't wake up.

Julie met them in the yard. One look at her son and the tears started. "We don't have time for any of that," Frank told her. "You get some blankets while I get the buckboard ready." Frank carefully lowered Phil to the ground. He pointed a finger at Katie. "And you help your mother, young lady."

"Yes, sir," the girl said softly.

Frank quickly hitched up the buckboard and spread hay in the back so Phil could ride more comfortably. Then he pulled around to the front of the house and placed the young man on the hay. Julie got in back with her son.

"Get up here and take the reins," Frank told Katie. "You take it slow and easy, girl."

"Yes, sir," she said, settling down on the seat. She twisted around to look at her mother. "I'm sorry, Mama," she said. "I really am."

"I know you are," Julie said. "It's all right, Katie."

"The hell it is," Frank said as he swung into the saddle. "But we'll talk about that later. Let's go," he ordered.

It was a quiet ride into town, with little conversation and only the occasional moan from the badly injured Phil.

The town of Heaven was just about to go dark for the night when they rolled into the main street. Frank rode ahead to alert the doctor. Within minutes, a crowd was gathering outside the doctor's office.

Doc Everett lifted the thin blanket that covered Phil and swore under his breath. "Who did this, Frank?"

"Gilmar and some of his men. They caught Phil with Betty Lou doing . . . ah . . . well, you know."

"Wonderful. I suppose that fool Gilmar thought he could undo what had been done by beating the boy half to death." He looked around him. "Some of you men standing around make yourselves useful and get the boy into my office. Come on, move."

"I'll arrange for rooms at the hotel, Julie," Frank told her. "You and Katie will need some rest and some place to freshen up."

"Thank you, Frank." She turned and went into the office. Frank waited outside, on a bench on the boardwalk.

John Simmons walked up and said, "You look tired, Frank."

Frank looked up. "I am, John. It's been a damn long day."

"How bad is the boy?"

"Oh, I don't think he's in any danger of dying. But he'll carry the marks of the beating for a long time."

"And many of the scars will be in his mind."

"That's sure true."

John Simmons walked on, leaving Frank sitting alone on the bench. The crowd gradually broke up, the men and women returning to their homes. Frank rose and walked into the doctor's office. Phil was on the examining table, the doctor working on cleaning up the numerous cuts on the boy's body.

"He'll live," Doc Everett said, glancing up as Frank entered. "I can't find anything broken. Not physically anyway."

"What'd you do with Julie and Katie?"

"I gave them a slug of laudanum and put them to bed in the clinic. Both of them went out quickly. Julie is emotionally exhausted."

"For a fact she can't take much more." He pointed toward Phil. "Is he conscious?"

"I'm awake, Mr. Morgan," Phil said softly. "But I sure hurt."

"I know you do, boy. Want to tell me what happened? That is, if it's all right with Dr. Everett."

"If you feel up to it, boy," the doc said.

"I do," Phil said. "Me and Betty Lou let things get out of

hand, I reckon. When . . . well, when we was done with it, we was layin' on the ground, holdin' each other, when all hell broke loose. Donnie and Katie was nearby. Katie screamed for us to run, but it was too late. Doc, what's the matter with my mouth? The words is comin' out funny-soundin'."

"Your mouth is swollen, boy, and you've lost a couple of teeth. If it hurts to talk, we can stop this right now."

"No, I want to tell it."

"All right."

"Anyways, Mr. Gilmar jerked Betty Lou up and threw her her clothes. Then he commenced to stompin' on me. I broke loose and run, but one of his hands put a loop on me and drug me back. Mr. Gilmar had a couple of his hands hold me while he beat me up some. Then they tied me to a tree and he used a whip on me. I disremember much of that 'cause I blacked out, it was hurtin' so bad. I remember you comin' up to me, Mr. Morgan, sort of. Then the ride into town. What happened to Betty Lou?"

"I don't know, Phil," Frank said. "But I'm sure she's all right."

"I bet her father put a belt to her," Phil said.

"He probably did."

"That's enough talk," Doc Everett said. "I'm going to move you to a bed, Phil. You try to get some sleep."

"I'm awful tired, Dr. Everett. Am I gonna die?"

"Don't be silly. Of course not. But you're going to hurt like the devil. I'll give you something for the pain and that will help you sleep."

"All right, sir. Mr. Morgan?"

"Yes, Phil?"

"Will you do something for me?"

"If I can, sure."

"Will you tell my mama I'm awful sorry for what happened, and will you try to find out what happened to Betty Lou?"

"I'll do my best."

"All right, Phil," Doc Everett said. "Enough talk. Let's see if you can get up and walk over to that bed in the corner. You're going to have to sleep on your stomach for a time, so get used to it."

When Phil was in bed and the lamps turned off, Frank and the doctor stepped outside the office. Doc Everett fired up a cigar and Frank rolled a cigarette.

"You sure Julie and Katie will sleep the night through, Doc?"

Doc smiled. "Probably until the sun is up. I gave them both some tincture of opium. They'll sleep quite well."

"All right. I think I'll head on back to my place. I'll be in first thing in the morning, and then I'm going to do some prowling around."

"You're not going to cross the line and head for Hell, are you?"

Frank still was amused at the names of the towns. He chuckled for a few seconds. "I might, Doc. The ranchers come over here to Heaven, don't they?"

"Never alone, Frank."

"Well, you can relax. I don't have any plans to ride to Hell."

"Besides, if there ever was a time Julie needed you, it's now. Think about that."

"You're right. I'll stay south of the road."

"Good. You want a drink, Frank?"

"Not now. It's a long ride back home. I best get going."

"I think I'll have me a toddy and then look in on Phil before I go to bed."

"Good night, Doc."

"Good night, Frank."

Frank was halfway across the street when Doc called after him. He turned around.

"You're an asset to this community, Frank. And you've found a good woman and a home. I hope you stay forever."

Frank smiled and waved. The ride back home seemed easier after that.

# FIFTEEN

Horse was well rested and ready to travel when Frank saddled him early the next morning. Frank made sure there was plenty of fresh water and food for Dog, and was in the saddle and heading for town long before dawn lightened the eastern sky. He was sitting on the boardwalk in front of the Blue Moon Cafe when the cook and waitress showed up for work and unlocked the front door. Frank was eating breakfast and working on his third cup of coffee when Doc Everett walked in.

"When you said early, you meant early, didn't you, Frank?" the doctor said, sitting down at the table with Frank.

"How is Phil?" Frank asked.

"Sore as hell. But he's talking and feeling a lot better. And before you ask about Julie, she's still asleep."

"Katie?"

The doctor sugared his coffee and grimaced, shaking his head.

"What does that mean, Doc?"

Doc Everett took a sip of coffee and added more sugar. "It means that I think she's about three months gone."

Frank set his coffee mug down and stared at the doctor. "If that's a joke, it isn't funny."

"It isn't a joke and it sure as hell isn't funny."

"Good God A'mighty!" Frank blurted out. "Katie told you?"

Everett smiled. "Let's just say I've seen a lot of pregnant women in my time, Frank."

"First Shelley is killed; then Phil is almost beaten to death, now this. All within forty-eight hours. I don't know how much more Julie can take."

"For a fact, she's had a lot to contend with."

"Are you going to talk to Katie, confirm this?"

"I thought I would. Perhaps you can take Julie out for a walk when she wakes up."

"I can do that. Sure."

"What do you know about this Donnie Bullard?"

"Some folks like him. Personally, I think he's a snotty little spoiled piece of cow crap."

"That's good enough for me."

"Don't let it be. I don't like his father, and I'm not above prejudice."

"Well, Julie doesn't like him either."

"That's understandable."

"Damn!" Frank whispered.

"You can't undo the pregnancy, Frank. All we can do is hope for the best for the girl."

"You think the boy will marry her?"

"Personally, no."

"Then the child will be a woods colt. That's a terrible thing to have hanging over someone's head."

The doctor shrugged his shoulders and took a sip of coffee. Frank spoke no more about Katie's situation while the men finished their breakfast.

"Don't worry about Julie today, Frank," the doctor said. "I'm going to keep her in town at least for one more day until I can send Phil home."

"All right. I'll head on back and milk the cow for her and check on the other livestock and feed the chickens. Then I'll do some prowling. Tell her I'll be back for her and the kids tomorrow afternoon at the latest."

"I'll do it."

Frank bought a sackful of biscuits from the waitress for his lunch and headed out. He saw to the morning chores at Julie's and then checked on his place, played with Dog for a few minutes, and then headed for the road, the dividing line between the two warring factions.

He prowled up and down the line until midafternoon, and did not see any hands from any of the ranches. "Laying low," Frank muttered just as he reined up and twisted in the saddle. The bullet that would have hit him squarely in the back missed him by about one inch and slammed into a tree.

Frank rolled out of the saddle, grabbed his rifle from the boot, and slapped Horse on the rump, sending the big horse trotting away. Frank knew he would not go far. Frank bellied down behind a tree, facing the direction the shot came from, and waited.

There was a wooded knoll about 150 yards away, the only good cover in the immediate area, and Frank felt sure that was where the sniper was located.

He chambered a round into his .44-40, wriggled around to the other side of the old tree, and chanced a quick look.

He could see nothing that might give away the shooter's position. He could do nothing except wait.

Whoever the shooter was, and Frank felt confident it was the back-shooter Orin Mathison, he wasn't about to give away his position by throwing any chance shots in Frank's direction.

Just then a rifle barked and a spray of dirt stung Frank's face. He backed away, thinking: *Orin's got him one of those telescopes on his rifle. Has to be.*

He worked his way down the slight incline, and began worming his way toward a small stand of scrub timber off to his right. He reached the timber and inched under the low branches, hoping he would not run into a big rattler seeking refuge from the sun.

There was no waiting snake, and Frank worked his way through the weeds until he had a good view of the timber where the shooter was hiding. He watched intently for a moment, and then the sniper moved, causing a flash of unnatural color to present itself.

Frank took aim and squeezed the trigger. The bullet must have come awfully close, for the shooter jumped quickly to one side. Frank put another round where he guessed the shooter would be, and that did it for the hidden gunman. No more shots came from the timber. Orin wanted no more part of this.

Frank waited for several moments, and then reset his back sights and worked his way out of the scrub timber. He located his horse, and cautiously made his way over and swung into the saddle, staying low until he had put some distance between the hill and himself. Then he made a long slow circle, coming up behind the hill and the timber. He found fresh tracks, and they were the same as the tracks he'd found several times before. There was no doubt in his mind the shooter was Orin Mathison.

Frank followed the tracks to the road and reined up. There would be another day for them to meet, he was certain of that. "Count on it, Mathison," he said aloud. "You and me got a score to settle."

He rode back to his place and stabled Horse, and he and Dog went into the house. Frank still had some biscuits left, and he fed those to Dog along with some jerky. Then he set about making supper for himself.

He was in bed sound asleep just after dark.


Frank awakened and lit the bedside lamp, glancing at his pocket watch. Three o'clock. He had gone to bed so early, he was well refreshed, and decided not to try to force himself back to sleep. He dressed, stoked up the stove, made a pot of coffee, and fried a half dozen slices of thick-cut bacon. He fixed a skillet of pan bread, and he and Dog had a pleasant early morning repast.

Frank decided to saddle up and do some early morning prowling; just checking on things in the south part of the connecting valleys.

He hadn't gone but a couple of miles before he began to smell dust in the air. A lot of dust, blowing in from the north. That meant a large number of either wagons or horsemen. At this time of the morning, it also meant trouble, for Frank didn't think it was wagons. He headed for the main road and town. He figured he was no more than five minutes ahead of the riders; maybe not that long.

Frank put Horse into a fast trot and hit the edge of the main street, yelling as loud as he could.

"What's going on down there?" a local hollered.

"A large group of horsemen on the way here!" Frank yelled. "I think it's trouble. Get up and get armed. I'll spread the word."

"I'll ring the fire alarm bell!" the local told him. "You keep yelling."

Frank rode through the town, hollering and shouting out warnings, urging the people to arm themselves.

On the ride back up the main street, Frank could see the night riders approaching, all of them carrying torches.

"They're going to try to burn the town!" Frank yelled. He jumped from the saddle, grabbed his rifle, and slapped Horse on the rump, sending him galloping into an alley—out of harm's way, Frank hoped.

The flickering, bobbing lights from the handheld torches drew closer as the first of several dozen night riders reached the north edge of town.

"They're crazy!" Lawyer Foster said, running up to Frank. He had on his britches with the galluses hanging down. Frank noticed that the man wore mismatched shoes and no socks. He was carrying a shotgun.

"Can you use that thing?" Frank asked.

"You bet I can," Lawyer Foster replied just as one of the hooded night riders fired the first shot, the bullet breaking a front window of a shop.

Foster lifted his shotgun and gave the rider a blast of bird shot.

The distance was too great and the load too light to be a killing shot, but it drew a yelp of pain from the rider.

Frank stepped out to the edge of the boardwalk just as those riders with torches began throwing them at the stores along the main street. Frank snapped off a shot that knocked a rider from the saddle and sent him bouncing in the dirt.

"Open fire!" Frank yelled to the citizens who had gathered along the street's boardwalks. "Or lose your town!"

"Fire, damnit!" Doc Everett yelled. Then he blasted away with a double-barrel shotgun.

The locals cut loose with rifles, pistols, and shotguns, the barrage emptying half a dozen saddles.

"We lost our surprise!" a gunhand yelled, his words slightly muffled behind the hood. "Let's get the hell outta here."

Frank was lining him up in gunsights as the last word left his mouth. Just as the hired gun wheeled his horse, Frank squeezed the trigger. The bullet hit the hooded man in the center of his back, and the man fell bonelessly from the saddle, his spinal cord severed.

The locals had reloaded their shotguns, and once again cut loose with loads ranging from bird shot to rusty nails. Several more saddles were emptied and several more hired guns got peppered with bird shot.

What was left of the bunch galloped out of town.

"You saved the town, Frank," Doc Everett said, walking up, holding a shotgun. "We're all in your debt."

Frank was punching out empty brass and reloading his Peacemaker. "I got lucky and smelled dust in the air, Doc. I just about didn't make it here in time."

"Help me!" a wounded night rider called from the street. "I'm hit hard."

Other downed riders joined in, calling for help.

"Well, I took an oath," Doc Everett said. "I'll go see what I can do."

"I'll join you," Frank told him. "And keep a gun on the others."

"Good idea. Come on."

Two of the night riders were dead, one was not long for this world, and the wounds of the others ranged from light to moderate.

"I'll send a telegram to the sheriff," Banker Simmons said. "And another to the governor, detailing what took place here this night. Then we'll see what happens."

"Save all the hoods for evidence," Frank said. "We'll need them for the trial."

Someone in the crowd laughed. "You don't really believe there'll be a trial, do you, Mr. Morgan?"

"They'll have to be if the governor gets the telegram."

"He won't," Doc Everett said, looking up from one of the wounded night riders. "One of his aides will intercept it and the governor will never see it."

"There's a good place for farmers and the like about fifty miles from here," one of the night riders who was only slightly wounded said. "Was I you folks I'd move over there."

"We're not moving anywhere," a local told him. "This is our home and here we intend to stay."

"Not for long," the night rider replied.

"How is Julie, Doc?" Frank asked, kneeling down beside the doctor.

"She's all right, Frank. And Phil is a lot better." Doc Everett stood up. "Some of you men start carrying these"— he paused— "white trash over to that vacant building where the millinery shop used to be. We'll use that for a hospital. And decide among you who'll take turns standing guard."

Frank walked over to the empty shop with the men and their prisoners, and then went over to the hotel to see about Julie and Katie.

Julie embraced him, holding on for a moment before pushing him away. "Phil's much better, Frank. Dr. Everett says he expects him to make a full recovery. Physically, that is."

"I'm glad to hear that. How is Katie?"

Julie's eyes searched his face for a few seconds. "The doctor told you, didn't he?"

"About Katie, yes, he did."

"What am I going to do?"

"We, Julie. What are we going to do?"

"You mean that, Frank?"

"Yes, I do. Well . . . we'll work it out, I reckon."

"It's going to take a lot of working out. What do you have in mind?"

"If the Bullard boy won't marry her, and that might turn out to be a bad thing for both of them, well, sending her away. I can afford it, Julie. I may not look like it or act like it, but I am not a poor man."

"I sensed that, Frank. I don't want her marrying that little brat. But sending her away . . . where?"

"I don't know. I'll ask Doc Everett. Maybe he'll know of someplace that takes in, ah, expecting young girls."

"It's shameful, Frank. I can't hardly bear to look other women in the eye."

"Don't feel that way, Julie. You didn't do nothing wrong. Besides, these things happen more often than gets talked about, you can bet on that."

"I suppose so. Frank? I just had a terrible thought. What if Betty Lou is, well, in a family way too?"

"Let's deal with one situation at a time. Good God. Let's don't even think about that other girl."

"Frank Morgan?" a man's voice called from the hall.

"Yes?" Frank's hand dropped to the butt of his Peacemaker.

"I'm friendly, Mr. Morgan. It's Jeff, from over at the livery. They's a boy outside, wants to talk to you and Miss Julie."

"A boy? What boy, Jeff?"

"Donnie Bullard."

# SIXTEEN

Julie insisted upon walking down with Frank and con-fronting Donnie.

"I don't think that's wise right now, Julie," he told her.

Her reply was to head for the door and step out into the hall. She looked back at Frank. "Are you coming?" Then she turned and walked on down the hall.

Frank plopped his hat on his head and went after her.

Donnie Bullard was standing on the boardwalk, his hat on his head.

*Just a scared kid,* Frank thought. *Fifteen years old and in a peck of trouble, and knows it.*

"Miss Julie," Donnie said. "I disobeyed my dad and run off from home to tell you I aim to do the right thing."

"What happened to your face, Donnie?" Julie asked.

"My dad, he hit me a couple of times when I told him

what I was fixin' to do. Then he forbade me from comin' to see about Katie."

"What do you think is the right thing to do, Donnie?"

Frank had stepped back into the shadows. This was between Julie and the boy.

"Well, me and Katie had talked abut it, ma'am. I aim to marry her."

Doc Everett had walked to within hearing distance and stopped.

"I see." Julie spoke softly. She looked at the boy in the faint glow of light from the lamps in the hotel lobby. "Your right hand is swollen and the knuckles raw, Donnie. What happened to your hand?"

Donnie shuffled his feet. "Well, Miss Julie, I hauled off and hit my dad after he punched me a couple of times and called Katie a dirty little whore. I mean, I knocked the stuffin' out of him. Knocked him flat on his behind, I did. Then I took off. I lit me a shuck outta there. That's how come my hand is kinda swole."

Julie had to cover her mouth with a hand to hide her quick smile at Donnie's explanation. Frank cut his eyes to Doc Everett, and saw that the man had a wide grin on his face.

"Well, Donnie, how do you plan on supporting Katie?"

"I reckon I'll get me a job, Miss Julie. I don't rightly know where, but I'll work. I'm not a bit lazy." He looked at Frank. "Mr. Morgan, ain't it?"

"That's right, Donnie."

"Could I work at your ranch, sir? I'm a right good hand."

"I'm sure you are, Donnie. And you've taken a big step toward becoming a growed-up man by coming here this morning. Your father should have been proud of you."

"My dad stood at the door of the ranch house and disowned me," Donnie said. "He screamed it out, real loud.

Everybody heard it, 'ceptin' the hired guns, who was already on the move to attack this town. He said if I ever set foot on .45 range again, he'd horsewhip me and leave me for the buzzards to eat my eyes."

"How about your mother?" Julie asked.

"She's scared of my dad," Donnie said. "She won't say nothin' against him."

Frank glanced at the eastern sky. Silver was just beginning to push away the blackness of night.

"I'm worried about Betty Lou Gilmar," Donnie said. "Scared about what her pa might do to her."

"That's a legitimate concern," Doc Everett said, finally stepping forward. "Ken Gilmar has a really bad temper."

"I know Betty Lou's been goin' to see Doc Woods of late," Donnie said. "Something's sure ailin' her."

"Oh, my Lord," Doc Everett muttered under his breath.

Julie looked heavenward and shook her head. "I wonder why," she said, her words laced with sarcasm. "Come on, Donnie," Julie said, holding out a hand. "Let's go see Katie. I'm sure seeing you will make her feel better."

"I'd better get back to the wounded," Doc Everett said, relighting the stub of a cigar. "I've still got some lead to dig out."

Frank stood alone on the boardwalk for a few minutes. Fresh dirt had been scattered over the blood spots in the street, and the locals had returned home to wash up, have breakfast, and dress and get ready for the day's business.

Frank looked up the street and watched as a paint pony walked slowly into view, the rider slumping in the saddle as if asleep or very weary. As the pony drew closer, Frank could see that the rider was a woman. He stepped off the boardwalk and into the street, walking toward the pony and rider—he could now tell that the rider was a girl in her teens. He grabbed the reins just as she began to fall from the saddle. Frank caught the girl in his arms. There was blood on the front of her red-and-white checkered shirt, and the back of the shirt was ripped and bloody.

"Get Doc Everett!" Frank yelled to a couple of men walking along the boardwalk. "Hurry!" Frank carried the girl to the boardwalk and set her down, holding her upright with one arm.

"Betty Lou Gilmar," Doc Everett said, walking up.

"Her face is all swollen and bruised," Frank said. "And her back is a mess."

"I see that. Can you carry her over to my office?"

"Sure."

Frank waited outside the doctor's office, and smoked a hand-rolled until Everett walked outside. "Her father beat that girl with his fists and then used a quirt on her back," Doc Everett said. "The rotten son of a bitch!"

"Nice family. How bad hurt is she?"

"Nothing is broken that I could tell."

"This is the girl who's been seeing the doctor in Hell?"

"The same."

"And?"

Everett sighed and tossed his soggy stub of a cigar into the street. "Oh, I'd say she was about three or four months along."

"I reckon we'll have us a double wedding."

"It better be quick, Frank."

"I'll talk to Julie about it."

"Then there is the matter of what the hell a couple of fifteen-year-old boys are going to do to support a family."

"They can farm and ranch."

"For you?"

"I reckon so. With all the sections I've bought, I've got a hell of a spread. Nothing like the acreage the folks up at the north end have, but I figure it's close to two thousand acres. Maybe a little more than that."

"Then you're really planning on staying?"

"I hope so, Doc. I'm sure going to try. If nothing else, I'll have me someplace I can return to now and then. For now, I'll arrange for a couple hundred head of cattle to be brought in for me and start the beginnings of a herd." He smiled. "I've heard about a couple more sections of land that's up for sale. I'll look into that."

Doc Everett looked at Frank for a few seconds, an odd expression in his eyes. He fished around in his jacket pocket and pulled out a fresh cigar and fired it up. "Good, Frank. You need someplace to return to now and then."

"You sound as if you don't think I can do it, Doc."

"Do *you*?" the doctor asked, then turned and walked away.

Frank watched the doctor go, then went in search of Julie. He found her with the kids, all four of them, in the doctor's small infirmary. Two of the beds were filled, with Betty Lou and Phil, both of them sitting up.

Julie looked up when Frank opened the door, and waved him in. "We're going to have a double wedding, Frank."

"That's, ah, wonderful, Julie. When?"

"As quickly as possible. Probably within two or three days. It'll be at the church."

"Well . . . I'll certainly be there."

"They'll all stay with me until they can find places of their own."

Frank nodded, not sure exactly what to say. Things were happening awfully fast.

"Are you hungry, Frank?" Julie asked.

"I could eat."

"Then let's leave the kids alone and have breakfast."

"Fine with me."

On the short walk over to the cafe, Julie said, "I don't know what else to do, Frank."

"There isn't anything else. Except hope for the best for all of them."

"Thank God you're here, though."

Frank experienced some sudden and strange emotions at that statement. He wasn't sure how to respond. He figured the best thing he could do was keep his mouth shut, so he did.

"My house is going to be crowded," Julie said.

"Sure will be."

"You and I can work something out, though, right?"

"Ah . . . yeah. I mean, sure we can."

"Good. That certainly takes a load off my mind."

Frank helped her up onto the boardwalk, thinking: *Life can sure get complicated in a hurry.*

# SEVENTEEN

After breakfast Julie returned to the kids, and Frank walked to the livery to check on Horse. He was just leaving the livery when he heard someone shout.

Frank stopped and looked up the street. About a dozen men were riding slowly up the main street.

"Gilmar and Bullard in the front," a local called. "And I don't think those men with them are regular cowboys."

Frank stepped up onto the boardwalk and walked toward the approaching riders. From long habit he had slipped the leather thong from the hammer of his Peacemaker the instant he spotted the riders. As they drew closer, Frank could pick out several men in the group with the stamp of hired guns on them. He knew one of the men personally: Al Chambers. Al was quick and mean and had a dozen kills to his credit.

On the other side of the street, John Simmons was walking toward his bank. He stopped and turned, facing the street when Gilmar called out his name.

"Kenneth," Simmons said. "I'm very surprised to see you in town."

"I'm come to fetch my daughter home, John."

"Well, that's up to her, Kenneth. Personally, I don't think she wants to return to your ranch."

"She doesn't have a damn thing to say about it!" the rancher snapped, reining up.

"She can't travel yet," Doc Everett called, stepping out of his office. "Won't be able to for several days. She's in a lot of pain and I've given her a sedative. So why don't you go away, and take your hired guns with you?"

"Why don't you go to hell, Doc?" Bullard said. "Nobody runs us out of any town."

Frank was standing on the boardwalk, in a silent but very deadly stare-down with Al Chambers.

"And I've come to take my son back home," Bullard said.

"No!" Donnie yelled from the second floor of the hotel. "You disowned me, remember?"

"Get your butt down here, boy!" the father yelled.

"Forget it!" Donnie yelled, and closed the window.

Suddenly, as if on a silent cue, both sides of the street were lined with citizens, all carrying rifles and shotguns.

"This town is dead," Gilmar said. "I'll destroy it and everyone in it."

The locals all raised their weapons.

"Easy, Ken," Bullard cautioned his friend in a low voice.

Frank and Al Chambers were looking at one another, engaging in a silent exchange of potentially deadly glances.

"Betty Lou!" the father yelled. "Get out here. We're going home."

"You go home!" the girl yelled from behind walls. "You go home without me."

The owner of the Lightning brand sat his saddle and cursed.

Al Chambers slowly swung out of the saddle and stepped up onto the boardwalk. Frank Morgan faced the man, the wide street between them.

"Donnie!" Bullard yelled. "Come on, boy. Stop this silliness now. It's time for you to come on home."

"Go to hell!" the son hollered.

The two ranchers exchanged glances. "This ain't workin'," Ken said. "I told you it wouldn't, Don."

"Take your hired guns and leave this town," Banker Simmons called. "You're welcome here anytime you want to come in peace."

Bullard pointed a finger at Simmons. "Nobody tells me what to do in this valley, Simmons. And that sure as hell includes you."

"Don't be a fool, Don," the banker told him. "We could have the most prosperous communities in this territory if you'd stop trying to fight growth."

The rancher cursed the banker.

"Yonder stands the reason these shopkeepers and sheepherders and clodhoppers all of a sudden got some courage," Al Chambers called. He pointed toward Frank. "Mr. Bullard, you and Mr. Gilmar pull your men back some, out of the line of fire. I'll take care of Morgan right here and now."

"Now see here!" Simmons said.

"Shut up, John," Bullard called. "You got your gunslick, didn't you? Well . . . we got a right to ours, don't we?"

"It's all right, John," Frank called. "I'll handle this. The rest of you citizens, stay out of this."

"Back up, boys," Gilmar called, waving a hand. "This is between Al and Morgan. We're out of it."

"No matter how it turns out?" a gunhand called.

"No matter what," Gilmar said. "That fair enough, John?"

"Fair enough," the banker said. "If that's the way Morgan wants it."

"It is," Frank called, stepping off the boardwalk into the street.

The ranchers and their hired guns backed away, leaving Al Chambers standing alone, facing Frank. The long lines of civilians on both sides of the street began moving aside, not wanting to get caught in the line of fire.

"I've waited a long time for this, Morgan," Al called.

"Well, your wait is over, Al. Make your play."

"All in good time, Morgan. I want to see you sweat some."

"Because I'm facing you, Al?"

Al nodded his head.

Frank laughed at him.

Al cursed him. "I'm gonna shoot you in the belly, Morgan. You're gonna die hard and long, you bastard."

Frank made no reply.

"Did you hear me, Morgan!" Al yelled.

"Of course I heard you, Al," Frank said. "Half the town did."

"Then drag iron, Morgan. Damn you, pull on me."

"After you, Al."

Al cussed him.

Frank yawned. "This is boring me, Al. If you don't do something pretty soon, I'm going to doze off right here in the street."

Julie and the kids were watching from a second-floor window. They were standing back so Frank could not see them and be distracted.

"Miss Julie," Donnie said. "Al Chambers is awful fast.

Him and some of the other gunfighters is gettin' triple
fightin' wages to deal with Mr. Morgan."

"I'm sure Frank knows that, Donnie."

"He's a real nice man, Miss Julie. I'd hate for something
bad to happen to him."

"So would I, Donnie."

Standing in the street, Al cussed and grabbed for his gun.
Frank hooked and drew, the motion so smooth and quick the
blinking of an eye would have missed it. The Peacemaker
cracked in the morning air. A hole appeared in the center of
Al Chambers's shirt. Al had not cleared leather. His .45
dropped back snugly into the holster, and Al staggered for a
couple of seconds, then sank to his knees.

"Jesus God," one of the hired guns whispered in awe.

"You bastard!" Al said. "You've killed me."

"You started it," Frank said, dropping his Peacemaker
back into leather.

Al tried to get to his feet. He struggled for a few seconds,
then sat back down in the dirt, blood beginning to leak from
his mouth. He cussed Frank, spewing the blood-tinged pro-
fanity into the quiet air.

The ranchers, Bullard and Gilmar, sat their saddles and
stared grim-faced at the scene before them.

Frank stepped back up onto the boardwalk just as Doc
Everett walked out of his office and over to the downed gun-
hand. The doctor squatted down and tried to open Al's shirt.
Al slapped his hand away.

"Leave me alone, you bastard!"

"With much pleasure," Doc Everett said, standing up and
backing away.

"Look at him, Doc," Ken Gilmar said.

"He doesn't want me to check him," the doctor replied.

Al fell over, facedown in the dirt.

"Maybe now you can check him out," Don Bullard suggested.

The doctor knelt down and quickly checked the fallen gunfighter. He looked up at the mounted ranchers. "He's dead."

"Couple of you boys pick him up and lay him across his saddle," Bullard ordered. "We'll bury him back across the line."

Frank was standing on the boardwalk, leaning against a support post, rolling a cigarette, watching the scene in the street.

Gilmar glanced over at Frank. "It isn't over, Morgan. Not by a long shot."

Frank shrugged that off. "It should be," he told the rancher. "You're fighting a losing battle. All that's going to happen is a lot of people, good and bad, are going to die."

"We didn't have nothing to do with them night riders who tried to burn the town," Bullard said. "You can believe that or not."

"You're saying it was all Trainor's doing?" Simmons called.

"I'm sayin' we didn't have nothin' to do with it, that's all."

Frank popped a match into flame and lit his cigarette.

Al Chambers's body was tied belly-down across his saddle.

"Let's go, boys," Bullard ordered, lifting the reins. He glanced over at Frank. "It ain't over, Morgan."

"I'll be around, Bullard." Frank replied.

The ranchers and their hired guns galloped out of town. Doc Everett walked over to Frank, while the locals lowered their guns and went back to their homes and businesses.

"You believe what Bullard said about the night riders, Frank?"

"No. His son said their confrontation took place just after the riders left to attack the town. Bullard's a liar."

"I've known that for years," Doc said sourly. "How do you feel, Frank?"

"No different than I felt ten minutes ago, Doc."

"I've seen a lot of death in my time," Doc said. "I've never really become hardened to it. My so-called callous attitude is meant to cover that up."

Frank smiled. "There's a question in there somewhere, Doc, right?"

"We've talked about this before, Frank. Killing doesn't seem to bother you."

"First time I shot a man, Doc, I nearly puked my guts out. I was just a kid, 'bout Donnie's age. Second time it was easier. My philosophy is simple. I use a gun to protect my life, my loved ones, my property. I won't take much talking down to, and I won't tolerate people putting hands on me. If I pull a gun, I'm ready to use it, and usually do."

"And if everyone shared your philosophy, Frank?"

"It would be a hell of a world."

Doc Everett grunted and said, "See you later, Frank."

"I'll be around."

Frank watched the doctor walk away back to his clinic, then stood and watched as the town got back to normal and stores began opening for the day's business. Dirt was raked over the bloodstains in the street, and Al Chambers became another short-lived memory in a Western town. The incident would be talked about for a few days; then something else would happen to push it out of the citizens' memory.

Frank walked over to the hotel to have a chat with Julie. They had a lot of things to discuss and not much time to do it.

# EIGHTEEN

Several of the town ladies met with Julie about the wedding plans, and Julie told Frank, in so many words, to go peddle his papers for a few days.

Frank did so gratefully, heading back to his place to check on things. Dog was glad to see him, and Frank spent some time playing and roughhousing with the big cur dog. He had just finished forking some hay for the horses when Harry Clay rode up. Frank greeted the man as he stepped from the saddle.

"Frank," Harry said. "Can I talk some business with you?"

"Sure. You want some coffee?"

"That would hit the spot, I reckon."

"I was thinking about it myself. Come on into the house and I'll make us a pot."

The men talked of small things while the coffee was boiling, then got down to business over mugs of steaming strong coffee.

"I got two sections of land, Frank. Good land, near 'bouts all of it, with good water."

"I know that, Harry. I've ridden over it."

"Me and the wife have talked it over and we want to pull out."

"Oh? I'm sorry to hear that."

"I got friends in Idaho who want me to come join them in a farming venture. I want to go."

"Idaho is right pretty country, Harry. I've spent some time there."

"You want to buy my land, Frank?"

"Well . . . I reckon I might, if the price was right."

"I won't hold you up on it. I'll make it fair."

"When do you want to leave?"

"The day we sign the papers."

"All right, let's talk about it."

Five minutes later, the men had agreed on a price. Frank and Harry Clay would meet at the bank the next day to finish the deal.

"This makes you the biggest landowner in the south section, Frank."

"I reckon that's true. For a man who doesn't know much about farming, I'm sure as hell land-poor."

Harry smiled. "For a man who might suddenly have a whole passel of kids to look after, you're gonna need it."

Frank laughed at that. "News does get around, doesn't it?"

"The boy and girl all right after them beatings?"

"Oh, yeah. They're both up and around and healing. They're young. They'll heal fast."

"Well . . . I'll see you at the bank in the morning then."

"See you there, Harry."

The price the men had settled on for the two sections of land was more than fair, and wouldn't even put a dent into Frank's finances, but he had to shake his head as Harry Clay rode away, thinking: *What am I getting into here?*

Before he could further question his wisdom as a businessman, Dog began growling low in his throat.

"What's wrong with you?" Frank asked.

Dog growled again, his ears laid back and the hair on his back standing up.

"Okay. I get the message." Frank picked up a rifle from the gun rack in the living room and walked to a front window, looking out. He could see nothing out of place or anything that might pose danger.

Still Dog continued to growl low in his throat.

Frank eared back the hammer on the .44-40. Something, or somebody, was definitely out there, and whoever or whatever it was presented danger. Dog didn't growl at friends. Frank looked at the big cur: Dog was baring his teeth in a snarl.

"Easy now," Frank said softly. "Settle down. You're staying in here with me."

Dog looked at him and growled.

"I mean it, you hardhead. Settle down."

Frank waited close by the window, his rifle ready. He had no idea who the person lying in wait outside his house might be. Frank knew he still had a bounty on his head, maybe more than one.

"I'll burn you out, you son of a bitch!" The shouted threat carried plain through the hot air.

The voice was familiar, but Frank couldn't put a name to it.

"I'll make you come out and face me!"

Frank waited while the as-yet-unknown man shouted out half a dozen very profane threats against his person.

"Oh, hell!" Frank muttered as he was finally able to put a face to the voice. "Not him again."

It was the loudmouthed young man from Butte, Rob something or another. Frank had been told by townspeople that Rob had ridden out as soon as his hip wound had permitted him to swing into the saddle.

"What the hell do you want, boy?" Frank shouted through the open window.

"I want to kill you!" Rob screamed the words.

"Well, you're not going to do that. Go home, hang up your guns, and live a long life."

"Hell with you, Morgan. I'm goin' to kill you!"

"Damn!" Frank whispered. He didn't want to have to kill the young man. It would suit Frank if he never had to use his gun again.

But he knew with his reputation, the odds against him ever being able to take off his gun and live in peace were long indeed.

"Go away, Rob," Frank called. "Do yourself a favor and ride out."

"After I kill you."

"Boy, that isn't going to happen. You're signing your own death warrant."

"You say, Morgan! I say different."

"I beat you before, boy. What makes you think this time will be any different?"

"It'll be different, Morgan. I know it will."

"All right, boy. I'm coming out. Just hang on." But instead of going out the front door, Frank quietly slipped out the back and began a wide circling, coming out behind the barn. Dog didn't like it, but he would stay put. Frank had taken off his spurs so he made no sound as he slipped up behind the young would-be gunman.

Frank tapped Rob on the shoulder.

"Huh!" Rob shouted, spinning around.

Frank butt-stroked him with the .44-40 and Rob went down and out cold.

When he came to a few minutes later, Frank had him tied to a straight-backed kitchen chair and was looking at him.

"What the hell am I going to do with you, boy?" Frank asked.

"Turn me a-loose!"

"Are you going to behave?"

"Turn me a-loose and find out."

Frank loosened the rope on Rob's wrists and backed up. "You're free."

Rob rubbed his wrists and glared at Frank.

"Now what?" Frank asked.

"Gimme my guns."

"Not a chance."

"I'll get some more guns."

"Why?"

"A man's got to have guns, Morgan."

"I'll agree with that. To defend himself. But not to go looking for trouble. That's what you do: hunt for trouble. Why? You think using a gun makes you a big man?"

Rob stared at him, offering no reply.

"I tell you what, Rob, and I'll try to make this as plain as I can. I'm real tired of messing around with you. I've put my life on the line three times messing with you. No more. This is the last time. If I see you again, I'm going to kill you. Do you finally and, I hope, for the last time understand that?"

The young would-be gunfighter slowly nodded his head. "I reckon."

"Good. You want some coffee?"

"Huh?"

"Coffee. Out of that pot on the stove yonder."

"You're offering me a cup of coffee?"

Frank sighed. "Yes. Do you want a cup?"

"That would hit the spot, for shore."

"Fine. At least we got that settled."

With the coffee poured and sugared, Rob said, "I reckon after I drink this, Mr. Morgan, I'll drift on out of here."

"Good. I've got enough to worry about without having to put up with you."

"I've decided to let you live."

"That's right nice of you," Frank said, the sarcasm lost on Rob. "That really eases my mind."

"I thought it would."

Frank decided right then that Rob wasn't playing with a full deck of cards. Maybe his mama had dropped him on his head when he was little.

"You want a grubstake to get you going, boy?"

"For a fact I ain't got no money."

Frank dug in his pocket and gave him twenty dollars. "That ought to get you a ways, boy. A long ways, I hope."

"Right nice of you, Mr. Morgan."

"Think nothing of it."

Frank sat out on the porch for a time after Rob had ridden out. He felt good about not having to face the young fool and shoot him.

"Stay gone, boy," he whispered. "And live a long life. And more importantly, stay the hell away from me."

Frank stepped inside to get himself another cup of coffee, Dog padding along with him. As he poured his coffee, Frank decided to fix a snack. He tossed some wood in the stove and put some bacon on to fry, then sliced some bread. He was pumping him some water at the sink when he saw movement in the timber at the side of the clearing. Dog's head came up at that instant and he growled, a snarl coming out behind the growl.

"Okay," Frank told him. "Settle down. It's that damn Rob again." He pulled the skillet off the stove and picked up his rifle, muttering, "Man can't even fix him a bite to eat. Damn!"

A dozen rifles opened up, the bullets breaking glass and shattering wood. Frank hit the floor belly-down. He shoved Dog behind the wood box and told him to stay there.

"It's about to get real interesting around here," he said.

# NINETEEN

Frank lay on the floor and let the riflemen blast away for a couple of minutes. The rounds busted windows and tore through parts of the house, breaking lamps and clanging off the stove. Dog lay safe behind the full firewood box, and Frank had crawled in front of a full book cabinet, the volumes stopping any rounds that blew through the walls of the house.

When the gunmen paused to reload, Frank crawled to a window and cautiously looked out. The first thing he saw was the leg of a man sticking out from behind a rack of cut firewood. Frank put a .44-40 round into the man's knee. Then, before the echo of the rifle died away, he quickly shifted position to the rear of the house.

The gunhand with the busted knee lay on the ground and hollered in pain.

"He's in the front!" someone yelled. "Blow it apart!"

The riflemen directed their fire to the front of the house, the rounds from rifles blowing through the several inches of wood. Frank had slipped to the back porch and had positioned himself behind a stack of firewood. He chanced a quick look around the edge of the stack and saw a man fully exposed, standing at the edge of the barn.

Frank put a round into the man's belly that doubled the gunslick over and set him on the ground on his butt, both hands holding his perforated midsection.

Then, before the rifle fire could be directed to the back porch, Frank crawled quickly into the kitchen.

"Help me!" the gutshot man yelled. "I'm hard hit and hurtin' somethin' awful."

Frank jumped to his feet and blew three quick rounds out the kitchen window. He didn't think he managed to hit anything, but he did send several gunhands diving for the ground.

He moved to the living room and peeked out through a bullet-torn hole in the wall. No one was leaving cover to help the badly wounded man. The man with the busted knee had crawled out of sight.

"Damn you all!" the gutshot man hollered. "Somebody come help me."

"Yeah," Frank whispered. "Somebody make a move. Please do."

Somebody did, jumping from behind cover and starting a run toward the wounded man. Frank brought him down, the .44-40 round dusting him from side to side and sending him tumbling to the ground. The man kicked a couple of times and then lay still, the blood leaking out, staining the ground.

"Three down," Frank muttered. "Come on, boys. Let's make it four or five. Somebody do something."

But the gunmen had suddenly become very cautious.

"We should have kilt him by now," a man called. "He should be shot full of holes."

"Well, he ain't," another man said. "And we got one down and wounded and two dead, or soon will be."

The gutshot man called weakly, "Don't leave me here, boys. I'm done for but I don't wanna lay here and rot. Bury me proper, you hear?"

"We'll plant you good, Sol. Don't you worry about that."

"Then gather up your dead and your wounded and get the hell out of here!" Frank called. "I won't fire on you."

"This ain't over, Morgan."

"Yeah, I know. You'll get me. I've heard it all before, many times."

"Morgan?" A new voice was added.

"Right here. I haven't gone anywhere."

"Get out while you can. That's a fair warnin'. This thing is bigger than you know. Ain't no reason for you to die for a bunch of sodbusters and ribbon clerks that don't really give a damn about you."

Frank knew that voice. He struggled for a moment, trying to put a name to it. Finally he gave it up. "This is my home."

"This is Dave Clayton, Morgan."

"Been a long time, Dave."

"Five or six years. Lomax is on his way in, and so is Jones. Thought you'd better know that."

Lomax and Jones were hired killers. Two damn tough hombres out of West Texas. "Tell your bosses they can bring in all the hired guns they can find, Dave. I'm not leaving."

"Ain't no law gonna interfere in this, Morgan."

"I know that."

"All right. You been warned. It's open season from now on."

"Works both ways, Dave. You better give that some thought."

"We're goin', Morgan. For now anyways."

"I hear you. Take your dead and wounded and clear out. I won't fire on you . . . this time."

The dead and wounded were collected and the gunmen rode away. Frank looked over at Dog, who was peering around the edge of the wood box, as if silently asking: What the hell is going on here?

"Come on out, fellow," Frank said, punching fresh rounds into his rifle. "It's all right." Frank slid the skillet of bacon back onto the stove, and then walked the length of the house, inspecting the damage done by the gunfire. Then he walked outside and around the clearing, kicking dirt over the bloodstains.

"I think, Dog," Frank said, "that it's time for me to go on the hunt. And I think I'll do just that. Starting right after I make me a little trip into town."

Frank left the big Appaloosa ground-reined about a mile from the main house of the Trainor spread, in a stand of timber. He slipped on moccasins, stowing his boots in the saddlebags. He took his rifle, a bandolier of ammunition, and a spare pistol, then slipped into a backpack.

"Now then, Colonel Trainor," Frank said with a smile. "It's your turn, you arrogant son of a bitch."

He checked his pocket watch: just after midnight. What was it someone had called this time of night? The witching hour? Something like that.

"Call it the mischief hour," Frank muttered. "And I'm the mischief maker."

He headed toward the complex of buildings, moving as silently as the night.

It was a few minutes before midnight when he reached

the buildings and slipped out of his backpack, laying it carefully on the ground. He opened the flap and in the faint light from the moon and starlit sky, smiled as he pulled out a three-stick bundle of dynamite, the sticks capped, fused, and tied together, ready to light. Frank had half a dozen single sticks ready to go, as well as several two-stick bundles and several more three-stick bundles.

He slipped to the rear of the bunkhouse and planted one of the charges with a long fuse. The three-minute fuse would give him time to get to the main house and plant a charge at the front door of Colonel Trainor's mansion. The huge house was made of stone, so Frank didn't think the charge would do much damage, except to Trainor's ego. As arrogant as Trainor was, Frank figured it would be amusing to give Trainor's ego a big boot in the butt.

After planting the charges, Frank slipped through the night to a stone fence Trainor had built around the several acres that contained his mansion and private barn. Frank settled down behind the low fence and waited for the fun to start.

The charge at the rear of the bunkhouse went first, the explosion shattering the tranquility of the night. Half of the roof collapsed and a major part of the rear wall blew inward, the concussion blowing out all the windows in the building.

"Good God!" Frank heard a man holler. "What the hell happened?"

"Somebody come get this crap off me!" another yelled. "I got part of the damn roof on my legs."

"My leg is busted," another moaned, the words just reaching Frank. "A damn beam fell on me."

The dynamite at the front door of the mansion blew and took the door out, blowing it off its hinges and into the fancy foyer of the home. Trainor must have been walking down the stairs from the second floor when the charge went off and the concussion had knocked him down. Frank heard a very audible thumping sound, much like someone bouncing ass-over-elbows down a flight of stairs. That was followed by a great deal of cussing.

Frank struggled to keep from laughing out loud as a very disheveled-looking Trainor appeared in what was left of the front entrance. He waved the dust cloud away and hollered, "What the hell is going on?"

Frank edged away from the fence over to the huge main corral, and opened the gate. He began screaming like a buck on the warpath, and several dozen horses bolted through the gate and were gone into the night.

The foreman, Tom Bracken, ran out of his quarters, dressed only in his long handles and hat. He was carrying his gunbelt. Frank put a .44-40 round at the foreman's bare feet and Tom hollered, dropped his gunbelt, and hauled his butt back into his quarters.

Frank lit a bundle of dynamite and tossed it into the center of the main compound. It landed in the bench area of a small gazebo, and blew just as several hired guns came running from the rear of the house into the clearing. The violent concussion knocked them rolling and sprawling on the ground.

"Get there and kill that son of a bitch!" Trainor yelled, waving his arms. "It's Morgan, goddamnit."

Frank put a round into the stone entranceway and got what he hoped for. The bullet flattened and part of it hit Trainor . . . right in the butt.

"Whooaa!" the arrogant rancher hollered, jumping up and down. "Holy crap!"

"Are you hit?" one of the hired guns hollered.

"Hell, yes, I'm hit!" Trainor yelled just as his son, Jules, came running down the stairs and into the foyer.

Frank put another round bouncing off the stone entrance to the mansion, and Colonel Trainor leaped into the foyer, colliding with his son. Both of them went down in a heap on the floor.

Staying low, the stone fence shielding him, Frank slipped around to the side of the huge house and chucked a sputtering stick of dynamite through an open window into the fancy living room.

The charge blew out all the windows and destroyed the expensive chandelier, bringing it smashing to the floor. The rolling shock wave from the explosion hit Trainor and his son just as they were crawling to their feet in the foyer. The concussion knocked them both down again and rolled them across the floor.

"Somebody kill that son of a bitch!" Trainor screamed. "A thousand dollars to the man who kills him."

Two hired guns jumped to their feet, six-guns in their hands, and came charging across the yard. Frank knocked a leg out from under one with a well-placed round, and the second one decided the charge was really foolish; he hit the ground and rolled behind some lawn furniture.

Frank lit two more sticks of dynamite and tossed them into the yard. A second before they blew, he was off and running into the night. He had done all he dared to do for this trip. As he ran he could hear Trainor screaming for somebody, anybody, to kill him.

"Goddamnit! What am I paying you men for? Get after him, you bastards!"

"Where is he?" a gunhand hollered. "I can't locate him."

Smiling, Frank melted into the darkness, carefully making his way toward his horse.

"All the horses is scattered, Mr. Trainor," the foreman yelled. "It'll take us a while to round them all up."

"Then get to it!" Trainor yelled. "And somebody get into town and get Dr. Woods for me."

"Where are you hit?" Tom yelled.

"In my ass, goddamnit!"

Chuckling softly, Frank reached his horse and rode away.

# TWENTY

The news of the assault on the Trainor mansion and the shooting of the colonel in the butt spread quickly all over the south end of the valleys. Actually, Colonel Trainor was not shot in the ass: a piece of rock knocked loose by the .44-40 round was what was found embedded in his butt. But to those in the south part of the valleys, the original story was just too funny to die.

Everyone in the town of Heaven felt sure it was Frank Morgan who assaulted the Trainor estate, but Frank never admitted it. He would just smile when asked about it.

Frank decided he would not replace the broken windows in his house; too much danger of them being shot out again. He boarded up the windows and left it at that.

The double wedding went off as planned, but without the attendance of anyone from the north end of the valleys. The kids went off to an undisclosed destination for a honeymoon, while Frank hired a crew of workmen to build a house for the kids on some of his property. The boys would work the land on shares.

"It's a fine thing you're doing, Frank," Julie told him. "I don't know what I would have done without you."

"The odds are against the kids making it, Julie. You know that. It's the least I could have done to make things a bit easier for them."

The big three ranchers in the north end built bunkhouses and line shacks for their remaining full-time cowboys and moved them out of the ranch areas. The old bunkhouses were now occupied by hired guns.

"It's going to blow wide open pretty soon," Frank said to Julie a few days after the wedding. "The Lightning, Snake, and .45 brands are hired on full with gunfighters, or men who think they're gunfighters. Mostly the latter. Although there are a few really bad hombres all mixed up in the bunch."

"And you think they'll do what?"

"I don't know for sure. But I suspect they'll start raiding farms and driving people out."

"Or killing them?" Julie asked in a whisper.

"Yes."

"Maybe we should just sell out to them and get out, let the ranchers have it."

"Nobody runs me out of anyplace, Julie."

"They've offered good money for the farms, or so I was told."

"Good money is nothing compared to what these farms will bring over the years. Nothing at all."

"Of course, you're right, Frank. I was just talking to hear my head rattle."

Frank put his arm around her and held her close. "And you were thinking about the kids too, right?"

She sighed. "Yes."

"They've made their own beds now, Julie."

"And now they have to lie in them, right?"

Frank smiled. "I 'spect they've been doing quite a lot of that the past few days."

"Oh . . . you!" She pulled away and poked him in the ribs.

Frank grabbed her and pulled her down on the sofa. One thing led to another. . . .


The Robert Clements family lived and worked a farm in an isolated area miles from their nearest neighbor and half a day's ride from the town of Heaven. The hired guns of the big three ranchers struck there one week after the assault on Colonel Trainor's mansion. The entire Clements family was killed and the house and barn burned. The incident was not discovered until two days after the occurrence. Frank was one of the half dozen men who rode out to the Clements place to help dig for the bodies.

"The oldest girl is missing," a local farmer, the Clementses' nearest neighbor, said.

"Laura?" a man asked.

"Yes. She was about fourteen or fifteen. Pretty girl."

"Them bastards dragged her off and took turns pokin' it to her," another farmer said. "I knowed it would come to this sooner or later." He shook his head. "My wife was scared somethin' like this was gonna happen. That's just about gonna do it for us. She'll insist we move on and I'm ready."

Frank stood for a time and listened to the men talk. "I'll see if I can pick up a trail," he finally said. "There is no more I can do here."

"I'll go with you," a farmer named Richard said.

Frank found tracks and began following them. Of course the hoofprints headed north. Frank found the body of the young girl a few miles from the burned-out home. She was naked and had been used badly.

"Dear God Almighty," Richard said, looking down at the battered body of the girl. "Looks like they broke her neck after they done it to her."

"Go back and get a wagon," Frank told the farmer. "Tell the others what we've found. Have someone ride into town and get Doc Everett and the preacher. We'll bury her alongside what's left of her parents."

"This is just about gonna do it for some folks, Frank," Richard said.

"Are you among them?"

"I don't know. Depends on what my old woman has to say about it."

"Give it some thought before you decide to leave."

"Oh, I will. But my woman won't. I'd better go get the wagon."

Frank waited until the men arrived with the wagon, and then took off, following the tracks. When he got to the crossroads, he headed west, toward a general store/saloon about five miles away. The old store was a favorite hangout for those hands north of the line. There were three horses tied out front, all wearing brands Frank was not familiar with. The horses all had bedrolls behind the cantles and full saddlebags.

Frank tied Horse in the rear of the store and walked into the saloon section through the back entrance. There were three men bellied up to the bar. The barkeep almost swallowed his cigar when he saw Frank. He got so excited he couldn't speak, only stammer.

"What the hell's the matter with you?" one of the gunslicks asked.

The barkeep pointed and the men turned their heads.

"Who wants to start it?" Frank asked.

"Nobody, Morgan," one of the men answered quickly. "We're ridin' out of here. We stopped here for a drink and supplies."

"You boys worked for Trainor?"

"No," another said. "Gilmar. But one's just as bad as the other. We packed up and give our notice soon as we heard what happened a couple nights ago. Don't none of us want no part of nothin' that evil."

"You boys the only ones leaving?"

"Far as we know, Morgan. Drawin' fightin' wages to protect range is one thing. Even runnin' out homesteaders is all right with us. But killin' and rapin' is something else."

"How many others who are taking fighting wages feel the same?"

The trio exchanged glances. "None," one finally said. "I reckon we're it."

"Then you boys made the right decision."

"I think so."

"Who raped and killed that young girl?"

Again the three men exchanged glances. "It was men from the big three ranchers. All mixed up."

Frank moved closer to the men. They could all see that Frank was ready for a showdown, and that made them nervous. One of the three was sure to get lead into Morgan if it came to gunplay, but they all knew that before Morgan went down, he was sure to get lead into all of them. No one wanted to risk that.

"Give me some names," Frank said.

The trio rattled off half a dozen names, one of them finally adding, "Jules Trainor."

"Trainor's son was in the bunch?" Frank asked.

"You bet he was. He's been part of nearly every raid that's

taken place against the sodbusters. He's kill-crazy, Morgan. He likes to hurt people."

"And his father ain't much better," another said.

"Yeah," the third hired gun said. "The apple sure didn't fall far from the tree in that family. The onliest one with any sense at all is Trainor's wife. But she's so addled on laudanum she don't know where she is a lot of the time."

"There are two other kids, Vinson and the girl, Martha. How about them?"

"Just as bad. Vinson is sneaky and the girl is wild as a drunk buck. She'll head for the bushes with just about anyone, if you get my drift. Somethin' is wrong with that whole family." He tapped the side of his head. "Up here."

Frank tossed some money on the bar. "You boys have a couple of drinks on me, and then ride out."

"We'll do it, Morgan. Thanks. And you have good luck in your hunt, 'cause you're sure gonna need it."

"Morgan?" one of the three said.

"Yes?"

"The colonel is killin' mad about you attackin' his mansion the other night." He smiled. "And about havin' to have Doc Woods dig out that piece of rock from his ass. He's done told his men to shoot you on sight."

Frank lifted a hand in farewell and went out the back door without another word. He rode a few hundred yards away, to a small stand of timber, and dismounted, waiting and watching the old general store. He felt that sooner or later some men from the big three would make an appearance. He would be ready when they did.

Frank watched as the three hands walked out of the store and rode away. They were the smart ones, for Frank intended to find those who killed the farm family and then raped and killed the girl. And when he found them, or any who sided with them . . . he would let his .45 Peacemaker mete out justice.

It wasn't the legal way, but there was no law in the valleys, and not much law outside the valleys . . . at least not for the farmers.

But there was Frank Morgan.

# TWENTY-ONE

It was not a long wait. About half an hour after the three men rode away, three others rode up to the general store/saloon. Jules Trainor was one of the three. The young man was dressed all in black, from his hat to his boots. His gunbelt was studded with silver dollars and he carried twin pistols, low and tied down.

"Quite a fancy outfit," Frank said. He stepped into the saddle and rode down to the store, reining up in front. He walked in nonchalantly and stepped up to the bar. "Whiskey," he told the barkeep.

Jules and the two men with him were so stunned at seeing Frank, they stood for a moment, speechless and staring.

"What's the matter, boys?" Frank asked. "Cat got your tongues?"

None of the three made any reply. Frank noticed there were scratches on Jules's face, maybe made by fingernails.

"What happened to your face, boy?" Frank asked. "You run into a briar patch?"

"Huh?" Jules blurted out.

"Your face, you stupid bastard!" Frank snapped at him.

Jules's mouth dropped open in shock. He was Colonel Trainor's son; no one had ever talked to him in such a manner. The two men with Jules started to step away from the bar.

"Stand still!" Frank said.

The pair froze in place.

"That's better," Frank told them. He lifted his glass of whiskey with his left hand and took a tiny sip. "This is rotgut," Frank said, tossing the glass on the bar, the booze spilling out. "Nobody but a rummy would drink crap like that."

"I'll pour you some of my special stock, Mr. Morgan," the barkeep said. "Sorry about that."

"Forget it," Frank replied. "I didn't really come in for a drink."

"Then why did you come in?" one of the gunnies with Jules asked.

"I wanted to get a good close look at the scummy son of a bitch who would rape and kill a young girl."

"Them's hard words, Morgan," the other gunhand said.

"If you don't like it, drag iron," Frank said, tossing the challenge out.

"You push hard, Morgan," his partner said.

"Yeah, I reckon I do," Frank said with a smile. "Now it's up to you."

"I didn't rape nobody," the gunslick said.

"Maybe not. But your pet pig there did. Didn't you, Jules?"

"She was askin' for it!" Jules shouted. "Ever'time I seen

that girl she was sashaying around, shaking her butt at me and battin' her eyes. Flirtin' with me. Then when I called her on it, she put up a fight."

"After you had a hand in killing her mother and father and brothers and sisters, you sorry piece of crap."

"To hell with you, Morgan!" Jules screamed.

Frank stepped away from the bar, his right hand near the butt of his Peacemaker. "Make your play, Trainor."

"I don't want to have to kill you, Morgan!"

"Oh, but I want to kill you, Jules. I want to kill you so bad I can taste it. You're a damned coward. No, you're worse than that, you're a mommy and daddy's boy. You hide behind your name. You're nothing but a rotten son of a bitch!"

"Don't force me to kill you!" Jules shouted.

Without taking his eyes off Jules, Frank asked, "You boys in on this?"

"We didn't have nothin' to do with no rape, Morgan. We left the girl with Jules and a couple of others and headed on back to the ranch after we set the place on fire. We thought the nesters would get out. I didn't like it when I heard they burned up. As for Jules, he can saddle his own horses and stomp on his own snakes. He's a growed-up man."

"What others? Give me names."

"You shut up, Storey," his saddle pard said.

"You go to hell, Garner. It was Mike Reeves and some guy called Cullen."

"You got a yellow streak in you, Storey," Garner said, stepping away from the bar. "I'm with you, Jules. Let's take him."

Storey backed away, holding his hands up in front of him. "I'm out of this, Morgan."

"Fine. You ready to die, Garner? If so, make your play."

"Damn you, Morgan!" Garner shouted. "Pull iron!" Garner's hand dropped to the butt of his gun.

Frank hooked and drew cleanly and swiftly. His bullet hit Garner in the chest, and the hired gun folded and sat down hard on the saloon floor, his own pistol still in leather.

"I'm gone, Morgan!" Storey said. "I mean, I'm clearin' out."

"Fine. Hit the trail and don't look back."

Storey walked out of the saloon and rode away.

Garner sat on the floor and cussed Morgan, both hands pressed against the bleeding hole in his chest.

Frank slid his Peacemaker back into leather and looked at Jules. "Your turn, Jules. Make your move."

"You leave me alone, Morgan!" Jules yelled.

"Kill the bastard, Jules," Garner moaned.

"I'm goin' home," Jules said.

"Back to hide behind your mommy's skirts, Jules?" Frank taunted him.

"You shut up! My dad will take care of you."

Frank laughed at him.

"You can take him, Jules," Garner said. "Do it!"

"Shut up!" Jules screamed at the dying gunman.

"Drag iron, Jules," Frank said.

"No!" Jules shouted.

Frank stepped toward the young man, smiling as he walked. "Come on, Jules. Show me how fast you are."

"You stay away from me, Morgan!" Jules yelled. "Damn you, now you leave me alone, you hear?"

Frank took another step. "You're real brave when it comes to beating up and raping young girls, Jules. But you got no guts when it comes to facing men, do you?"

"I'm as much a man as you! And I'll kill you someday, Morgan!" Jules's shrill words were almost a scream.

"Why not today, Jules?" Frank told him. "The Indians would say it's a good day to die. Are you afraid to die, Jules?"

"Kill him, Jules," Garner said as he collapsed on the floor. "Kill him for me. I'm done for, boy. Kill him."

"You shut up!" Jules screamed. "Don't tell me what to do."

But Garner couldn't hear him. He was dead.

"Just you and me now, Jules," Frank said. "You better draw. And you'd better make your first shot count."

Jules backed up.

Frank moved toward the young man. The bartender stood and watched in silence. He wasn't about to get involved in this fracas.

Jules backed up against the wall. He was trapped.

Frank smiled at him. "Now, you damned worthless piece of crap. Now what are you going to do?"

Jules lunged at Frank, in hopes of knocking him down and getting to the open door of the building. Frank slugged him, a hard right to the mouth that put Jules butt-down on the floor, his lips bloody.

"How many times did you hit that young girl, Jules?" Frank asked.

"Goddamn you!" Jules screamed, crawling to his knees. "They wasn't nothin' but nesters. They got what they deserved. They ain't worthy people."

Frank put the toe of his boot in Jules's belly, knocking the wind out of him and laying him back on the floor, gasping for breath. Frank reached down and hauled the young man to his feet. He reached down and jerked Jules's guns from leather, hurling them across the room. Then he proceeded to beat the crap out of Jules Trainor.

When he finished, Jules Trainor's looks had been forever

altered. The young man's face was ripped and mangled. His nose was flattened against his face. One ear was hanging down, held by only a thin strip of skin.

Jules lay on the saloon floor, puking from all the blows he'd taken in his belly. He was crying in pain and frustration and humiliation.

The bartender had not moved during the brief one-sided but brutal and bloody fight. Now he said, "Good God A'mighty. Morgan, you better haul your ashes out of this state. The colonel is sure to come gunnin' for you."

"I hope he does. I really hope that arrogant bastard does."

The barkeep pointed toward Jules. "What am I supposed to do with him?"

"Throw him out in the road if you want to. I don't care. Right now, pull me a beer. I'm thirsty."

"You better clear out now, Morgan. And I mean right now. I'm tellin' you that for your own good."

"Why should I?"

"'Cause a bunch of them boys drawin' fightin' wages from the .45, the Snake, and the Lightnin' ranches like to come here for a drink near'bouts ever' day, that's why."

"Good. I'll just wait then. Now pull me that beer."

"Oh, Lord," the barkeep moaned, shaking his head. "My place is gonna be shot all to pieces, I just know it."

"We'll all make sure you get compensated for any damages."

"Compen . . . what?"

"Paid."

"Oh. How can you pay me if you're dead?"

"I don't plan on being dead."

"Trainor yonder didn't plan on gettin' his gizzard stomped out neither." The bartender pointed to the nearly unconscious Jules. "But he damn shore did."

"Are you going to pull me that beer?"

"Shore, shore. Right now. Don't get your dander up, Morgan. I'm just a poor store owner, that's all. I ain't got no di-rect hand in none of this."

"Fine. I'll be sitting over there." Frank pointed to a table by the window. "Bring the beer to me."

"Yes, sir. Right away."

Jules moaned on the floor and tried to get up. He didn't make it, falling heavily back to the boards.

"I hope he don't die in here," the barkeep said. "That would be bad for business. Not to mention my health."

"He'll probably bleed on your floor some more. But you can mop that up. He's not going to croak."

Frank's beer was placed on the table, and the barkeep moved quickly back behind the counter. "Mr. Morgan?"

"What?"

"Don't you think we ought to do something for young Trainor?"

"What do you have in mind?"

"Patch him up, or something."

"Go ahead."

"I ain't no doctor."

"Then leave him lay where he is."

"You 'bout the coldest man I ever seen."

"So I've been told."

"Son of a bitch!" Jules mumbled through smashed lips and loose teeth.

"Are you talking to me, buffalo turd?" Frank asked.

"I'll kill you," Jules said.

"Sure you will."

"My daddy will horsewhip you and then hang you."

Frank laughed at him and took a swig of beer.

"Oh, Lord, Morgan!" the barkeep said.

"What's the matter?"

"Riders coming from the north. I hear them."

"Good," Frank said. "Now it'll get interesting."

"You're crazy, Morgan!" the barkeep said. "They'll kill you."

"I doubt it." Frank finished his beer in two swallows and stood up, walking to the front door and looking out. "Only four of them."

"Only four?" It was then the barkeep noticed the short-barreled .45 tucked behind Frank's gunbelt, at the small of his back.

"Help!" Jules hollered weakly and very mush-mouthed. "Help me, boys."

"They can't hear you, you pissant," Frank told him. "And nobody is going to help you. So why don't you just shut your dirty lying mouth."

"My daddy will get you for this, Morgan!" Jules gasped.

But Frank had already stepped out onto the wide porch.

The Snake riders reined up in front of the store and sat their saddles, staring in silence at Frank.

"Any of you named Reeves or Cullen?" Frank asked.

"I'm Reeves, Morgan," a stocky rider said. "What's it to you?"

"Where's Cullen?"

"Back at the ranch, if that's any of your business, which it damn shore ain't."

Before Frank could speak, another Snake rider asked, "Where's Jules and Storey and Garner?"

"Garner's in the bar part of the store, with ants crawling across his dead eyes. Storey lit a shuck out of the country. Mama's little boy Jules is inside, on the floor, where I stomped his face in and kicked a few of his teeth out."

"You're a goddamn liar, Morgan!" the Snake hand said.

"No two like you could kill Garner and make Storey take water."

"Kill him!" The weak voice of Jules could be heard from inside. "Kill the bastard for me, boys. He hurt me bad."

"Your play, boys," Frank said calmly.

Two of the Snake hands reached for iron.

# TWENTY-TWO

Frank's .45 boomed twice. He had drawn and fired in less than a blink of an eye. The two Snake riders who had grabbed for iron tumbled from the saddle. One had been shot through the heart; the other one had taken the slug in the center of his forehead.

The two remaining riders, one of them Reeves, wheeled their horses and got the hell out of there. They did not look back, and Frank let them go.

Frank walked back inside the saloon and up to the bar. "Now you have two more to plant. You can have their guns and whatever's in their pockets for your trouble. That sound fair enough to you?"

"I reckon so, Mr. Morgan," the barkeep replied in a shaky voice. Frank noticed the man's hands were shaking.

"Their horses too, if they're not riding Snake stock." He

looked down at the bloody mess that was Jules. "Now I have to figure out what to do with you."

Jules cussed him. "My daddy will get you for this."

"You've got a one-track mind, Jules. And you're boring me."

"I wish you'd get him out of here and to a doctor, Morgan," the barkeep said.

Morgan laughed at that. "If this piece of crap sees a doctor, it won't be me taking him."

"He's hurt bad."

"He just can't be called a pretty boy any longer, that's all. Get up, Jules. I'm going to send you home to your mommy and daddy."

"Help me up."

"I'll stand here and kick you until you get up or you die. The choice is yours."

Jules cussed him once more, but managed to struggle to his feet.

"Outside, pretty boy," Frank told him.

Jules staggered out onto the porch.

"Over by your horse," Frank said.

When Jules stumbled over to his horse, Frank said, "Now strip, Jules. Right down to your skin."

"What?"

"You heard me. Strip, or I'll rip those fancy clothes off of you."

Jules was crying when he said, "My daddy will kill you for this, Morgan."

"I hope he tries. I ought to heat up a runnin' iron and brand you for raping and killing that girl, you damn punk. Strip!"

A couple of minutes later, Jules was stark naked.

"You had this horse a long time, Jules?"

"Five years or so. Why?"

"Then he knows his way home, right?"

"Sure, he does. He ain't stupid."

"Good. Mount up." Frank used Jules's belt to tie the young man's hands to the saddle horn. "Have a good trip, craphead." He slapped the horse on the rump and watched as the animal galloped away, Jules cussing and swaying in the saddle.

"He's gonna have a sore butt when he gets home," Frank said. "But it's probably the only justice he'll get for what he did."

"You're a dead man, Morgan," the bartender said matter-of-factly from the porch. "Colonel Trainor will never rest until he sees you dead. Sendin' Jules home like that will be the last straw. Man, are you crazy?"

"I've been called worse," Frank said. He pointed to the dead men sprawled in the dirt and horse crap in front of the store. "You'd better get them planted."


It took only hours for the news of what Frank Morgan had done to sweep through the southern half of the valleys. Many of the residents thought Jules got what he deserved. But more than a few thought what Frank had done was too harsh.

Maynard Higgins and George Miller were the most vocal against Frank. The farmers met with a few others of like mind to condemn Frank for his actions.

Frank shrugged off the criticism.

"They're scared, Frank," Julie told him. "Scared of retaliation."

"If they're going to stay here and live, they'd either better learn to fight or die well," was Frank's reply.

"They're farmers, not gunfighters. They're worried about their wives and kids and having to start over somewhere."

Frank looked at her for a silent moment, sensing that something between them had been lost, and probably would never be recovered. "What do you want me to do, Julie?"

"Whatever you want to do," she said coolly, then turned away.

The subject was closed, Frank reckoned. No point in pursuing it any further. "All right." He walked out of the house and mounted up, riding back to his place.

Dog greeted him as Frank dismounted. "You and me again, Dog," he said. "Least I think that's the way it's turning out. Sure sounded that way to me. And you know what? Maybe that's for the best. 'Cause I don't know for sure what is it I've done to get myself on her bad side. I just flat don't understand women."

Dog sat and looked at him, wagging his tail.

"But what the hell am I going to do with all this property? I never intended to be a farmer. What the hell do I know about raising beets and potatoes?"

Dog walked off and plopped down in the shade of a huge old tree.

"You like it here, huh? Is that what you're telling me?"

Dog looked at him, yawned, then curled up and went to sleep.

"Wonderful," Frank muttered.


The kids came back from their honeymoon and Frank put the boys to work in the fields. He also hired the same crew of carpenters that built his house to build a house where the old Jamison shack once stood. They could share it. The kids were grateful and showed it. Julie smiled at him and said that was very nice of him.

Frank had received warmer greetings from soiled doves.

"I got me a hunch we won't spent the winter here, Dog,"

he told the big cur. "It's already gettin' chilly, and I'm not tallkin' about the weather."

Frank made a deal with the boys, with Lawyer Foster drawing up the papers and Julie and Banker Simmons present, about working the land.

Frank told Simmons later, "Least when I pull out I'll know my interests will be taken care of."

"Women are notional, Frank. Julie is a good woman. Give her time. You two can work this out."

Frank shook his head. "I don't think so, John. She's had second thoughts about me, and none of them good."

"What brought it on?"

"What I did to Jules and my killing those three men at the old store. At least that's a big part of it."

"Jules got what he deserved and those three men needed killing."

"Yes. But Julie damn sure doesn't see it that way, and neither do about half of the farmers in the valley."

"Give them time to think about it, Frank."

"As usual, I've run out of time. It's no big deal. Hell, I'm used to it."

The lawyer started to speak, and Frank held up a hand, silencing him. "I see Julie's point, and understand why the others feel the way they do too. What I did just may have terrible consequences for the people here in the south end of the valleys."

"Perhaps, Frank. And perhaps still more people will die, on both sides of this issue. But this is still a young country, and west of the Mississippi is still wild and woolly. Where there is no law, or the law is in the pocket of the rich and powerful, people have but two choices: bow down and become slaves, or fight. Just maybe you've shoved some steel into the backbones of these people. Have you thought about that?"

"Maybe. But maybe they didn't want their backbones reinforced."

"I think most did, Frank."

Frank offered no immediate reply. He stood on the boardwalk and silently rolled a cigarette.

"You're going to pull out, aren't you, Frank?" the lawyer said.

"Looks that way. But before I do, I'll see this thing through to its end."

"And that means? . . ."

Frank looked at the banker, and John Simmons suppressed a shudder. He could plainly see death in the gunfighter's eyes. "I suppose it's come to that," Simmons finally said.

"Yeah," the Drifter said. "I reckon it has."

# TWENTY-THREE

Frank cleaned his guns carefully. He put his short-barreled .45 behind in a holster on the left side of his gunbelt, and stowed another fully loaded Peacemaker in his saddlebags. He loaded up his .44-40, and put several boxes of cartridges for pistol and rifle in his saddlebags. He made sure Dog had plenty of food and water; enough to last him several days. Then he wrapped up some jerky and biscuits and stowed those away. Finally he filled a canteen with fresh water from the well.

"You stay here," he told the big cur. "I'll be back. Might be a few days, but I'll be back. You stay here. Right here! You understand?"

Dog licked his hand, and then walked away and lay down in the shade of a tree.

Frank mounted up and rode away, toward the crossroads.

He reached the crossroads at the same time as a freight wagon. He smiled when he saw it was driven by Luke, the man he'd met on his first day in the valley.

"Howdy there, Frank Morgan!" the freighter called as he halted his team.

"Luke. You sure you want to be seen speaking to me?"

"Why not? I ain't one of those who are highbrowin' you. I'm not sayin' all of them are, but them that is ain't nothin' but a pack of yellow-bellied hyenas."

"Hard words, Luke."

"Bull!" the freighter snorted. "Them's true words, Frank Morgan. And you know it. They want the protection your gun and your guts gives them, but they only want so much. Jules Trainor is a cruel young man. Mean-spirited to man and beast alike. He's beat or shot more than one dog and horse to death just for the fun of it. And that young girl who's in an early grave wasn't the first he's raped, believe me. His no-good daddy's been gettin' him out of trouble ever since he was old enough to wear long pants."

Frank smiled at the considerable heat behind the man's words. "That was quite a speech, Luke."

"I reckon it was. But all the words was true ones." He looked hard at Frank. "I got me an idee you're goin' bear-huntin', Frank."

"You might say that."

"Plenty of grizzlies to choose from around here."

Frank nodded his head in agreement.

"You cross this road and you're in bear country, Frank."

"I know that."

"You wasn't plannin' on goin' to Hell, was you?"

"No. Just heading that way to see what I might scare up."

"You want me to give you a hand?"

"How do you mean?"

"Well, this load I'm carryin' is goin' to Hell. I might sort of pass the word around that you're on the prod, if you know what I mean."

Frank thought about that for a moment. "That ghost town north of here would be a dandy spot for a ruckus."

"Shore would, for a fact."

"I think I'll head that way."

"I'll pass the word. Frank?"

Frank looked at the man.

"They might come all in a bunch."

"That's a possibility."

"That don't worry you?"

"Do me a favor, Luke?"

"Name it."

"If I don't come back, will you take care of my dog?"

"It would be a pleasure."

"I'd appreciate it. He's a good dog."

Luke smiled. "But I got me a hunch you'll be back."

"I hope to do just that."

"You and Miss Julie have a spat?"

"Not really," Frank said with a faint smile. "All of a sudden she decided she wasn't really happy with me."

"Some of them other women in the valley got to her, Frank. And if she let them, she ain't the one for you. My first wife left me when I become a freighter. Said she didn't like being left alone so much. Just took the kids and hauled her ashes. My second wife left me after I killed three men who was tryin' to rob me on a lonesome road. Said I should have been more com-passion-ate. I had to go find me a feller to explain that to me. Didn't make no sense then, don't now. Frank, it'll take me a couple hours to get to Hell. Give them hired gunhands an hour to get to the ghost town. I wish you the best of luck."

Frank lifted a hand and the big wagon rolled on north. Frank headed for the ghost town.

* * *

Frank tucked his horse in a cul-de-sac a few hundred yards from the old town. There was some graze there and some water in a tiny creek. Horse would be all right. Frank walked into the deserted town and began looking around.

There wasn't much left.

The town had only prospered for a short time, so Frank had been told, before everyone just up and pulled out one day. Like many a ghost town in the West, no one really knew exactly what had happened. The town was one of the first in the area, and then one day all the inhabitants were gone.

What remained were the rotting shells of eight or ten buildings. Frank walked into the old saloon, picked a chair up off the floor, dusted it off, and sat down by the window. Resting there, he took himself a little nap.

He slept for about half an hour, then got up and shook himself like a big dog, getting the cobwebs out of his head. He took a sip of water from his canteen, then walked out onto the boardwalk and rolled a smoke. Autumn was definitely in the air, a very pleasant breeze blowing, and the nights were turning cooler. Frank sat down on the edge of the boardwalk and smoked and thought about some things . . . especially his life. Not especially about any regrets he had, and he had a few, but about what he was going to do about the rest of his life. The town of Heaven was not going to be his home; Frank sensed that with an odd feeling of both sadness and relief.

For a few weeks he and Julie had shared something special. Then it had vanished like a puff of smoke. *Probably for the best,* Frank thought, *for I am no family man. I'm a drifter and have been for most of my life.*

Frank had once read about some fellow way back centuries ago who was asked if he was afraid of something that faced him. No, the man said. He wasn't afraid of anything in the future, only what was behind him.

*Does that fit me?* Frank pondered as he sat on what was left of the boardwalk in the crumbling old town.

Frank abruptly stood up and shook his head. No time to be thinking deep thoughts. Not with what was facing him on this day.

But the thought kept pushing at him: *Why am I doing this?*

*Why don't I just mount up and ride out? Don't even bother to look back.*

*I don't owe these farmers anything. Hell, about half of them don't even like me.*

Frank walked the dusty main street, trying to shake the curious thoughts from his mind, his spurs softly jingling as he paced. He was suddenly very conscious of the .45 Peacemaker on his hip and the short-barreled .45 tucked behind his gunbelt at the small of his back. Odd, for the guns had nearly always been a natural part of him.

Gunfighter. Killer. Manhunter. Those words sprang into his head, words he'd heard used to refer to him dozens of times in the long years that lay behind. Bloody years. Lonely years.

Frank walked back to the saloon and picked up his rifle and canteen, once more stepping out onto the boardwalk. He took a sip of water, stood for a moment, and then walked across the wide street, over to some now-nameless old shell of a store. With an almost visible physical effort, Frank pushed all thoughts except survival from his mind. He began to take stock of where he was, carefully looking all around him.

He checked his pocket watch. It wouldn't be long before the first of the hired guns and bounty hunters would come riding in, anxious to be the one to get lead into Frank Morgan.

"Well, come on, boys," Frank muttered. "Let's get this dance started."

Frank smoked one more cigarette before he heard the sounds of a horse walking slowly over the rocky old road that led to the town. Frank stood up and slipped the hammer thong from his Peacemaker. He waited under the shade of the boardwalk awn-ing . . . the part of it that was still standing, and it was tilting precariously.

Within moments he saw the lone rider slowly ride up to the edge of the single long street and dismount. Frank stepped out into the street.

"Morgan?" the man called.

"That's me," Frank said.

The man walked up the center of the street and stopped about fifty feet from Frank. A young man, maybe twenty-five at the most.

"I'm called Lucky Seven."

"Strange name."

"I was born on the seventh day of the week and the midwife said if I lived a week I'd be lucky."

"You pull on me, Lucky, and your luck is gonna run out."

"Naw, I don't think so, Morgan. I feel really lucky today. 'Sides, I've killed seven men and that's my lucky number."

"You're a fool, young man. How much is Trainor paying you?"

"I don't work for Trainor. I hired on with the .45 brand."

"For how much?"

"Enough. You ready to die, Morgan?"

"Something we all have to do."

Lucky stood and stared at Frank for a moment, a puzzled look on his face. Morgan did not appear to be at all tense. No sign of nervousness about him. "What's with you, Morgan? Don't you know you're going to die right here in this dirty street?"

"Not me, Lucky. It isn't my day."

"You think you're fast enough to get me?"

"Yes, as a matter of fact, I do."

"Then you're the fool."

"I guess that remains to be seen, doesn't it?"

Frank's calmness was beginning to unnerve Lucky. The other men he'd faced in his brief career as a gunslinger had all appeared shaky and nervous moments before the actual shoot-out. Not Frank Morgan. He just stood there patiently, with not a sign of tension. *Damn him!*

"Well, do something, damn you!" Lucky yelled.

Frank just smiled at him. "After you, Lucky. It's your show."

"Are you ready, Morgan?"

"Hell, Lucky, I've been ready. Anytime you want to stop running your mouth, just hook and draw."

"By God, I will!"

"I'm waiting."

"You got any last words, Morgan?"

Frank laughed at him.

"Don't you laugh at me, damn you! Don't you make fun of me. I won't stand for that. You hear me?"

"Of course I hear you, Lucky. I'm not deaf."

"Well, then . . . you stop it."

"Stop what?"

"Damn you, Morgan. There you go again."

"Come on, Lucky. Do something before I fall over from old age."

"That's it, ain't it, Morgan? You're so damn old you done lost your nerve. You're afraid to draw on me, ain't you?"

Again, Frank simply smiled at the man.

"Pull iron, you old bastard!" Lucky screamed the words. "Damn you, draw on me."

"You first, Lucky," Frank said calmly. "I believe in giving a man an even break . . . sometimes, that is."

"Don't you do me no favors, Morgan. You hear me? I'm Lucky Seven. I'm fast. And I'm gonna kill you!"

"Then have at it, Lucky. Do something, for God's sake. You're about to put me to sleep with all this talk."

"You're a son of a bitch!"

"Is that the best you can do, Lucky? That's pitiful."

Lucky's hand dropped to the butt of his pistol and he pulled iron. Frank smoothly cleared leather and his Peacemaker boomed, the .45 slug slamming into Lucky's chest and knocking the young man off his boots. Lucky sprawled in the center of the dusty, tumbleweed-littered street. He had not gotten off a shot.

Frank walked the short distance up to the dying man and looked down at him.

"You bastard!" Lucky said. His fingers dug in the dirt for his gun.

Frank kicked the young man's pistol away from him. The fancy engraved .45 sailed away and landed behind an old horse trough.

"I hate you, Frank Morgan," Lucky gasped, then closed his eyes and died.

# TWENTY-FOUR

Frank left the body of Lucky Seven in the street, walked over to the boardwalk, sat down, and stared at the corpse. *Another life cut short at my hand,* he thought. But he could not dredge up even one tiny bit of remorse for his act.

*All I wanted to do was settle down here and live out the rest of my life in peace,* Frank thought. *I didn't start this damn war . . . but I'm not going to run away from it.*

Frank punched out the empty brass in his Peacemaker and loaded the empty chamber. He usually carried the hammer over an empty chamber, but now was no time for that bit of precaution. Other gun-handlers would soon be arriving. Frank retrieved his rifle and canteen and leaned the weapon against the outer edge of the boardwalk. He took a sip of water and waited.

It was not a long wait.

Frank stood up, picking up his rifle at the sounds of fast approaching horses. He saw the dust first as the riders stopped at the edge of town.

Three riders came slowly, cautiously into view. They were still too far away for Frank to recognize them, if he knew them at all. He stepped back onto the boardwalk as soon as one pointed at him.

Frank waited.

The three riders dismounted and split up, one going to the left, behind the buildings, one to the right, behind the buildings, and one walking slowly up the broken boardwalk across the street from Frank.

"You boys are playing a fool's game," Frank called.

"The ranchers put up quite a purse for you, Morgan," the only hired gun visible shouted. "Thousands of dollars to the man who kills you."

"What ranchers?" Frank asked.

"All of them. Every rancher north of the crossroads."

"That's good enough for me," Frank called.

The gunhand snapped a quick shot at Frank, the bullet slamming into the wood behind him. Frank returned the fire, and he didn't miss. The .44-40 slug doubled the man over, putting him down to his knees. He slowly toppled over and off the boardwalk, landing in the dirt of the street. He did not move.

Frank stepped back into the open door of the building and quickly made his way to the rear of the store. He waited by the long-broken-out window. He could see what remained of the outhouse, now just a jumble of rotting boards.

"He got Layton!" The faint shout reached Frank.

"Dead?" the gunhand coming up behind Frank's position called.

"I reckon so. He ain't movin'."

"Morgan ain't gonna stand and fight eyeball-to-eyeball."

"Would you?"

There was no reply to that.

Frank eared back the hammer on his rifle and waited.

"You see him, Chase?" The shout came from across the street.

"No. I don't know where he went. He's a sneaky one." The hired gun called Chase was very close to Frank's position.

Frank slipped to the open door.

"You be careful."

"You bet I will," said Chase.

Frank stepped out onto what remained of the loading dock and put a hole into Chase's chest. The bounty hunter's boots flew out from under him, and he was dead before he stretched out on the ground.

"Chase?" the one remaining gunny called.

Frank levered a round into the chamber and moved as silently as possible to the front of the rickety old store.

"Did you get him, Chase? Answer me, boy!"

Frank waited, as patient and silent as death.

The last of the trio made a run from one side of the street to the other. Frank nailed him, the .44-40 round turning him around in the street. The hired gun banged off several rounds, all of them blowing holes in the dirt, then slumped to the ground, groaning and cussing. His six-gun slipped from suddenly weak fingers.

Frank stepped out of the building and off the boardwalk, walking over to where the man lay dying. He looked down at him, saying nothing.

"You're slick, Morgan," the man whispered.

"Not really," Frank replied. "You were just too anxious."

"I reckon. But there was big money involved. Makes a"—he stammered and coughed up blood—"a man reckless."

Frank stood quietly and let the man talk.

"They's a whole bunch coming after you, Morgan. I hope they kill you. I hope you die hard, you bastard."

Frank just smiled at him.

"You'll get yours someday, Morgan. I'm just sorry I won't be around to see it."

"You got anyone you want me to notify?" Frank asked.

"Hell, no!"

"That's too bad."

"Who the hell do you have that gives a damn about you?" the gunhand challenged.

"I have one or two who might give a small damn," Frank replied. "But not much of one."

"Serves you right."

Frank had to smile at that.

"Something funny, Morgan?" The man coughed out the words. Before Frank could reply, he said, "I'm lung-shot, ain't I?"

"Yeah, you are."

"Side-to-side, right?"

"That's right."

"I guess you're just gonna leave me to die right here in the middle of the damn street, ain't you, Morgan?"

"Where do you want me to take you?"

"How the hell do I know?" The man coughed up pink blood. He was definitely lung-shot. "Don't make no difference nohow, Morgan. Do it?"

"Not much of one."

"I got me a good horse. Take care of him. Will you do that for me?"

"Sure. That big black?"

"That's him. He's a good one. And . . . I bought him legal. I didn't steal him. Paper is in my saddlebags."

"I'll take care of him."

"Thanks." The man closed his eyes. He never opened them again.

Frank left him and walked to the end of the street, reloading as he walked. He found the horses and led them over to where he'd left Horse. Horse laid his ears back and let the newcomers know who was boss immediately. Frank left them to work it out, and walked back into the falling-down old town. He sat down in the dark shadowy shade of the boardwalk, took a sip of water, and rolled a cigarette.

He waited, rifle across his knees, very conscious of the heavy smell of death in the air; it clung to everything.

"Morgan!" The shout cut the air. "You there, Morgan?"

Frank did not move or reply to the call. In the sun's slow move toward the western horizon, the place where Frank rested under the awning was now dark. The newcomer, or newcomers, as the case probably was, could not see him.

"Damn, Jerry!" another voice called. "They's two bodies in the street."

"I see them," the first voice said. "But I can't make out who they are. For a fact, Morgan's in there somewhere."

"I'm goin' to swing around, come in from the other end of town."

"All right. Sing out when you're in position. I ain't movin' till you holler."

"Yeah. Morgan's a sneaky one. I think he's maybe part Injun. I'll give you a shout in a few minutes."

Frank waited motionless. He was wearing dark trousers and a dark blue shirt. He blended in well with the deepening shadows.

Frank listened as the rider made a wide loop around the ghost town. He was riding slowly, pausing often to check out the area. Frank guessed that Jerry had not moved.

"In place!" The shout came from the opposite end of the street.

"All right, Ed. Let's go collect that bounty."

*Jerry and Ed,* Frank thought. *Sounds like a vaudeville team. All we need now is some dancing girls in short dresses.*

Suddenly, and with no warning, Frank thought about his son, Conrad. He wondered how the young man was doing. Wondered if he ever thought about *him.* Hell, Frank wasn't even sure where Conrad was. Probably back East somewhere.

He pushed those thoughts away. No time to be thinking about anything except staying alive.

Frank heard a board creak in protest somewhere to his left. Sounded like it was near. But in the warm, still air, he couldn't be sure.

"Jerry?" The voice was so close it jarred Frank. "I don't think he's here. There ain't no sign of him."

"I shore ain't cut no sign myself." That voice came from Frank's right. But from across the wide street.

"Is that Layton in the street?"

"Yeah. One of 'em. I can't see for shore who the other one is."

"I seen one in the back. Didn't take the time to see who it was."

Frank slowly moved his head, looking to his left. Ed was a dozen or so yards from him, walking carefully and slowly up the broken and warped boardwalk, a six-gun in his right hand.

"You looking for me, Ed?" Frank asked, lifting his rifle.

"Jesus!" Ed shouted, snapping off a shot into the shadows. The shot missed Frank by several feet.

Frank's shot did not miss. The .44-40 bullet ripped into Ed's chest and knocked the man off the boardwalk. Ed rolled in the dirt and tried to rise to his boots. He didn't make it, falling forward onto his face in the dirt. He cursed Frank, coughed up blood, then trembled once and sighed as life left him. A moment later, Frank heard the sound of a horse galloping away. Jerry had pulled out.

"The buzzards are going to have a feast later on," Frank muttered, shoving fresh loads into his rifle.

Frank waited for a few minutes, sitting in the shade of the awning. No more hired guns showed up. "They'll be along," Frank whispered. "I'll be very surprised if they aren't."

Frank stripped the saddles and bridles from the horses and turned them loose. Then he returned to his shady perch and ate a biscuit and sipped water from his canteen. He longed for a cup of hot, strong coffee. He settled for a cigarette.

He waited, sitting by the street of death in the old ghost town. Silent slow minutes passed before Frank heard the approaching horse. A single rider appeared on the edge of town. Frank recognized him: Jess Malone.

"Well, now," Frank muttered. "All by himself too."

Frank wondered where Jess's running buddy, Peck Carson, was.

"Not far away, I'll wager," Frank muttered.

"Morgan!" Jess hollered. "I see the bodies. Looks like you've been busy."

Frank stepped out into the sunlight. "There's several more you can't see, Jess," he called.

Jess walked his horse up the street, stopping and dismounting about a hundred feet from Frank. "You want to talk some before I kill you, Morgan?"

"You're dreaming, Jess. The only way you'll see me dead is if your buddy, Peck, shoots me in the back."

"Peck ain't with me. He's back at the Snake nursin' a bad hang-over."

"I'm real sorry to hear that, Jess. If it's the truth, that is. With any sort of luck, he won't recover."

"It's the truth, Morgan. I may be a lot of things, but I ain't no liar."

"With all these dead men around you, you're going to pull on me?"

"That's right, Morgan. More than that, I'm goin' to be the one to tote your stinkin' carcass back to the Snake and collect me a big pile of bounty money."

Frank laughed at him. He knew that Jess was very quick on the draw, but Frank also knew that *he* was faster.

"By God, Morgan!" Jess flared. "Don't you laugh like a jackass at me." Jess began walking toward Frank.

"You better get back on your horse and get the hell gone, Jess. That's the only warning you're going to get from me."

"Damn you and your warnin', Morgan." Jess kept walking, closing the distance between the two men.

Frank stood in the middle of the street, waiting. He was more conscious than ever before of the dead men around him. Overhead, circling darkly, the buzzards had begun to gather, sensing a feast.

"I'll be known as the man who killed Frank Morgan!" Jess shouted.

"Wrong," Frank said.

"Now!" Jess yelled, and pulled iron.

# TWENTY-FIVE

Jess cleared leather a half second behind Frank, and got off a shot. The bullet tore up dirt about ten feet in front of Frank. Frank's shot was true, striking Jess in the chest and knocking him down to one knee. Jess lifted his .45, trying for a second shot. Frank put another round into the man's chest. Jess toppled over to one side, losing the grip on his six-gun. He tried to rise but could not, collapsing and dying in the dirt.

Frank walked slowly up to the dead man and stood for a moment, looking down at him. Then he turned and walked away. Frank found Jess's horse and pulled saddle and bridle from the animal, turning him loose. He walked over to Horse and mounted up, taking the reins of the big black he had promised to look after. He rode away from the death town, leaving the bodies sprawled where they died. The buzzards began their slow descent toward the corpses. Frank did not look back.

It was after dark when Frank reached his house. He stabled the horses, rubbing them down and forking hay for them. He put some grain in the feed box and then went into his house, Dog padding along beside him.

Frank was tired and hungry and longed for a pot of coffee. He put water on to boil and then washed up, anxious to get the stink of death off him. The hot water and soap helped some. He sliced some bacon and laid the strips in the skillet to fry. He pulled off his boots and slipped his tired feet into moccasins. When the meager supper was ready, he ate the bacon and sopped up the grease with slices of bread, then took his mug of coffee outside. He sat down wearily in a rocking chair on the porch and rolled a cigarette.

"It was a sorry day, Dog," he said to the big cur after taking a swig of the hot, strong coffee. "I left another string of dead men behind me. But what the hell did I accomplish by doing so? What did I prove? Am I the better man by doing what I did?"

Dog lay by his side, careful to keep his tail from under the rocker. Dog was smart; he had learned that quickly and somewhat painfully early on.

"The fastest gun in the West," Frank said. "That's me. What an honor. After doing what I do best, I come home and talk to my dog." He reached down and patted Dog. "No disrespect intended," he added with a smile.

Dog wagged his tail.

Frank drank his coffee and smoked his cigarette, then fixed another cup and returned to the rocking chair on the porch. Dog had curled up on the porch and was sleeping, at peace with the world.

"We'll be on the trail again before too much longer,"

Frank said to the silent night. "I can sense that. I've had a lot of practice knowing when I've worn out my welcome."

Frank finished his coffee and went to bed. He slept soundly and dreamlessly, and was up an hour before dawn. Dog went out with Frank, both of them tending to their morning business; then Frank washed up and put on water to boil. He sat outside on the porch, enjoying the early coolness while he woke up with a cup of strong coffee. Frank was drinking coffee, finishing up the pot, when the sun cracked the silver gray wide open and brought the day forth.

"I think I'll ride into town and get me a good breakfast at the cafe, then a bath and a haircut, Dog. You keep an eye out for trouble, and if you see any, you run like hell and get under cover, you hear me?"

An hour later, Frank rode into the town of Heaven and dismounted in front of the Blue Moon Cafe. The cafe was crowded with men and humming with conversation until Frank walked in; then it fell as silent as a tomb.

Frank took a seat at a corner table and ordered breakfast. Slowly the conversation among the patrons resumed, but at a much lower hum than before. John Simmons came in, spotted Frank, and joined him at the table, waving at the waitress and ordering coffee.

"You stirred up the pot yesterday, Frank," the banker said. "Two deputies from the county seat were on their way home from prisoner-chasing, and saw the buzzards over the ghost town and went to take a look. One of them stayed to keep the buzzards off while the other one rode into town for a wagon."

"They brought the bodies here?"

"What was left of them, yes."

"The deputies must have ridden by just after I rode out."

"I guess so. Anyway, the townspeople, most of them, are awfully upset about the situation."

"And they would like for me to leave?" Frank asked with a half smile.

"Many of them, yes, Frank. I'm sorry, but that's the mood right now."

"Well, it won't get any better, John. I've seen this happen before."

"You're probably right about that."

"And what's going to happen when I pull out?"

"I tried to tell this very group of men in the cafe right now that things will only get worse if you leave. But they weren't having any of it. They want you gone."

Frank's smile widened. "Then why don't they tell me face-to-face?"

The banker chuckled at that. "I think you know the answer to that, Frank. They're scared of you and they're scared of the ranchers." John looked around him. "Here come the two deputies now."

"Let them come. Here comes my breakfast. They can talk and I'll eat."

"Morgan!" one of the deputies brayed from the doorway.

"I can hear you," Frank said as the waitress placed his breakfast in front of him. "I'm not deaf."

"We want to talk to you," the second deputy said.

"So talk. I'll eat."

"We wired the sheriff and he wants to talk to you, Morgan. You'll have to come with us."

"I don't think so, boys," Frank said, buttering a biscuit. "I don't have a damn thing to say to your sheriff."

"Morgan," the first deputy said. "You're pushing."

Frank laid down his knife and set his biscuit on the side of his plate. "Your sheriff is bought and paid for by the ranchers, boys. And you probably are too. All of you knew the ranchers were hiring guns to make war against the farmers. You know about the killings and burnings and rapes and did nothing about them. You're both white trash, and that's probably too good a description. Now get the hell out of my sight or get ready to drag iron. Get out of here. Tuck your damn cowardly tails between your legs and get the hell gone. Now, goddamnit!"

The deputies almost tore down the door getting out of the cafe. Frank picked up his fork and resumed eating.

One of the townspeople in the cafe began chuckling. "Seeing that was worth the price of a stage ticket. Good for you, Morgan. I don't have much use for your kind, but that performance deserves a round of applause."

"But it don't change nothin'," another man said.

"Relax, boys," Frank said. "I'm planning on pulling out in a few days. Maybe a week. No more than that. I've got some loose ends to wrap up and some banking business to take care of. Then I'm gone."

"Don't you men know what the ranchers are going to do when Frank is gone?" John said, flaring up, twisting around in his chair.

Heavy boot steps rattled the boardwalk and the front door was flung open. "The gunslingers is comin' into town!" the man yelled. " 'Bout a dozen of 'em."

"Damn you, Morgan!" a local yelled at Frank. "See what you've done? I hope you're happy."

Frank stood up, his breakfast half finished, and stepped out of the cafe, Banker Simmons with him. A dozen or so riders reined up in front of the cafe just as the rest of the cafe crowd filed out to stand on the boardwalk.

"We're lookin' for you, Morgan," a gunny said once the dust had settled.

"You found me."

"We're not lookin' for no trouble," another gunhand said. "We just wanted to tell you we're pullin' out."

"Oh?" Frank said.

"Yeah, Frenchy here"—he gestured toward a rider—"is from Louisiana. He says you got you a mojo hand or a juju or some sort of that Cajun voodoo goin' for you. I don't rightly know what the hell he's talkin' about, but some of what he says makes sense. You got the luck goin' for you, that's all I know. No human man leaves half a dozen dead men for the buzzards and rides away without a scratch. So that done it for us. Maybe they'll be another time, maybe there won't. But for this time, we're gone."

"This all that's leaving?" Frank asked.

"Half a dozen pulled out yesterday. Might be some more, I don't know." He lifted a hand. "We're gone. I personal hope I don't never see you no more, Morgan. Not never again."

The riders wheeled about and rode out of the town.

"Well, I'll be damned," a local said.

Frank walked back into the cafe to finish his breakfast. "Hotten my coffee, will you?" he called to the waitress. "Maybe now I can eat in peace."

Frank spent the rest of the morning with Lawyer Foster and Banker Simmons. They worked out an arrangement for the newlyweds to farm and ranch Frank's land, in exchange for fair compensation for their labors.

"It's a good deal for the kids," Lawyer Foster said. "More than fair really."

"They deserve a chance," Frank said. "I can afford to give it to them."

"What about Julie?" John asked.

"What about her?" Frank questioned. "We had a bit of a fling, I guess you could say, and now it's over. With the addition of her holdings, the kids are going to be working a lot of land; far more than anyone else in the south part of the valleys. It's going to be a hell of a responsibility for the young people. As for Julie, well, there are provisions in this arrangement for her to be well taken care of. There's no more to say."

The lawyer and the banker exchanged glances.

"Is there more?" Frank challenged.

"Not if that's the way you want it, Frank," John said.

Frank pushed back his chair and stood up. "Then we're finished. I'm going back to my place. The kids can move in next week."

"That's when you're pulling out?" Foster asked.

"There is nothing here to hold me. Is there?"

The banker and the lawyer said nothing.

Frank smiled. "See you boys later."

As Frank stepped out of the bank, he saw Ortiz lounging in the shade of a store awning across the street. He looked up the street. Viola Trainor's carriage was in front of the livery. Frank walked across the street and stepped up on the board-walk.

Ortiz smiled at him. "The man who set more souls free to roam the ghost town. How are you, Frank?"

"I'm well. And you're looking the same."

"A month or so older than when last we met."

"How is Jules?"

Ortiz chuckled. "He's all right. Still a bit sore in the butt area from his ride home. But his hate for you is vile."

"He knows where to find me."

"He's practicing his draw daily, for several hours."

"He can practice all he wants too, Ortiz. But when that crazy-in-the-head young man braces me, I'll put lead in him."

Ortiz lifted his hands and shrugged his shoulders. "What can I say? I am not his keeper. What he does, he does."

"How's the colonel?"

"Aflame with hate. For you, of course."

"I'll put lead in that arrogant bastard too."

Ortiz laughed. "Ah, Frank, when men such as you and I are gone, the West will be a boring place, will it not?"

Frank smiled. "It won't be the same, that's for sure."

Ortiz looked over at the apothecary shop. "There is my charge, Frank. She now has enough drugs to keep her in a mild stupor for several weeks. I must be going. Is it true you are leaving the valley?"

"Yes. In a few days, maybe a week. But I'm leaving for sure."

"I may give up my extremely boring position and drift myself. But I will drift south, toward a home I have not seen in years."

"Are your parents still alive?"

"I don't know. And that is a disgraceful thing to have to admit." He lifted a hand. "Good luck to you, Drifter."

"Same to you, Pistolero."

Frank watched as the Mexican gunfighter mounted up and the carriage rolled past, Ortiz riding shotgun. Frank looked up and down the street. *Nice little town,* he thought. *I'll miss it, even though I know it's not the place for me. It's filled with good people, most of them anyway. But not my sort of people.*

He smiled at that last thought. *What do you want, Frank?* he silently questioned. *A town filled with aging gunfighters?*

Preacher Philpot and his wife strolled past on the boardwalk, both of them averting their eyes so they would not have to speak to Frank. Frank didn't press the issue. It wouldn't have solved anything by pushing.

He stepped off the boardwalk and mounted up. Lawyer Foster and Banker Simmons waved to him as he rode out, heading for home.

*Home?* Frank thought sourly. *No. A place to stay for a few more days, that's all it is. It isn't a home.*

Frank began to feel better as he cleared the edge of town and put the buildings and the townspeople behind him. *Not my kind of people,* he thought again. *But where the hell do I find my kind of people?*

As he rode, he mentally toyed with the idea of heading back East, looking for a place there. He quickly rejected that germ of an idea. It wouldn't take long before his true identity would be discovered and he'd be faced with the same problems. No, there was a place for him in the West he loved. He just had to keep looking, that's all.

*Money sure as hell hasn't brought me much happiness or contentment,* he thought. Then he shook that away and smiled, thinking: *But I've helped some deserving kids, that's a fact. Maybe that's what money is really for.*

On his ride back to his place, Frank met and passed several local farmers and their families, heading into town to shop. None of them spoke to him or waved at him. Their actions began to amuse Frank and his dark mood lifted. He was feeling much better as he rode up to his place and Dog ran out to greet him.

"Well, someone is glad to see me," he said, as he paused to pet the big cur. "I can always count on you, can't I, fellow?"

Dog barked happily and licked his hand.

"You feel like traveling?" Frank asked.

Dog jumped around and wagged his tail.

"Yeah? Well, me too. Two drifters, that's us." He looked up as a buckboard rattled down the road and turned into Frank's place. Julie was at the reins, her blond hair shining in the sun.

"This ought to be interesting." Frank muttered. "And final."

# TWENTY-SIX

"I owe you an explanation, Frank," Julie said.

"I'll make it easy for you, Julie. I'm too violent. It sickens you. You can't bear to be around me anymore. Am I on the right track?"

"Yes," she said softly. "But you're a good man, Frank. There is a decent streak in you. I've seen it. If only you would take off those guns."

"I'd be dead in a month."

"You won't even try, Frank? Not even for us, for what we had?"

Frank shook his head. "You want to be a widow again, Julie?"

She stared at him for a moment, her eyes turning chilly. "You can live with the gun or you can live with me, Frank. But you can't have it both ways."

"I'm sorry you feel that way."

"I will be eternally grateful for everything you've done for the kids and for me, Frank. And a part of me will always love you."

"Good-bye and good luck, Julie."

That startled her. She was visibly shaken when she said, "That's all you have to say about it, about us?"

"There is nothing else to say. Would you like me to see you home?"

"I can manage quite well, Frank."

Frank touched the brim of his hat. Julie spun around and walked away, back to her buckboard. She drove away without a backward glance.

Frank walked back into the house, Dog padding along beside him. He made a pot of coffee and filled a cup, then sat on the porch in his rocking chair and smoked and drank his coffee. *Odd,* he thought, *I don't feel any great sense of loss about Julie. Actually, I don't feel anything. Maybe that means there wasn't anything of substance between us to build on. That's a good thought to maintain,* he concluded.

"Better to find out now than later," Frank said aloud. "Later would have really been a big mess."

Dog looked up at him, then left the porch in a run, to bark and chase at some chattering squirrels in the side yard.

"The next few days just might prove to be interesting," Frank muttered. "It will all depend on what Trainor and the other ranchers have up their sleeves now that many of the hired guns are pulling out."

Frank went back into his house and fixed another cup of coffee. "To hell with it," he said as he sugared and stirred. "I'm better off alone."

\* \* \*

Frank stayed close to his house the rest of that day. The dozen or so gunfighters who had pulled out made up less than a quarter of the men the three ranchers had hired to fight the farmers. Frank was sure there would be more attacks . . . but when and where those attacks might occur was something he could not answer.

"It's none of my affair any longer," he murmured. "The people have spoken, so to speak. The locals don't want me around, so I guess that means they can damn well handle their own troubles."

But he knew if called upon for help, he would not hesitate.

Late that afternoon, Frank was sitting out on the porch enjoying the cool breeze that was blowing down from the distant mountains. He heard the sounds of horses coming down the road, and took his Peacemaker and laid it in his lap. The horses turned into his road, and Frank tensed when he recognized three men from the Snake brand; three hired guns.

"Take it easy, Morgan," one called. "We ain't here to make no trouble."

"Ride on in and have a seat on the porch then."

"New, we'll just say what we come to say and then head on out."

"You boys pulling out?"

"You betcha," another gunny said. "And we ain't alone. 'Bout a dozen more pullin' out right behind us. In the mornin', I think."

"Why?"

"This ain't workin' out, Morgan," the third rider said. "I don't mind ridin' over crops or killin' hogs or whatever, but burnin' people to death and rapin' young girls and abusin' women ain't my style. I don't hold with that."

"Good for you."

"But the ones that are stickin' are mean, Morgan. They got no inner feelin's 'bout nothin'. They'd as soon kill a child as look at one."

"I'll keep that in mind. Thanks for telling me."

"We heard you was pullin' out too. That true?"

"Yep. Next week probably."

"Maybe we'll see you around someplace, have a drink."

"Maybe. You boys sure you don't want some coffee? I just made fresh."

"Well . . . sure! Why not? It's a long ride for us."

Frank rose from his chair as the gunhands dismounted, and all three were quick to notice the Peacemaker. One smiled and said, "Don't worry, Morgan. We done drawn our time and was ordered off Snake range. Old Colonel Fancy-Pants give us a good cussin', he did."

Frank smiled. "I bet he did. That man doesn't like to lose. Have a seat. I'll get cups and the pot."

"'Preciate it, Morgan."

Over coffee and cigarettes, one of the hired guns said, "This is a nice place, Morgan. Peaceful. Damned if I don't think I could make a go of it if I had me a place like this."

Frank smiled. "And hang up your guns too?"

The man returned the smile. "Folks like us can't never do that. Yeah, for a fact, I see what you're gettin' to. Damn shame, though."

"Where are you boys heading now?"

"South. Down Texas way. Folks in West Texas are hiring; payin' fightin' wages." He shrugged. "It's what we do. It's a job of work."

The guns-for-hire finished their coffee and stood up. "You watch yourself, Morgan," one said just before swinging into the saddle. "Trainor is turnin' 'bout half crazy. Course with him, that probably wasn't no long journey.

Whole damn family's crazy, 'ceptin' for Viola, and she's so addled on drugs she don't know where she is most of the time. But there's no tellin' what the colonel's apt to do in his frame of mind."

"I'll keep that in mind. You boys take it easy."

Frank watched them ride away, then poured him another cup of coffee and returned to his rocking chair. Dog came around from behind the house and lay down beside the chair. "Only the real bad ones are left, Dog," Frank said as the late afternoon shadows began to slowly creep over the land. "Someone's going to be coming after me, bet on that."

Dog looked up at him, as if to say, "What else is new?"

"Yeah," Frank whispered to the dying day. "Right."

Frank sat for a few more quiet minutes, finishing his coffee. "I think, ol' fellow," Frank said, "I'll just take me a ride into town come the morning. But I'll take the long way in and check on Julie and the young people. Give them some warning about what might be coming at them. I'll leave early, before good light."

Far away, an owl hooted.

"Now some Indians would say that was a bad sign," Frank said. "While some others would say it was a good omen. I guess we'll just have to wait until tomorrow to find out."

# TWENTY-SEVEN

Frank was on the move an hour before dawn, arriving at Julie's place just in time to smell the coffee boiling and the mouth-watering aroma of bacon sizzling in the skillet and fresh-baked biscuits just out of the oven.

But he doubted he would be invited in.

Julie met him at the door, and her eyes were glacier cold and her tone not much warmer. "You're out very early, Mr. Morgan."

Frank sat his saddle and smiled at her. She was behaving like a little schoolgirl. But damned if he was going to tell her that. "Yes, I am, Miss Julie. I came to tell you of some new developments in the valley war."

"I'm listening."

Frank quickly brought her up to date, closing with: "I'd advise the boys to pack iron wherever they go."

"Of course, you would, Mr. Morgan. That's how you settle everything. With violence."

Frank sighed. "Where are the kids?"

"The boys drove their wives into town for an early appointment with Dr. Everett. They have to get back as quickly as possible. It's harvest time here. Or weren't you aware of that?"

"Yes, Julie. I know it's time to harvest. I may not know much about farming, but I do know that."

She stood in the door and glared at him.

"I have a cup in my saddlebags, Julie. Could I trouble you for a cup of coffee? Or would that be too much bother?"

"Give me your cup. I'll rinse it out for you and bring the coffee out to you."

"Do you mind if I dismount?"

"Not at all. Just stay out here. I'll bring your coffee out to you."

"Of course." Frank swung down from the hurricane deck and gave her his tin cup.

"I suppose you'd like some bacon and biscuits too?"

"That would be right neighborly of you."

She frowned at him, then turned and walked back into the house without speaking and closed the door.

The line about hell having no fury like a woman scorned sprang into Frank's mind. He thought: *Whoever wrote that sure must have pissed off some lady. The fellow damn sure knew what he was writing about.* He couldn't recall who penned that line.

Julie stepped outside with a plate of food and a cup of coffee. She handed it to him without speaking, then turned to walk back into the house. Frank's words stopped her cold.

"Julie, don't you think you're behaving a bit childish?"

She spun around, her eyes glowing with a cold fire. "I'm not the one who refuses to change, Frank."

"Really, Julie? I'm one hundred percent wrong and you're one hundred percent right. Is that the way you see things?"

That made the woman so mad she began spitting like a cat. Frank backed up a step, the plate of bacon and biscuits in one hand, the cup of coffee in another. "Easy now, Julie," he said with a smile he could not stop. "You wouldn't hit a nice, gentle person like me, would you?"

"Oh . . ." she sputtered. "You . . ." She fought to find words. Unable to speak at the moment, Julie spun around and flounced back into the house, slamming the door.

Frank breathed a silent sigh of relief, and took his food and coffee over to a homemade bench under a tree and sat down. "I will never, ever understand women," he said after taking a sip of coffee. "Horses and dogs, yes, but not women."

Frank ate his bacon and biscuits and sipped his coffee. Before he could finish his coffee, the front door was jerked open and Julie came storming out, marching up to Frank. Frank quickly looked around; he was hemmed in.

"Give me the damn plate!" she demanded.

Frank handed her the empty plate.

"Just leave the cup on the bench when you're finished."

"It happens to be *my* cup. Unless you want something to remember me by."

"Frank!"

"All right, all right. Just making a small joke." He drained his tin cup. "I'll be on my way, Julie." He stood up and started toward Horse.

"Frank?"

He turned around.

"I appreciate everything you've done. More than I can ever put into words. I want you to understand that."

"All right, Julie. I do."

"But I can't live the way I know you think you must. Do you understand that?"

"I guess so."

"I'm sorry. So very sorry."

"Me too, Julie. Me too." He mounted up and rode away, without looking back.

Frank rode into town and reined up in front of Doc Everett's office. Donnie and Phil were sitting in the waiting room. "Boys," Frank said. "Is everything all right with the girls?"

"Yes, sir," Donnie said. "Everything is fine. They're getting dressed now. The nurse is in there with them. Doc Everett is seeing another patient."

"Crops look real good."

"They're going to be bumper," Phil said. "Why do you have to leave, Mr. Morgan?" he abruptly asked.

"Because it's time, Phil. That's the best answer I can give you."

He nodded his head. "I know that Mama is not real easy to get along with at times."

"She's a good woman, Phil. She just really doesn't know anything about a gunfighter's life, that's all."

"It must be tough to hang up those guns, Mr. Morgan."

"It's almost impossible, Phil. Look, good to see you, boys. Tell the girls I said hello and we'll see each other again before I pull out."

Frank left the office and sat down on the shady side of the street, out of the glare of the morning sun. Once again the thought came to him that this was really a nice town. The town was clean and free of trash. The streets were graded often; a water wagon was used when needed to cut down on dust. *This town is probably going to make it,* Frank thought. *Those in the north part of the valley will not succeed in de-*

*stroying the town of Heaven, no matter how many gunfighters they bring in. The good people will prevail.* Frank was suddenly certain of that. *Maybe someday I can come back and live out my remaining days here. I would like that.*

Frank watched as a dozen or so horsemen appeared on the edge of town. He stared, trying to identify them, then tensed when he recognized Don Bullard and Ken Gilmar, accompanied by some of their hired guns. The group rode en masse up the main street, stopping when they reached the center of town, across from where Frank was sitting under the awning, in the shade. One of the men pointed at the buckboard in front of Dr. Everett's office.

Frank watched as Doc Everett came out of his office to stand and glare at the ranchers and their paid shooters.

"Our kids in there, Doc?" Ken Gilmar asked in too loud a voice.

"What if they are?" the doctor questioned. "What business is that of yours?"

"They're our kids, damn you!" Don Bullard yelled. "That makes it our business."

"They're married legally and in the sight of God," Doc Everett came right back. "As far as I know, that makes them adults according to the laws of this territory."

"We don't give a tinker's damn about the laws of this territory. I want my boy out here right now!" the owner of the Diamond .45 hollered. "Don't make me walk all over you to get him, Doc!"

"And I want my girl out here!" the Lightning owner shouted. "And by God, I'll tear that office down if I have to."

"Both of you can go to hell," Doc Everett said calmly. "And take your damned hired guns with you."

"I'm warnin' you, Doc," Ken said. "Don't make this no shootin' issue."

"You going to shoot me, Ken?" Doc Everett challenged. "Shoot me down in cold blood? I don't carry a gun and you all know it."

"Doc," Don said in a calmer tone of voice. "We're not going to shoot you. You know better than that. But we're the parents of that boy and girl in yonder. We got a right to talk to our kids."

"You both disowned them. You gave up your rights when you did that."

"Them was hard words spoken in heat. You know we didn't mean it."

Doc Everett said nothing as he stood on the boardwalk, staring at the heavily armed group of men.

Frank felt eyes on him and studied the mounted men. He met the eyes of two men: Lee Brown and Able Wainwright, two gun-handlers out of Arizona. Frank knew that both of them were experienced and both of them were fast and better-than-average shots.

Donnie Bullard and Betty Lou Gilmar Wilson stepped out of the doctor's office. Donnie was carrying a rifle and Betty Lou was toting a pistol. A .44, it looked like to Frank.

"What are you kids doin' with them guns?" Don asked.

"That depends on you, Dad," the son replied. "It's all up to you."

"And you, girl," Gilmar said to his daughter. "You ain't never shot a pistol in your life. You try to fire that thing and you're apt to blow your own foot off."

"I've been firing a pistol for two years, Daddy," Betty Lou said. "Phil taught me with a pistol that Donnie loaned him. And I'm a pretty good shot."

"Is that right?" the father demanded.

"That's right, Daddy. And I'll tell you something else that's right. This is your grandbaby I'm carrying. A part of me and I'm a part of you."

The Lightning owner put both gloved hands on the saddle horn and took a deep breath. He sat his saddle and stared at his daughter.

"So you're not comin' home with your pa, right, girl?"

"I'm going home with my husband, Pa. And you and Mother are welcome to visit us anytime you like."

"Is that right?"

"Yes, Pa. That's right."

"Well, damn!" the rancher said, and took off his hat and shook his head. "You do have a fair amount of sand in you, girl. You take after me, I reckon."

"I reckon I do, Pa."

"Pa," Donnie said. "Let me tell you something."

"Go ahead, boy," Bullard said.

"I never wanted to be just like you. I mean . . . you're a good man in your own way. But I knew what I wanted to be the first time I seen a field of wheat in the sun. And when me and Katie first started battin' eyes at one another, I knew I was gonna farm the land with her. For the rest of my life. I love this country and I love the land. I like to see things grow. And I like the people south of the line. I'm proud to be a part of them."

"You through, boy?" Don asked.

"No, I'm not, Pa. You won't beat us. You can't. 'Cause we're in the right, and you're in the wrong. And if I have to, I'll shoot you personal. God forgive me for sayin' that. But I will, Pa. I mean it."

"I believe you do mean that, son."

"I do, Pa. Standin' right here beside my wife."

The two ranchers looked at each other for a moment. Then both of them slumped in the saddle. Don Bullard was the first to speak. "It's over," he said. "The war is over, far as I'm concerned. You, Ken?"

"I'm done," he replied. He looked around him at the hired

guns. "Any of you boys that have time comin' see the foreman and pack your gear. This war is over."

"Same with me," Don announced. "I got no more use for pistol-handlers. Draw your time and ride."

"Hell, Trainor's still hirin'," Lee Brown said.

"After we finish up in this town," Able Wainwright, his saddle pard said.

Lee cut his eyes to Frank. "Yeah. You be right about that."

The other gun-handlers silently turned their horses and rode out of town. Lee and Able dismounted, tied up at a hitching post, and walked to the saloon.

*Two more looking for a reputation,* Frank thought just as John Simmons walked up.

"By golly, Frank," the banker said. "I believe the war is just about over."

"Tell the women to gather up their kids and get off the street," Frank told him.

"What?"

"Brown and Wainwright. The two gunhands who walked over to the saloon."

"What about them?"

"They're going to brace me. Clear the street."

"Are you sure, Frank? They've just been dismissed by their employers. I heard Don and Ken tell them."

"This has nothing to do with money, John. Clear the street."

John walked away and Frank waited on the boardwalk, in the shade. When Brown and Wainwright had knocked back enough whiskey to bolster their nerve, they'd step out and challenge Frank.

Don Bullard and Ken Gilmar had walked into the doctor's office with their kids. The boardwalk on both sides of the street was rapidly clearing of foot traffic. Frank waited. His wait was not long; *maybe three quick shot glasses of bad whiskey,* he thought as the batwings were pushed open and Lee and Able stepped out.

"You ready, Morgan!" Lee hollered, Able standing beside him.

"Make your play," Frank said.

The two gunmen grabbed iron.

# TWENTY-EIGHT

Frank drew, fired, and jumped to one side just as both men cleared leather and their .45s boomed. Frank's shot hit Able in the side, and he grunted and went down to one knee. Lee's shot tore out a chunk of wood from the awning support post. Frank fired again, the bullet from his .45 striking Lee in the chest, high up and on the left side. Lee staggered back and fell over a bench in front of the saloon. He crawled to his feet just as Able got off his second shot, which missed. Frank's next shot didn't miss, the slug taking Able in the belly. Able Wainwright sat down on the boardwalk, dropping his pistol. The cocked weapon went off, and the round struck Able in the foot, blowing off part of his boot and taking part of his foot with it. Able started howling in pain and frustration.

"Kill that bastard, Lee! Kill him!"

Lee got to his feet and raised his pistol just as Frank fired. This time the bullet caught Lee in the center of the chest and put him facedown on the boards. He did not move.

"Damn your eyes, Morgan!" Able shouted, squirming around, trying to find his gun.

"Don't do it, Able," Frank shouted. "Give it up and live."

"Hell with you, Morgan. Trainor's still payin' a big bounty for your head. Where's my damn gun?" he shouted.

"Leave it alone, you fool!" Frank shouted. "I don't want to have to shoot you again."

"You kilt Lee, you bastard!" Able found his pistol and cocked it, sitting up and pointing the weapon at Frank.

Frank drilled him through the heart, the .45 slug knocking Able back and laying him down on the boardwalk.

Frank slowly walked across the street to stand in front of the two fallen gun-handlers. Doc Everett walked out and looked at both men.

"Dead as they'll ever be. You had no choice in the matter, Frank. You gave them a chance to live, they refused it."

"Are you all right, Mr. Morgan?" Betty Lou asked, rushing out of the doctor's office.

"I'm fine, Betty Lou. I was sure proud of you and Donnie, standing up to your father."

Donnie and Phil and Katie all came out and gathered around Frank. "The war's over, Mr. Morgan," Katie said. "You don't have to leave now."

Frank's smile was sad. "Yes, I do, honey. I've played out my string in this town. Believe me, I have to go."

"That isn't fair!" she cried.

"Not much in this world is, girl."

"Some of you men carry the bodies over to the undertaker," Doc Everett said, motioning to a crowd of locals that had gathered around.

Bullard and Gilmar stepped out of the office, walking up

to Frank. "You did what you had to do, Morgan," Bullard told him. "You gave Able more chances than I would have given him."

"For a fact," Gilmar said. He looked at Bullard. "We'd better get back. We've got some firing and hiring to do."

"Sure do," his friend replied. "It'll be a relief to get back to the business of ranching."

Frank walked away, into the saloon and up to the long bar. Chubby was polishing glasses. "Drink, Frank?"

"Coffee, if you've got any fixed."

"Fresh pot. Made it myself. I'll get you a cup."

Leaning against the bar, Frank sipped his coffee while some of the locals quietly filed back into the saloon, several farmers among them, including a couple who had expressed a dislike for Frank from the git-go.

"Be nice when all the pistol-handlers finally get out of the valley," one said in a voice that was a tad too loud.

"Sure will," another replied. "Be nice and peaceful . . . for a change."

"Don't pay them no mind, Frank," Chubby whispered.

"Kind of hard not to, Chub. Don't worry about it. I've got a real thick skin."

"I wish you would change your mind about pullin' out, Frank."

"Can't do that," Frank said, setting his coffee cup on the bar. "I'm pulling out in a few days. Tell you the truth, more and more I'm looking forward to it."

"I don't blame you a bit. Way some of these people is actin' is disgraceful."

Frank smiled. "I'm used to it."

"You gonna stick around and see what Trainor will do now that his big rancher friends have called a halt to the war?"

"If he's going to do anything he'd better do it quick, Chub."

"I think he will, Frank."

"We'll see." Frank nodded at the barkeep and walked out of the saloon. He mounted up and rode out of town, heading back to the peace and quiet of his farm.

Colonel Trainor sat in the study of his ranch house, the rage in him building steadily. His foreman, Tom Bracken, had just left the ranch after announcing he was quitting. Tom had been with Trainor for years; now he was gone, leaving after Trainor had refused to join Bullard and Gilmar in calling off the war with the farmers in the south end of the connecting valleys. And to make matters worse, the few remaining cowboys on the Snake payroll, those not drawing fighting wages, had walked out with Tom.

"The hell with all of you!" Trainor had shouted as the working cowboys rode away. "I don't need any of you yellow bastards!"

Trainor's dark thoughts were interrupted by a knock on the study door. "What is it?" he yelled.

The door pushed open and Orin Mathison stepped in. "You wanted to see me?" the back-shooter asked.

Trainor didn't hesitate. "You want to earn five thousand dollars, Mathison?"

"Stupid question," the man said. "Of course I do."

"Kill Frank Morgan and the money is yours."

"Morgan is out of this fight, Trainor," Orin said. "He's leaving the area in a few days. Killing him won't solve a thing."

"Goddamn you!" Trainor yelled, jumping up from his leather chair. "Do you want the money or not?"

Orin shrugged his shoulders. "Sure, I do. Half now."

"What?"

"You give me half now, half when I finish the job."

"Why, you . . ." Trainor fumed.

"Take it or leave it," Orin said calmly, stopping the rancher's tirade. "That's the deal."

Trainor calmed himself and slowly nodded his head. "All right, Mathison." He walked to a huge safe and opened it, taking out a wad of paper money and counting out twenty-five hundred dollars. He laid the money on a table. "There's your money. Take it and go do your job."

Orin smiled one of his very rare smiles. "With pleasure." He turned and walked out.

"I'd a done it myself," Jules said, walking into the room. "For nothin'."

"You had your chance, boy," the father said. "I heard all about it from the barkeep at the old store. You're yellow. Now go away and play with rag dolls or something."

"Rag dolls?" the young man yelled.

"You heard me. Just get out and leave me alone."

Jules cursed his father and stormed out, slamming the door behind him.

Trainor returned to his chair and sat down. "For five thousand dollars I could get the King of England killed," he muttered. "Frank Morgan ought to be a lot easier than that."

If the graveyards all around the West could talk, there would be dozens of hollow, muted voices contradicting Trainor's remark.

Frank was sitting on the front porch of his house, drinking coffee and enjoying the cool of late afternoon, when Dog's head came up fast and he growled low in his throat.

Frank was out of the chair instantly and in the house, hustling Dog in with him. He grabbed his rifle and shoved Dog behind the wood box.

"Stay there," he told the animal. "If somebody is sneaking up on us, I got me a pretty good idea who it is."

Dog laid his head on his paws and stayed put. But every few seconds he would bare his teeth and growl low.

Frank moved to the front of the house and chanced a peek out one of the few windows that hadn't been shot out and boarded over. Frank jerked his head back just as a rifle cracked and more window glass was blown all over the living room floor.

"I think you've lost your touch, Orin," Frank yelled, putting his hunch as to who it was into words.

"It ain't over yet, Morgan," Orin hollered. "Matter of fact, it's just now startin' between you and me."

"Then come on and face me, Orin."

"I'd rather do it this way."

"I'm sure you would. The coward's way is oftentimes the easiest way."

There was a moment of silence before Orin spoke. "I know what you're tryin' to do, Morgan. It won't work. You can't make me mad enough to slip up."

"I'm not trying to make you slip up, Orin. I'm telling the truth. It's known all over the West. You're a coward."

"That's a damn lie!" Orin shouted.

"I think it's the truth."

"You go to hell, Morgan!"

Frank had just about pinpointed Orin's location. But instead of chancing a shot that would probably miss the man, he decided to continue goading the back-shooter.

"Only a coward kills children, Orin. The lowest of the low. Wherever you go you leave a trail of slime. You crawl out from under a rock. That's where you make your home. You live in a pool of filth."

"Goddamn you! Shut up, Morgan!"

Frank smiled at the almost frantic tone in Orin's voice. "What sort of night creature was your mother, Orin? Some sort of *thing* that has no name?"

"My mama was a good woman, Morgan. Don't you be bad-mouthin' her. You son of a bitch, I won't stand for none of that."

"I hear you were born in a whorehouse. Is that right?"

Orin screamed out his anger. No words, just a howl of wild rage.

"I guess the rumors are true. You don't know who your daddy is, do you?"

"That's a vicious lie, Morgan. I'll kill you for sayin' that. My daddy was a good decent man. He loved my mama."

"I heard your daddy was a circus freak, Orin. A sideshow operator got him out of an asylum. Is that right?"

Orin cursed Frank until he was breathless.

"That's the truth, isn't it, Orin? Your mother was a fifty-cent whore and your father was a sideshow freak."

Orin Mathison jerked in frustration and cussed Frank heatedly.

"What's the matter, Orin?" Frank yelled. "It's not your fault you take after your whore mother and your freak father."

"Goddamn you!" Orin screamed, jumping up and exposing his upper body. That was all Frank needed. He put a .44-40 round into Orin's belly. The back-shooter rose up in pain and shock. Frank shot him again, the slug striking the man in the chest. Orin fell forward, landing on his face at the edge of the clearing. He jerked a couple of times, his hands digging into the dirt, then cried out once. After that, he did not move again.

Frank slipped out of the house, using the back door, and circled around, coming up on Orin from the timber. He watched the man until he was certain Orin Mathison was dead. Frank went through Orin's pockets and put the twenty-five hundred dollars into his own pocket, then found Orin's horse and tied the man belly-down across the saddle. "Have a good trip back to the Snake, Orin," Frank said.

He slapped the horse on the rump and the animal galloped off. The Snake horse would head for familiar pasture.

Frank walked back into the house and set about making another pot of coffee. While the water was heating up, Frank set out a bowl of biscuits and meat scraps for Dog and pumped fresh water for him.

Frank took a cup of his fresh-brewed coffee out onto the porch and sat down in his rocker. The sun was sinking into the far western horizon.

"It's going to be a beautiful sunset," he said aloud.

The man known as the Drifter sat in his rocking chair and sipped his coffee as dusk silently settled around him.

# TWENTY-NINE

Frank rode into town the next day and deposited the twenty-five hundred dollars in his farm account.

"The kids can use this to buy seed and equipment or baby clothes and food," he told John Simmons. "Whichever comes first," he added with a grin. Then he told John where he got the cash.

"So Orin Mathison is really dead," the banker said softly.

"Stiff as a board," Frank said.

The banker smiled. "I'll bet the colonel is boiling mad."

"He's going to pull something very soon, you can bet on that."

"You know he's hired a lot of those gunfighters who were dismissed from the Diamond .45 and the Lightning ranches."

"I heard. Doesn't surprise me a bit."

A teller stuck his head into John's office. "Sorry to bother you, Mr. Simmons, Mr. Morgan. But you both should see this. A whole bunch of riders coming into town."

Frank and John stepped out onto the boardwalk just as a dozen riders reined up in front of the general store. Frank personally knew one of them. A puncher turned gunfighter from Wyoming, name of Paul Robinson. Paul looked at Frank and held out his hands.

"We're friendly and peaceful, Frank. Just come into town to buy supplies for the trail. Hell don't welcome us no more. We're not even gonna have a drink 'fore we leave. We've quit this war."

"Glad to hear it, Paul." Frank called. "Have an easy trail."

"Thanks, Frank. You too. No hard feelin's?"

"None at all."

Paul nodded his head and smiled. "It was just a job of work, Frank. Nothin' personal."

"That's good enough for me, boys."

The riders dismounted, hung their gunbelts on the saddle horns, and walked into the store.

"The colonel still has a lot of gunmen riding for him," John remarked.

"But not as many as before," Frank replied. "And these boys probably won't be the last ones to leave."

"And you'll be leaving shortly yourself?"

"In a few more days."

The banker sighed audibly. "There is no point in me continuing to try to persuade you to stay, is there?"

"No, John. No point at all. Seems like everything I've tried to do since coming here has backlashed on me."

"Well, now, Frank, I have to take issue with that statement."

Frank chuckled at that. "I thought you weren't going to continue your pestering me to stick around."

The banker smiled. "All right, Frank, all right. But you've

done a lot of good here. Don't sell yourself short on that account. You'd only be lying to yourself."

Frank looked up the street at the approach of a buckboard. "Here comes a lady who might disagree with you about that."

With Julie Wilson handling the reins, the buckboard rattled slowly to a stop in front of the millinery shop. She stepped down and walked into the ladies' store.

"She didn't see you, Frank," John said.

"Maybe so. But I think she did. She just wants to avoid confrontation, that's all."

The gunfighter and the banker stood on the boardwalk and watched as the hired guns exited the general store, stuffed their newly purchased supplies into their saddlebags, and rode out of the town, taking the southerly route.

"I wonder where they'll go," John said.

"Anywhere there is a need for a hired gun, a bounty hunter, or a marshal. The West is settling down, but slowly. In ten or fifteen years their kind, my kind, will be only a bad memory."

"We're going to get us a newspaper in Heaven, Frank. I got that word yesterday. We're growing, changing with the times."

Frank was suddenly conscious of the weight of the .45 on his hip. "You're telling *me*?" he said with a smile.

John laughed and slapped Frank on the back. "See you later, Frank."

"All right, John."

Frank stood alone for a moment, watching the people of the town as they walked along the boardwalks. They greeted each other warmly, often stopping to chat for a time. No one spoke to him. People who walked past him averted their gaze to avoid eye contact. Frank had started to step off the boardwalk and ride out when a young boy ran up to him.

"Mr. Morgan?" he asked.

"That's me, son."

"Two men down on the other side of the livery give me a dollar to tell you they're waitin' for you."

"They have names, son?"

"Yes, sir. Peck and Rondel."

Frank gave the boy a silver dollar and thanked him. Then he began the walk down to the livery. Ever since Frank had killed Jess Malone back in the ghost town, he'd wondered how long it would take for Peck Carson and his partner, Rondel, before they made a play for him. He didn't have to wonder any longer.

He slowed his walk as he approached the end of the business district of stores and shops, and cut down an alley, coming out behind the livery. He pressed up against the building and listened and waited.

He could hear nothing. He edged closer to the huge rear doors, picking up a stone along the way. When he was at the doors, he tossed the rock into the semidarkness. The rock bounced off the rump of a horse and the horse kicked and whinnied.

"What the hell caused all that?" a man asked.

"He's here. Shut up and listen, Rondel."

"Front or back?"

"How the hell do I know? You watch the back, I'll take the front."

"I figured he'd come walkin' down the middle of the street and call us out, damnit," Rondel whispered.

"Well, he didn't."

Frank waited, motionless as he pressed against the outside wall, his Peacemaker in hand, hammer back and ready.

A couple of minutes ticked by.

"Maybe that wasn't him," Rondel said. "I can't hear nothin'."

Frank figured the gunman was maybe two feet away from where he stood by the open doors of the livery.

"Maybe it wasn't," Peck called from the front of the building. "Maybe that damn kid just stuck the dollar in his pocket and went off to buy some candy."

"You can't trust nobody no more. Kids is shore different from when we was kids, ain't they, Peck?"

"For a fact. Hell, let's amble up the street and find him."

"The kid?"

"No, damnit! Morgan."

"Oh. Okay."

Frank listened as the men moved to the front of the livery. He stepped into the dark rear of the huge barn and came up behind them in front of the livery.

"You boys looking for me?" Frank called.

Peck and Rondel spun around, both of them cussing and dragging iron as they turned.

Frank put lead into Peck first, doubling the gunman over. Frank's Peacemaker boomed a second later and Rondel went down, his chest suddenly bloody, Rondel's pistol cracking and spitting fire and smoke, blowing a hole in the ground and sending up a cloud of dust. Down on one knee, Peck cursed Frank and lifted his .45. Frank shot him again, the bullet taking Peck in the center of his forehead. Peck stretched out on the ground, his gunfighting days over.

"You sneaky bastard," Rondel gasped as Frank walked up to the fallen gunfighters. "You killed me."

"Looks like it," Frank replied, kicking Rondel's pistol away from him. "You boys should have ridden out with the others."

Rondel had no reply to that. He was dead, his lifeless eyes wide open and staring up at the blue of the sky.

John Simmons was the first to arrive at the scene. He ran up the street and stood panting and sweating next to Frank.

Frank calmly punched out the empty brass and reloaded.

"You killer!" a woman screamed from the boardwalk. "Why don't you get out and leave us in peace!"

John turned and looked at the woman. "Be quiet, Mrs. Mid-dleton. Frank was merely defending himself."

"He stalked those men!" a man yelled from the other side of the street. "Mrs. Middleton is right. I seen it all."

Frank looked at the banker, sadness in his eyes. "It won't be long now, John. Believe me, I've been through this before."

"I'm sorry, Frank," the banker said, his shoulders slumping in defeat.

"Don't be. Actually, I'm looking forward to some trail dust."

Dr. Everett came strolling up, and glanced briefly at the two dead men sprawled in the dirt. "I'm really going to miss you, Frank. However, not as much as the local undertaker and grave-diggers."

Frank shook his head and grimaced at the doctor's dry and very macabre sense of humor. "For sure, Doc, the undertaker ought to have quite a collection of guns and saddles and boots by now."

A group of local men began gathering around, staring at the bodies. One said, "I'm gettin' mighty tired of gunplay in our streets."

Doc Everett glanced at him and replied, "Jim, did anybody ever tell you that you are sometimes a real pain in the ass?"

"Who stuck a bee down your drawers, Doc?" the local asked. "Hell, I ain't said nothin' but the truth."

Doc Everett frowned but made no reply.

"I'm going," Frank said.

"Good," someone in the gathering crowd of men and a few women muttered.

"Are you all right, Frank?" Doc Everett asked. "You're not hit?"

"No. I'm fine. I'll see you men."

Frank pushed his way through the crowd and walked to his horse. He rode out of town, very conscious of the many eyes on him from the people gathered on both sides of the street. They were standing silently, staring at him.

Frank got the saddle pack for the packhorse out of the barn and inspected the rigging. It looked all right. Dog sat on the ground, looking up at him and wagging his tail in anticipation. Frank smiled at the dog's actions.

"You're ready to travel, aren't you, boy?"

Dog barked excitedly.

"All right, all right. A couple more days and we'll pull out. That's a promise."

Frank lit lamps in the house, for the rooms were dark due to the many boarded-up windows. He fixed his bedroll, tied it tight, and packed his saddlebags. He packed his gear for traveling without any real sense of regret, for he was ready to put the valley behind him. More than ready really.

When he was finished, he looked around the house, checking for anything he might have missed. The only articles that were left were those that would go into his packsaddle. And not many of those.

"We're just about all set, Dog," he said. "Not much more to do. But we're going to find us a real home one of these days. I promise you that." *Someday*, Frank silently added. *Somewhere, I hope.*

Back in the kitchen, Frank pumped a big pot of water for coffee and set it on the stove. He looked around. He would leave the dishes and most of the pots and pans for the kids.

"I wonder if I'll ever see this place again," he murmured. "And do I give a damn whether I do or not?"

He decided he didn't.

The coffee was ready, so Frank fixed a mug and went outside to sit in his rocking chair on the porch. He sipped his strong coffee and smoked a cigarette.

Dog lay down beside the rocking chair.

"We almost made it here, Dog," Frank said. "We came close. But I think in the future what we need to look for is a place about twenty-five or so miles from the nearest town, and don't make any friends. Don't get close to anyone. I think that's the trick. That's what we'll do. We'll look for a small ranch where I can raise horses and run a few head of cattle. And mind my own affairs and stay the hell out of everybody else's business."

*That's not asking too much, is it?* Frank silently questioned.

*Is it?*

# THIRTY

"Where are you going, boy?" Colonel Trainor asked, sitting on the front porch, drinking a cup of coffee and enjoying the cool of early morning.

Jules never stopped walking across the front porch of the mansion. "What do you care? I'm nothin' to you."

"I asked you a question! Don't get smart-mouthed with me. Answer me!"

Jules did not reply. He walked straight to the barn, saddled a horse, and rode out of the compound.

"Hell with you then," Trainor muttered. "Good-for-nothing yellow little pup."

Jules headed for the town of Heaven. He'd by God show his father he wasn't yellow. He'd ride straight into that damn town and shoot it up, maybe kill him some local yokels. Yeah, that was a good idea. The doctor, the banker, and maybe that damn lawyer, Foster. That would get his father's attention for a fact.

Frank had ridden into town to get a slab of bacon for the trail. He had everything else he needed, and had made up his mind he was pulling out the next morning. He'd say his good-byes in town, then ride out to say good-bye to the kids and Julie, and that would be it. He'd shake the dust of this area off him. He'd already given the Appaloosa to Phil.

Colonel Trainor had changed his mind about Jules, and he and a crowd of hired guns had ridden after him. The boy might be a coward, but he was still a Trainor.

It was nine o'clock in the morning when Jules rode into town. Frank was in the general store. Doc Everett was having coffee in the cafe. John Simmons was at his desk in the bank. Lawyer Foster was standing outside his office, chatting with a friend. The druggist, Sam Bickman, was mixing some medicine for a customer. Reverend Philpot was lumbering along the boardwalk, savoring the thoughts of the horrible punishment that awaited sinners and the wondrous joys of those he had shown the way to salvation. Julie had just rolled up in a buckboard and was going over her list of things she had to buy in town.

"What is that crazy Jules Trainor doing in town?" the clerk asked, looking out the window.

Frank instantly tensed as Jules dismounted and tied up at a hitch rail. He stepped up onto the boardwalk just as Reverend Philpot came ambling along, rattling the boards and shaking windows as he walked.

Jules walked right into the more-than-ample preacher. It didn't move Philpot an inch, but the impact almost knocked Jules off the boardwalk.

"Watch where you're goin,' you big fat tub of crap!" Jules snarled at the preacher.

"Watch your mouth, young man," Philpot thundered. "You are speaking to a man of the cloth."

"Go to hell, fat man," Jules said, and started to walk on.

Philpot grabbed the young man by the arm and spun him around. "You need a good thrashing!" he shouted.

Jules jerked free of the man's grasp. Cursing loudly, he gave Philpot a hard shove. The push sent the preacher stumbling backward. Philpot lost his balance and went crashing through a store window.

"Good Lord!" the store owner shouted as several women customers started screaming in fright.

Philpot struggled to get his weight up off the floor, all tangled in piles of men's long-handled underwear, britches, and shirts. "Help!" he hollered. "Somebody help me!"

Jules looked in through the broken window. "I ought to shoot you, you fat pile of horse crap!" he yelled. "By God, I think I will!" He jerked one .45 out of leather and banged off a shot, the bullet gouging out a hole in the floor next to Philpot's ample rear end.

Philpot was off the floor as fast as greased lightning. The customers would all later recall they had never seen the preacher move that fast.

"Wahoo!" Jules shouted, and banged off another shot. The bullet ripped through the floor between Philpot's feet, and the preacher started picking them up and putting them down. Huffing and puffing like a locomotive with a full head of steam, Philpot charged through the store, several steps ahead of the store owner and the customers. He was out the back door in two blinks of an eye.

Jules turned and put a shot into the barber pole across the street. The red-and-white striped pole began spinning wildly. The barber and the man in the chair both hit the floor.

Yelling like a wild man, Jules walked out into the middle

of the street, both hands filled with .45s, and started shooting. Julie fell out of the buckboard and landed on her rear end in the street. She scrambled under the buckboard, and managed to get up onto the boardwalk and into the general store. She spotted Frank.

"Do something!" she yelled.

"Do what?" Frank asked. "What do you want me to do: shoot the kid? I thought you wanted me to hang up my guns?"

Jules let another round rip, and the bullet busted out a window and clanged off a cook pot on a shelf. The store owner hollered and vanished behind a display of canned goods.

Julie gave Frank a very dirty look and dropped to the floor, crouching behind a counter.

Frank walked to the door and took a look out. Jules had walked up the street, cussing and shouting. "You can all get up now," Frank said.

"Hell with you!" the store owner said. "That damn kid's crazy."

Julie crawled to her feet. "Go out there and disarm that person, Frank!"

"Why?" Frank asked. "I'm leaving. The good citizens wanted me out of their town. So I'm pulling out. This is none of my affair."

"I can't believe you're saying that!" Julie said.

"You want me to repeat it?" Frank asked.

"You're impossible, Frank Morgan!"

"Guess so," Frank replied with a shrug.

"I see you, Morgan!" Jules yelled. "I'm gonna kill you!"

"Now that makes it my affair," Frank said. He looked out at Jules. "Boy, put up those guns before you hurt somebody."

"To hell with you, Morgan. Step out here and face me and

I'll holster them, and then we'll see who's the fastest gun-handler."

"Why don't I just say: Okay, you win. Would that satisfy you?"

"Huh?" Jules hollered.

Frank sighed, thinking: *Jules is sure enough not totin' a full load in his brain box.* "Jules, I don't want to fight you. Can't you understand that? I don't want to have to shoot you. Go on home, boy."

"You get out here and face me, Morgan. Or I swear I'll start puttin' lead in every local in this damn sheep-dip town."

"And what would that prove, Jules?"

"Huh?"

"Jules, that would just prove that you really are a coward. Nobody but a coward shoots an unarmed man or women or children."

"I ain't no damn coward, Morgan!" Jules screamed.

Frank looked over at the shopkeeper, who was peeking over the counter. "Tell me, why doesn't someone in this town knock his legs out from under him with a shotgun?"

"How do I know?" the shopkeeper said. "You shoot him. You're a gunman, aren't you?"

"I thought it would come to that."

"Do something, Frank!" Julie said.

"Right. Sure." Frank sighed. He looked up at the north end of the street just as Colonel Trainor and his crowd of hired guns rode into view. "Here comes Jules's father. Maybe I won't have to do anything."

"Jules!" Colonel Trainor hollered. "Put away those guns, boy."

"Go to hell!" the son told the father.

Trainor walked his horse up the street, stopping about fifty feet from his son. "You're making a fool of yourself, boy. Somebody's going to kill you if you don't stop this right now."

"Nobody's gonna kill me!" Jules shouted. "This whole town is scared of me. I got them all buffaloed."

"Morgan's in town," one of the gunfighters called to the colonel. "Yonder's his horse."

"Morgan!" Trainor yelled. "Don't kill my son. The boy is addled some. He needs some help. You hear me?"

"I ain't neither addled!" Jules screamed. "You get out here, Morgan, and face me like a man. I want this thing settled 'tween us."

"There is nothing between us, Jules," Frank called. "Not a thing. Listen to your father, boy. Go on back home."

Jules's reply to that was to put a round through the window of the store. Julie and the storekeeper hugged the floor.

"That does it, Jules," Frank called. "I'm coming out." Frank dropped his hand to the butt of the Peacemaker and slipped it in and out of the holster a couple of times. He knew from long experience the talking was over.

"Then get out here and face me!" Jules shouted.

Frank stepped out of the store onto the boardwalk.

"Kill that bastard!" Colonel Trainor yelled, pointing at Frank.

Frank jumped back into the store just as the dozen mounted gun-handlers opened fire.

# THIRTY-ONE

Frank managed to snap off one shot that knocked one hired gun out of the saddle. Then he had to dive behind a counter filled with sewing notions and hug the floor as the main street of town erupted in gunfire.

When there was a few seconds' lapse in the howling bullets, Frank jumped to his feet and ran to the storeroom, then out the back door. He stood on the loading dock for a moment, then jumped off and headed for the alley.

"Morgan!" The shout came from behind him just as he reached the mouth of the alley.

Frank instantly spun, dropped to one knee, and fired, his bullet hitting the man in the hip and spinning him around. Frank fired again. This time the gunman hit the ground and did not move. Frank ran up the alley, and almost collided with another of the Snake gunhands. Frank jammed his

Peacemaker in the man's belly and let it bang. The man's mouth opened in shock and pain and his eyes widened. He dropped his gun and sank to his knees. Frank grabbed up the man's pistol, and eased up to the mouth of the alley just as a shotgun boomed. He looked out and saw that Jules was down in the street, his legs bloody. He couldn't tell what citizen had found the courage to pick up a gun and join the fight, but he would bet it was either Lawyer Foster, Banker Simmons, or Doc Everett.

"Damn you to hell!" Jules screamed out at the man who'd shot him. "I'll kill you! I swear I will."

Frank ran back down the alleyway and circled around, coming out at the far south end of town. He paused for a moment, catching his breath and listening.

"Where is he?" he heard a man shout. "He's disappeared."

"Curly's dead," another man shouted. "He's in the alley. Morgan shot him in the belly. Must have been close up 'cause his shirt's still smokin'."

"Any sign of Morgan?" a third voice called.

"Not a trace."

"Find him!" Colonel Trainor screamed. "Find the son of a bitch and kill him." Then, almost as an afterthought, Trainor said, "And someone drag my idiot son out of the street and carry him over to the doc's office."

"You can carry that fool back to Hell!" Doc Everett shouted from his office. "Don't bring that putrid piece of coyote crap over to me."

"And kill that damn doctor too!" Trainor shouted.

Doc Everett's shotgun boomed and a hired gun hollered, more in shock than pain. "He damn near got me that time. Hell with this. I'm outta here, boys. See you."

"You get back here, you coward!" the colonel hollered.

"Go suck an egg!" the gunhand yelled.

"I'm with you, Lee," another man yelled. "Let's get outta here."

Frank waited at the edge of the main street. Two down, at least, and two leaving. The odds were being cut down.

"Morgan!" a man called. "I'm gone with them other boys. You hear me, Morgan? I'm gettin' my horse and ridin' out. Don't shoot."

"Poole!" Trainor yelled. "Don't you quit on me, you yellow bastard!"

"Hell with you," the hired gun replied. "I'm gone from here."

*Three gone,* Frank thought. *Come on, boys. The rest of you ride out of here.*

"Colonel?" The shout came from across the street from Frank's location. "This is Bell. Me and Granville is still with you."

"Good, Bell," Trainor shouted. "How about you other boys?"

"We're with you, Colonel," Frank heard someone shout.

"Who is we?" Trainor called.

"Vance and Meeker."

"Good men. They'll be extra money for you after this is over. Anyone else?"

"Barker here, Colonel," another hired gun called. "I'm with you."

"All right!" Trainor yelled. "Let's finish this, men. Get Morgan!"

Frank had listened to the men buy into this life-and-death game. He didn't know any of them; had never heard of any of them. He smiled knowingly. The more experienced gunhandlers had all pulled out. They were gone. He shifted positions and chanced a look into the street. Jules apparently was not badly hurt. He had more than likely been hit with a load of bird shot. He had crawled unassisted to the edge of the boardwalk. He had managed to hold on to one of his pistols.

Frank waited, not wanting to give away his position.

"You men in town!" Trainor called. "Stay out of this! This is between me and Morgan. When this is over, I'll pull back across the line and you can have your goddamned pigs and chickens and potatoes. You have my word on that. And I have never gone back on my word. You all hear me?"

"We hear you, Colonel." The shout came from the Blue Moon Cafe. "This is Sutton. Now, I can't talk for everybody, but there's a half dozen of us in the cafe. We're out of it. We'll hold you to your word."

"Good man," Trainor yelled. "You won't regret your decision."

*He's a good man, all right,* Frank thought bitterly. *Cowardly bastard.* Frank slipped to the rear of the buildings and began his move toward the center of town, pausing when he heard one of the gun-handlers call: "Morgan might have slipped out of the town, Colonel. He ain't on this side of the street."

"Then he's on the other side of the street," Trainor yelled. "He didn't leave. Morgan doesn't run. Check it out."

Frank heard boot steps behind him. He turned, his Peacemaker raised. The man spotted him, leveled his pistol, and opened his mouth to yell.

Frank drilled him in the belly. Then he stepped up to the man and kicked his pistol away.

"Who is that?" someone yelled.

"Barker's over on the other side. Barker? You hear me? Answer me, Barker!"

Barker groaned.

"I don't hear nothin'."

"I think he's been hit."

"Check it out," Trainor called.

"Too dangerous," a man called.

"Damn you!" Trainor shouted. "I said check it out. You work for me, you do what I tell you to do."

"Then I don't work for you no more."

"What's your name?"

"Meeker. And I'm goin'. See you, boys."

"Bell, Granville, Vance. One of you check out the other side of the street."

"I'll do it, Colonel. I'm closer."

"Is that you, Bell?"

"Yes, sir."

"Good man."

Frank drilled Bell before he got halfway across the street. Bell stumbled and fell face-first into the dirt.

Trainor emptied his pistol into the mouth of the alley, hitting nothing but air. "Get him!" the ranch owner shouted.

"Forget it," a gun-handler called. "Me and Vance is haulin' our butts outta here. He's all yours, Colonel."

"You're all craven cowards!" Trainor shouted. "Worse than that yellow pup I have to call my son."

Jules stirred at that remark and managed to sit up by the boardwalk. He fumbled with his pistol and struggled to reload it.

Frank waited near the mouth of the alley. He was unable to see Jules from his position. "All right, Trainor," Frank called. "It's down to you and me now. What's it going to be?"

Trainor cursed him, loud and long.

"That doesn't tell me a thing, Trainor," Frank shouted. Trainor offered no reply.

"What's he up to now?" Frank muttered.

"Frank?" Doc Everett called. "Trainor ran across the street. He's in the store with Julie."

"Shut up, you damn quack!" Trainor shouted. "Stay out

of this." He stepped out of the store, onto the boardwalk, pushing Julie in front of him. Trainor had one arm around the woman's neck, holding her close to him for protection.

"Look out, Frank!" Lawyer Foster shouted. "He's got Julie hostage."

Frank took a half step out of the alley for a better look. "You're the coward, Trainor," he called. "Hiding behind a woman."

Trainor cussed Frank, the townspeople, and the farmers.

"Let her go, Trainor," Frank said. "Then me and you will step out into the street and settle this thing. Just you and me. How about it?"

"You'd like that, wouldn't you, Morgan?" Trainor shouted. "You're a professional gunman. I'm just a rancher trying to make a living."

"Trainor, you won't get away with this. You've gone too far by using Julie as a shield. The people in this town will testify against you for this. Give it up before she gets hurt."

Trainor snapped off a shot at Frank. The bullet went wide, slamming into the building behind Frank. "How about that, Morgan?" Trainor called.

"I think you're a lousy shot," Frank called. "Let Julie go, Trainor."

Trainor laughed at the suggestion.

"He's crazy, Frank," Doc Everett called from his office doorway. "Something has snapped in his head."

"Just like his son," Frank muttered. "They're both crazy as a lizard."

Jules began laughing almost hysterically. "Now who's the coward, Daddy?" he shouted. "Now who's crazy? I never hid behind no woman. You're the damn coward, not me."

"Shut up!" the father screamed at his son. "You half-brain pup."

Jules laughed again, spittle leaking from his mouth.

"Help me, Frank," Julie pleaded.

"I'll help you, Miss Julie." Jules called. "I'll show you I'm no coward."

"You?" the father said, laughing. "What the hell could you possibly do to help anybody?"

"This," Jules said. He lifted his pistol and shot his father. The bullet hit his father in the side and tore through the man, blowing out the other side.

Colonel Trainor dropped his pistol and staggered backward, releasing his hold on Julie. He turned awkwardly and looked at his son as Julie ran sobbing back into the store. "Why . . . you miserable little . . ." He tried to take a step, and collapsed on the boardwalk.

Jules laughed at him. "That's funny, Daddy," the young man called. "I bet you can't do that again."

Frank stepped out of the alley and slowly walked toward Jules. He took the pistol from Jules's hand and stood looking down at the young man. "All right, Jules," he said. "It's over now."

"Tell Daddy to get up and make me laugh again," Jules said. "Tell him for me, will you, Morgan?"

"Yeah, I'll do that, Jules."

Doc Everett ran up and knelt down beside Colonel Trainor for a moment. He looked at Frank. "He's dead, Frank."

"Check out the kid, will you, Doc? His legs are a mess."

The townspeople began slowly gathering around.

"We really wasn't gonna side with Trainor, Mr. Morgan," one of the men said nervously. "We was just talkin', that's all."

Frank looked at the man for a moment. The man looked away, refusing to meet Frank's hard eyes. None of the men or women who had gathered around would meet Frank's level gaze. Frank shook his head in disgust.

Frank handed Jules's pistol to Lawyer Foster and turned to walk away.

"Where are you going, Frank?" the attorney asked.

"As far away from here as I can get," the Drifter said.

# THIRTY-TWO

Weeks later, with winter's chill strong in the air, Frank had stopped in Cheyenne for supplies, a bath and haircut, and a drink and meal. Spiffied up, he fed Dog and walked over to the saloon for a drink. He spotted a familiar face sitting alone in the back of the bar. He took his drink and walked over to the table.

"Hello, Drifter," Ortiz greeted him. "Have a chair."

"Hi, Pistolero," Frank replied, sitting down. "You're a long way from the ranch."

"I quit about a week after you pulled out. I'm heading home to see my parents . . . if they are still alive."

"And hang up your guns?"

Ortiz smiled. "As much as possible. You?"

"Just drifting. What happened after I left the valley?"

"Jules recovered from his physical wounds. But his mind

is gone. He was being committed to an asylum when I left. He had turned into a babbling idiot. We had to keep him in chains like a wild animal."

"Mrs. Trainor and Jules's brother and sister?"

Ortiz shrugged. "Viola is a hopeless addict. Martha and Vinson are . . ." He paused. "Worthless."

"Julie?"

"Already making eyes at the editor of the new paper in town. And the town is going to change its name. I don't know what. Who cares?"

"Not me," Frank said. "My lawyers will probably tell me . . . when they catch up with me, that is."

"So our trails cross here for the final time, hey, hombre?"

"Looks like it."

"I am glad you and I did not have to meet in gunplay."

"So am I, Pistolero. So am I."

"But aren't you the least bit curious as to who would have been victorious?"

"I would have been, naturally."

Both gunfighters shared a good laugh at that.

"So," Ortiz said. "Today we will have a drink or two, then get something to eat, and tomorrow we shall say our good-byes."

"Sounds good to me."

The Drifter and the Pistolero clinked glasses and silently toasted one another.

"I hope that someday you find a place to hang up your guns, Morgan."

"And you too, Ortiz."

The next morning, Ortiz headed south and Frank and Dog headed southwest. Northern Arizona was a good place to spend a few winter months. Maybe, Frank thought, he could stay out of trouble there.

He laughed at that. "Not likely," he said aloud.

For a sneak preview of
the next book in the series—

THE LAST GUNFIGHTER:
SHOWDOWN
(coming in July 2002)

—just turn the page . . .

The town had grown quite a bit—it had been no more than a wide spot in the road the last time Frank Morgan had ridden through. About ten years back, he thought with a smile. He didn't remember the name of the town.

*Still not much to it,* he thought, looking down at the buildings from a hill. *But maybe there's a barbershop with a bathhouse.* Hard winter was fast approaching and Frank was out of supplies and needed a bath, a rest, and a meal he didn't have to fix himself. He looked down at Dog, sitting a few yards away.

"And you need a good scrubbing too, Dog," he told the cur.

Dog wagged his tail without much enthusiasm at the mention of the word "bath."

A few weeks had passed without incident since Frank had left the valleys of contention and the twin towns of Heaven and Hell. But peaceful times were coming to a close, and events were now in motions that would forever change the life of the gunfighter known as the Drifter.

They were events that Frank could not have altered even had he known about them. Events that had taken place in a private men's club in New York City, a club to which only the very wealthy could belong.

Frank had intended to head southwest when he left the valley, but instead he headed northwest. Why, he didn't know; he just did. He rode slowly toward the town, passing a weather-beaten sign that read: SOUTH RAVEN.

Frank shook his head at the name. "I wonder where North Raven is."

It took him about a minute to ride the entire length of the town, passing a general store, a saloon, a leather and gun shop, a barbershop/bathhouse/undertaker combination, a small cafe, a stage office/telegraph office and several other stores. He finally reined up in front of the livery stable.

Frank swung wearily down from the saddle. An old man walked out of the shadows of the livery, sized Frank up for a few seconds, and said, "Howdy, boy. You look plumb tuckered out."

"I am," Frank replied.

"Come a ways, have you?"

"A good piece, for a fact. Did I miss the hotel coming in?"

The old man chuckled. "Ain't nary. But they's rooms for hire over the saloon."

"Where's North Raven?"

"You're funny, boy, you know that? There ain't no North Raven. Never has been. Town is named for the local doctor. He's from the South. That's how the town got its name."

"What part of the South?"

"Alabama. Raven was a doctor in the Confederate Army. I think he was a colonel."

"There were a lot of them, for a fact."

"You was a Rebel?"

"I was."

"I was on the other side. That make a difference to you?"

"Not a bit. War's over."

"We'll get along then. I hate a sore loser. You want me to take care of your horse?"

"And my dog. I'll stable them and feed them."

"You don't think I can do that?"

"I don't want you kicked or bitten."

"I'll shore keep that in mind. Them animals got names?"

"Horse and Dog."

The liveryman smiled. "That ain't very original."

"It suits them."

"I reckon so. You look sort of familiar to me, boy. You been here 'fore?"

"Can't say I have. But I appreciate you calling me 'boy.'"

"I'm older than dirt, boy. Everybody's younger than me." He stared hard at Frank for a few seconds. "I've seen you 'fore. I know I have. It'll come to me."

"Let me know when it does. Is there anyone in town who does laundry?"

"The Widder Barlow. The barber'll get your stuff to her."

"All right. My gear will be safe here?"

"Shore will. I got a room with a lock on the door."

"The cafe serve good food?"

"Best in town," the liveryman said with a wide smile.

"It's the *only* cafe in town," Frank reminded him.

"That's why it's the best!"

Frank smiled and led Horse into the big barn, Dog following along. Dog would stay in the stall with Horse. Frank left his saddle in the storeroom and walked across the street to the barbershop. He arranged for the washerwoman to launder his trail-worn clothes, and then took a long soapy bath in a tub of hot water. He dressed in his last clean set of long-handle underwear and clean but slightly wrinkled jeans and shirt, then got a shave and haircut. He stepped out onto the boardwalk smelling and feeling a lot better, and walked over to the cafe for some lunch.

"Beef stew, hot bread, and apple pie," the waitress told him. "It's all we got, but it's good and there's plenty of it."

"Sounds good to me," Frank told her. "And keep my coffee cup filled, please."

Frank ate two full bowls of the very good stew and drank several cups of coffee before his hunger was appeased. He walked across the street and signed for a room, then went into the bar for another cup of coffee and to listen to the local gossip, if any. The patrons fell silent when he entered, everyone giving him the once-over. Frank ignored them, and took a table in the rear of the room and ordered a pot of coffee.

"I know who you are," a man said from across the room.

Frank sipped his coffee and offered no reply to the statement.

"What are you talkin' about, Ned?" another man asked.

"The gunfighter who just walked in," Ned said.

"What gunfighter?"

"Frank Morgan."

*"Frank Morgan!* Here in South Raven? You're crazy."

"That's him what just walked in, Mark," Ned stated. "Sittin' over yonder drinkin' coffee."

Frank took another sip of the strong coffee and remained silent.

"Is that true, mister?" Mark asked. "Are you Frank Morgan?"

"Yes," Frank said quietly.

"Oh, my God!" another patron blurted out as the front

door opened, letting in a burst of cool air. "He's here to kill someone."

"I don't think so," the old liveryman said, stepping into the saloon. "Seems like a right nice feller to me." He walked to the bar and ordered a beer. "Your name come to me, Mr. Morgan. I knowed it would."

Frank lifted his coffee in acknowledgment.

"I seen Doc Raven right after you stored your stuff. Told him 'bout you. I reckon he'll be along anytime now."

"Why are you here in our town, Frank Morgan?" another bar patron asked.

"To spend a couple of days, resting my horse," Frank said. "To eat a meal I didn't cook and to get my clothes washed. Is that all right with you men?"

"Shore suits me," the liveryman said.

"You're not lookin' to kill no one?" Mark asked.

"No."

"By God, it is you," a man said, stepping into the saloon from a side door. "I thought Old Bob was seeing things."

"Told you it was him, Doc," the liveryman said. "Dr. Raven, Mr. Morgan."

Frank nodded at the man. "Do I know you?"

"No," the doctor replied. "But I've seen your picture dozens of times and read a couple of books about you."

"Don't believe everything you read," Frank told him. "According to those books I've killed about a thousand white men, been wounded fifty times, been in gunfights all over the world, and been received in royal courts and knighted by kings and queens."

The doctor laughed. "And you're still a young man."

"I'm forty-five, Doc. And feel every year of it."

The doctor sat beside him. "May I?" he asked, lowering his voice. "I've got something to say."

"Something that concerns me?"

"I would certainly say so. It's been in the works for . . . I'd guess six months at least. Probably longer than that. You're about to become the prey in what some are calling the ultimate hunt."

Frank's eyes narrowed for a few seconds; that was the only betrayal of his inner emotions. "You want to explain that? And also, how did you find out about it?"

"I have a doctor friend in New York City. We went to college together; graduated just in time to serve in opposing sides during the Northern aggression against the South. He wrote me months ago asking if I knew you. Of course, I told him I didn't. In his next letter, which was not long in coming, he told me about a group of wealthy sportsmen who had each put up thousands of dollars for this hunt. To be blunt, the money goes to the man who kills you."

"The authorities haven't stepped in to stop this . . . nonsense?"

"Obviously not. The so-called sportsmen are on their way West as we speak."

"The West is a big place, Doc. How do they propose to find me?"

"I understand the group has hired private detectives to do just that."

Frank hottened up his coffee and sugared it. "Doc, this is the damnedest thing I ever heard of. Hell, it's *illegal.*"

"Of course it is. But you're a known gunfighter. In the mind of many people, the world would be a better place without you in it."

Frank sighed heavily. "This is going to bring out every two-bit gunslinger west of the Mississippi."

"Well, we have a couple of gunfighters right here in this community. They'll be in town later on today, you can bet on that."

"You know that for sure?"

"It's Friday, Frank. And they always come in for drinks on Friday."

"Ranch hands?"

"They occasionally hire on to some ranch, when they're not stealing cattle or horses."

"I'm surprised anyone will hire them."

"Oh, they're careful not to steal from any of the ranchers in this area. But they've already heard about the other money being offered for your head."

"Sounds like everyone in the West has heard of that," Frank said sourly. Then he took a sip of coffee and smiled. "But no one's collected it yet."

"Obviously," Doc Raven replied. "But don't sell these two men short, Frank. I'm told they're fast and good shots to boot."

"Young?"

"Mid-twenties."

"The worst age. They're full of piss and vinegar and think they're ten feet tall and bulletproof."

"That's an interesting way of putting it, but accurate, I would say."

"Doc, if I could have one wish granted me by the Almighty, it would be that I could live out the rest of my years in peace and never have another gunfight. And that's the God's truth."

Doc Raven stared into Frank's pale eyes for a few seconds. He took in the dark brown hair, peppered with gray. The thick wrists and big hands. "I believe that, Frank. But it doesn't change anything."

"No, it doesn't. Doc, do you have a marshal here?"

Doc Raven smiled. "No. We had one, but he died several years ago. Not much goes on here, Frank. It's a very peaceful town."

"If you want it to remain peaceful, then I'd better move on," Frank said.

"Nonsense. You're welcome to stay here for as long as you like."

"The mayor and town council might have something to say about that."

"I'm the mayor, Frank. And we don't have a town council."

"Interesting. How about a bank?"

"A small one, located in the stage office."

"Do you own it too?"

Raven laughed. "As a matter of fact I do. Would you like to open an account?"

"Not really. I have ample funds with me."

The doctor pushed back his chair and stood up. "Enjoy your stay in South Raven, Frank. I've got to see about a patient. We'll visit again soon."

"I'm sure."

The doctor walked out of the saloon and into the crisp fall air of southern Idaho. Frank poured another cup of coffee and rolled a cigarette.

Old Bob, the liveryman, came over to Frank's table, a beer mug in his hand, and sat down. "The doc tell you about the Olsen boys?"

"The horse thieves?"

Bob laughed. "That's them. They're cousins, and worthless. But both of them are pretty good with a pistol."

"Maybe I can avoid them."

"Doubtful, Mr. Morgan. Them two is lookin' for a reputation."

A man turned away from the front window of the saloon. "Here comes Brooks and Martin. They're reinin' up now. Oh, Lordy, the lead is goin' to fly for sure."

"The Olsen boys?" Frank asked.

"That's them," Bob said.

The front door opened and two young men swaggered in, both of them wearing tied-down pistols.

Bob pushed his chair to one side, giving Frank a clear field of fire. Frank sipped his coffee and waited.

# THE FIRST MOUNTAIN MAN SERIES BY
# WILLIAM W. JOHNSTONE

## *Available Wherever Books Are Sold!*

Visit our website at **www.kensingtonbooks.com**

# THE MOUNTAIN MAN SERIES BY
# WILLIAM W. JOHNSTONE

## THE ASHES SERIES BY
## WILLIAM W. JOHNSTONE

## *Available Wherever Books Are Sold!*

Visit our website at **www.kensingtonbooks.com**